EMMA HEAT

Emma Heatherington lives in Donaghmore, Co Tyrone, Northern Ireland with her three children – Jordyn, Jade and Adam. She loves country music, red wine, bubble baths and cosy nights in by the fire. Find Emma on Twitter @emmalou13 and on Facebook emmaheatheringtonwriter.

Crazy For You

EMMA HEATHERINGTON

Harper*Impulse* an imprint of
HarperCollins*Publishers* Ltd
77–85 Fulham Palace Road
Hammersmith, London W6 8JB

www.harpercollins.co.uk

A Paperback Original 2014

First published in Great Britain in ebook format by Harper*Impulse* 2013

Cover Images © Shutterstock.com

Emma Heatherington asserts the moral right to
be identified as the author of this work

A catalogue record for this book
is available from the British Library

ISBN: 978-0-00-759161-9

This novel is entirely a work of fiction.
The names, characters and incidents portrayed in it are
the work of the author's imagination. Any resemblance to
actual persons, living or dead, events or localities is
entirely coincidental.

Automatically produced by Atomik ePublisher from Easypress

For my mum, Geraldine Mc Crory (1954 – 1991)

Your creativity and love for life lives on through us all

Missing you always xxx

Chapter 1

Good Things Come To Those Who Can't Wait

Daisy Anderson scowled at her suitcase as she scurried barefoot through the hallway of her first-floor apartment. Moving towards the bathroom door in a fit of bad temper, she turned on her heels and firmly kicked the giant case for the fourth time that morning.

"Who wants to go on holiday anyway?" she shouted as she kicked it once more for luck, then howled in pain as she realised that repeat attacks were hurting her own toes more than the huge lump of green canvas that lay sprawled across her floor.

On its opened surface, a red and white-striped bikini with the label still attached stretched across two pairs of pastel-coloured flip-flops that would now never see the light of day. Unopened bottles of sun-tan lotion in descending factors were squashed among handy-pack facial wipes and bite-size shampoo bottles, and to add insult to injury, her brand-new passport sat as neat as a pin in the case's netted pocket, sadly surplus to requirements.

Daisy hobbled away miserably on her injured foot and plunged herself into a pathetic lukewarm bath.

I should be in Spain now, she thought sorrowfully. *I should be lying on a sun-drenched beach, smothered in delicious coconut sun-tan lotion, with hot white sand sticking between my toes.*

In the glorious heat of the Costa Dorada, she and Lorna had planned to rise at dawn to bag two of the best sun-beds by the pool. They were to go Dutch on evening meals and then starve on sunlight during the day as they nursed multi-coloured cocktail hangovers. Scuba-diving lessons had been considered, even though they were both petrified of deep water, as had salsa lessons even though they both had two left feet.

Instead, back in the dismal excuse of a Belfast summer, where disaster seemed to be her middle name, the only thing gripping Daisy's sore toes were the chilly chrome bath taps she kept turning on and off in hope of some warm water.

"Come on. Please warm up, just a little. Don't you feel sorry for me?" she asked, spotting her warped reflection in the taps. Sinking her shoulders beneath the gloomy water, she let out a shiver. It was only Monday and so far this was panning out to be the worst week of her life. Failing her last twelve theatre auditions, being dumped by her agent and watching women with chubby ankles force their feet into discount-priced shoes had done little to cheer her up.

Lorna, on the other hand, had come out of the whole failed holiday saga smelling of roses, or seaweed, or some fancy treatment at a posh hideaway in southern County Down. When the online holiday company crashed into cyberspace, her latest boyfriend whisked her away on a luxury last-minute spa break to make up for her 'dreadful disappointment.'

So while Lorna had bagged herself a mid-week 'dirty weekend' out of the disaster, Daisy faced seven days of pure misery in her cramped apartment without even her best friend to bitch with. She could always unpack the darned suitcase, she supposed. Or she could go back to work in Super Shoes and save her holidays for later in the month. That would be the sensible thing to do. She could always slice off her sore big toe, for that matter.

Closing her eyes tightly, she tried to imagine that the limp, bubble-free bath water was the dazzling blue waters of the

Mediterranean Sea but despite her most concentrated efforts, it wasn't working.

"Saved by the bell," she mumbled when the phone sang from the hallway. She tugged out the bath plug and wrapped herself in her favourite fluffy red robe. Frantically tying it at the waist, she shuffled along the tiled floor, dodging puddles and trying not to slip under her damp feet.

"Hello… shit!" said Daisy as the phone bounced off the wall. She picked up the receiver again. "Sorry, sorry," she said. "I dropped the phone."

"Whoops-a-Daisy," said the voice on the other end, which wasn't instantly recognisable.

Not distinctly male *or* female for that matter.

"Hello?' she replied, desperately trying to place the mystery person on the other end. He or she sounded a bit dodgy, or American, or both.

"It's *me*. Like, *hello*. Jeez, has it been so long that you don't even recognise my voice?"

Daisy's mind was blank. She was stuck. Really stuck. She was useless with names, but normally caught voices straight away. If Lorna had given that freaky Ricardo dude from the video store her number, she was dead meat. It sounded a bit like him, but she was only in there yesterday hiring out *Titanic* as an excuse to cry her lamps out, so what would he be phoning *her* for?

"Of course I do," she said in her chirpiest voice trying to buy a few more seconds. "What's the craic…?"

"Jack?"

"Jack, of course. Hi Jack. How's tricks?" she said, pulling her wet hair back and making faces at herself in the mirror.

She didn't know any Jacks.

"We used to say that all the time, remember? What's the craic, Jack? And then, you'd say, not much…"

"Not much, Butch!" squealed Daisy. "Omigod is that..?"

"It's me, you dimwit."

3

"*Gay Eddie*? How the hell are you? Wow! This *is* a blast from the past."

The caller didn't reply and Daisy's excitement was marred by a two-second pause that seemed to last a lifetime. She could feel her face go hot.

"I'm so sorry," she said. "I must have picked you up wrong. I thought you were an old friend of mine, Eddie Eastwood? We used to have this really weird rhyming slang when we were younger and…"

"It *is* me, stupid," he sniffled. "I'm just a bit emotional at hearing your voice. God, Daisy, it's been way, way too long."

Daisy dabbed the black mascara rings under her eyes with a facial wipe from her suitcase and made a mental note to remind Eddie he was from Donegal, not downtown L.A. The wipe smelt funny and she realised it was one for warning off mosquito bites. Chance would be a fine thing.

"Hey, Ed. Come on. Don't be like that. We do catch up from time to time. I only emailed you last week, didn't I?"

"Forwarding jokes to me in San Francisco doesn't count for correspondence, Daisy. I haven't seen you in almost four goddamn years and I desperately need to talk to you. Is it OK if I come over?"

Daisy plonked herself down on top of the bulky suitcase, ignoring the discomfort of the bulging bag of toiletries she threatened to destroy under her posterior. To give him his dues, Eddie always had amateur dramatics down to a fine art. But Eddie couldn't just 'come over'. He lived a million miles away, for goodness sake. This *was* serious. Or was it? With Eddie, most of the time, it was very hard to tell.

"Sure. Fly over right away. Ed. I'll see you in about ten or twenty hours' time. At least I'll be dressed by then."

Eddie gave out a dramatic deep sigh.

"Em, well, you see I'm sort of… I'm, I'm actually outside your apartment."

"What???!"

4

"I'm in the car park. Sorry, Daisy. I can come back later if now doesn't suit…"

Daisy raced to the window. She couldn't see any desperado loners lurking about, and as usual the quiet suburban apartment block was as silent as a graveyard. Everyone else in the world was at work after all.

Or on holiday.

"Very funny. You really had me there, Mr America. I am actually standing here like a prat, looking out of my window for you. Good one."

"I know you are. I can see you. You're wearing what looks like a huge red, fuzzy blanket. Look over here. I'm in the yellow car."

Daisy gulped. Was he serious? A canary-coloured Mini Cooper convertible shone boldly like a beacon among the scattered vehicles in the cobbled Stranmillis car park. It had to be his.

Small, brassy and as gay as Christmas.

A long arm waved out of the driver's side window, which even from a height and through pouring rain was noticeably perma-tanned and laden with bling.

"I don't believe it! When did you get home? Come on, come on up quickly."

"You're a darling, Daisy Anderson," said Eddie with new rigour. "I'll be with you in two shakes and all will be revealed."

Daisy flicked the switch on the kettle and then immediately changed her mind. This wasn't a tea or coffee moment. This was an occasion. It wasn't every day an old friend like Eddie turned up unexpectedly like this. She would treat him to a slap-up brunch at Deane's Brasserie and pretend she was as lively and sophisticated as the place itself. Plus, she once snogged one of the waiters and she wouldn't mind another glimpse of him while she was there.

She quickly grabbed a bottle of sparkling white wine from the fridge and set out two of her finest champagne flutes – her only champagne flutes, and uncorked the bottle with a feeling of teenage rebellion.

5

Fumbling through her own and then Lorna's CD collection, she quickly settled on a George Michael compilation. That should make him feel at home, she thought, congratulating herself at how considerate she'd become in her late twenties.

The doorbell finally buzzed and Daisy ran towards it, laden with celebratory drinks to welcome her childhood neighbour into her humble abode.

"Come in if you're good looking," she shouted into the intercom and sat the drinks on the phone table. She then bounded towards the doorway and wrapped her arms and legs around Eddie's muscular frame as soon as he crossed the threshold.

"You *have* been working out, my boy. What an unbelievable hunk!" She smothered his cheek in kisses knowing it would turn his guts. "And a *real* Californian tan to match. Yum."

Eddie almost buckled under Daisy's tight grasp and lifted a glass of wine from behind her back.

"You could at least have got dressed," he said jokingly in a transatlantic drone. "You weren't going to go on holiday like that, were you?"

Daisy let go of Eddie's brown neck and took a gulp of her wine. She tugged him eagerly by his snow-white t-shirt into her living room before answering.

"Actually, I *was* due to fly out to Salou today for a week in the sun with my room-mate Lorna, but then the damn holiday company went bust at the last-minute and now…"

"I know."

"Oh, "she said. "Duh, I suppose the sullen suitcase is a bit of a give-away…"

Eddie sat down and flicked through a glossy magazine before eventually meeting Daisy's eye.

"No, I know about your holiday plans falling apart."

"How?"

"It's a long story."

"I have all day. It's not like I have a plane to catch or anything."

6

Daisy curled her feet underneath her and watched as Eddie flung the magazine into a chrome rack by the television and braced himself.

"Well, you see…" He cleared his throat, as Daisy thought, for added effect. He never could tell a story and get straight to the point.

"I *see*…," nodded Daisy.

"It's…well, it's my Mum," he said, avoiding her eye. "By the way, what *is* this wine? It's quite good."

"It's white and cold, that's all I know. What about your mum? Don't tell me it's…"

Eddie took his time to answer and drained back the dregs of his glass like he was swallowing nails.

"It's come back, Daisy," he murmured, and stared out of the window onto the roof of the opposite apartment block. "The cancer's back."

Now it was her turn to sigh. She felt her heart hit the floor, bounce back up into her mouth, then settle to form a huge lump in her throat.

"Oh, Eddie, I am so, so sorry. I didn't know. When?" Daisy moved towards her friend and draped her arm around his shoulder. He smelled flowery and fresh. Not manly in the slightest, but nice and clean all the same.

"She's riddled with the bastard. I just found out yesterday. She, er, she doesn't have very long."

Daisy watched Eddie's eyes fill up with tears and she felt the same overwhelming urge to comfort and protect him as she did when they were at high school and the other kids taunted him for his feminine ways. She hugged him tightly, letting his hot tears fall onto her face, his sun-bleached hair brushing softly against her cheek.

"Is she at home?" asked Daisy when his gentle sobbing subsided.

"Yes. She's at home for the rest of her time, whatever that means. We wouldn't have it any other way and your mum has agreed to

7

help nurse her through it. She told me about your non-holiday."

Eddie fought within him to hold back tears.

"This is awful," said Daisy. "Were you still in America when you found out?"

He shook his head.

"Well, it's was a bit of a fluke, really," he said. "I wanted to surprise our Jonathan for his birthday and got a great last-minute deal on a flight home yesterday, but instead I arrived, full of *Happy Birthdays*, only to hear the worst news possible."

Daisy retraced the events of the past few days. She had been so wrapped up in her own self pity that she just about managed to text her own mother the day before to inform her of her ruined holiday after the holiday company had crashed at the eleventh hour. If she'd bothered to phone home more often she would have known all about this and would have raced there straight away, instead of worrying about a lack of warm water or a range of wasted bikinis and flip-flops with the labels still on them.

"Is there anything I can do?" asked Daisy, ditching the empty champagne flutes into the sink and pouring two goldfish bowl-sized glasses of wine instead. She hated that silly question used so often in such horrible circumstances. What would be the perfect answer? Find a cure for cancer?

"Actually, yes. There *is* something you can do," said Eddie, taking another gulp of wine. "You see, Daisy, that's why I'm here."

"It is? Oh, great." She'd walk over hot coals right now if it meant easing Eddie's pain.

"But you haven't heard what it is yet."

Daisy slung an arm around Eddie and rested her head on his broad shoulder.

"I said I'll do *anything*. Even help Jon, if need be, and you know how much I can't stand your big brother. No offense."

Eddie threw up his eyes in disbelief. "Yeah, yeah. Well, you know the way I've never actually got around to telling Mum of my, er, of my…you know."

8

"That you're gay? You *still* haven't told your mum you're gay? Oh, come on, Eddie! I thought you told her ages ago…"

Daisy bounced away from his side and Eddie stared back, his faced stern with determination.

"No. I haven't told her and I won't tell her. Ever. She has enough on her plate."

Daisy felt an urge to shake him but felt sorry for him at the same time.

"Christ, Eddie. I don't bloody well believe this. It's who you are. You can't deny it forever and let's face it, you're as camp as a row of tents and all that. I mean, it's so bloody obvious." Daisy heard her voice raise a notch in disbelief. "She's bound to know. You should be honest with her. Tell her the truth. We're almost twenty-seven and not getting any younger, unfortunately."

Eddie pursed his lips and looked again out of the window.

"OK, so that's not going to happen," continued Daisy in an uncharacteristic flap. "Tell me then. Where do I come into the equation? Do you want *me* to tell her the truth? I thought I'd quit being your minder years ago. *Oh, hello Isobel. Long time no see. I just called to say that your youngest son has decided to come out of a very cobwebbed closet.*"

Eddie looked directly into Daisy's eyes. "Don't be like that. I just want you to come home with me for a few days, that's all, and…"

"Oh." Daisy retracted and sat down. She felt guilty now. "I'm so sorry. Is that *it*? Of course I'll come home with you. It's about time I bit the bullet and spent a few days in Killshannon and if it helps you get through all of this…"

Eddie looked stunned and it dawned on Daisy that she was missing a vital component of his plans.

"There was an '*and*' in there, wasn't there?"

He nodded slowly.

"So what else would I have to do?" She sat up straight in her chair, poised and ready to take the challenge.

"Well, it's just… You see, I told Mum…" Eddie looked away

again.

"Go on..."

"Well, I sort of told Mum I had a *girlfriend*."

"You what?"

Eddie knew he had only one chance at selling this fantastic, but crazy idea to Daisy so he just spat the rest of it out.

"...and she was delighted. Over the moon. In fact, it made her day. It made the rest of her life, to be honest. Daisy, I told her that *you...* are my girlfriend."

Daisy's mouth fell open. She couldn't speak. She should be in Spain now, but instead she was here in Belfast listening to the most ridiculous thing she'd ever heard. She didn't know whether to laugh or cry. She should be on the beach drinking sangria with Lorna and eyeing up gorgeous lifeguards and meeting ugly sea creatures face to face under water. Not putting on a façade for her gay friend and his poor dying mother.

"And...," said Eddie, quickening the pace of his speech into a wild gallop. "I sort of told her, that we were... that I was going to ask you to marry me."

Daisy sunk into the sofa and stared dizzily at the blond bombshell in front of her, whose eyes were shut tightly in preparation for her response.

"Oh, this is *crazy*. Get me another glass of wine, you absolute shit," she said through clenched teeth.

"Anything you say, Daisy. I swear. If you do this for me I'll be your slave forever."

Eddie fumbled around the tiny kitchen until he found the fridge and then glugged some more wine into Daisy's glass.

"You see," he continued as Daisy stared at the floor. "Mum really wants me and Jonathan to each settle down with a wife and children and it would make her so happy if she thought I was at least going in the right direction."

Daisy tried her best to let Eddie's crazy notion sink in. She'd imagined being asked to accompany himself and his mother on a

10

luxurious weekend at a health spa, or asked to take her swimming with dolphins, or go skydiving just so he could try it out himself, but this? This was downright mental. Could they really pull it off?

Her own mum would be admitted to a nearby clinic with shock. And Lorna would think she'd finally lost her marbles, with no hope of ever retrieving them. As for Jonathan? Well, his reaction could go any which way but it wouldn't be pretty. It would look like she was deliberately driving that final nail into the coffin of their dead and buried relationship.

Eddie paced the apartment's shiny floor in anticipation of Daisy's response. She sat there in silence, her face twitching in thought, so obviously weighing up the pros, if there were any, and cons of the situation. Anything was better than an outright no, he supposed.

"Well?" he asked eventually. "It's quite simple really, isn't it? You are a trained actress after all.'

"Simple? Is it now, Einstein? For your information I gave up acting two months ago in order to enter the real world and sell shoes so I can pay my bills. It's about time you stood on planet Earth yourself."

Eddie wasn't listening. "So, so simple," he said. "And from what I can see, you're all packed and ready to go. Say something, Daisy. Say yes."

Daisy smirked back at him and her suitcase caught her eye from the hallway. It was smirking too. She stuck out her tongue at it.

Minus the bikinis and plus a few woolly jumpers, she *was* just about ready to go. Somehow, she didn't think she'd have any need for skimpy swimwear in the back end of Donegal.

"I must be crazy. I must be stark-raving mental to even contemplate this…"

"You beauty! I knew you would. I just knew it…"

"Just for one week, though. After that, we're finished. Split up. Over forever. Deal?" she said in a muffled voice as Eddie hugged her with delight on the sofa.

"Deal!" said Eddie. "I'll make it up to you. I'll take you on a super-duper holiday, all expenses paid…"

"Now you're talking."

"And shopping! I'll take you shopping till you drop."

"I hate shopping."

"That's right. No shopping then. Eating then. Lots of eating out, every single night for as long as you want."

The grin on Eddie's face would have made anyone smile.

But Daisy didn't smile. She burst into hysterical laughter at the thought of the sheer madness she was about to allow into her life. Going home to village life in Donegal as the girlfriend of a man that everyone, apart from his mother, knew was gay. Facing sniggers from nosy neighbours and country cousins who had never ventured out of their comfortable village boundaries. Had she totally lost the plot?

Sod it. It would be fun, if nothing else. It wasn't as if she lived there anymore, and her mother would understand. She would have to tell her the truth from the outset, of course.

"Can I just make one teeny *weeny* suggestion?"

"OMG, what is it now?"

"That, er, red thing you're wearing…"

"Yes? It's my favourite dressing gown. I'm going to change out of it now, don't worry. Why?

Eddie fingered the bally, fleecy texture of the robe and then let go in mock disgust.

"It's just that, I don't think there's too much room left in your suitcase for it," he said. "And my hired car *is* very small. You're just going to have to leave it behind."

Daisy sashayed along the narrow corridor and back towards him, swinging the fabric so that it brushed across his designer stubble.

"Christ, you're naked underneath!" squealed Eddie. "Don't do that! Get dressed!"

"I could turn you yet, my boy," said Daisy, raising an eyebrow

12

seductively.

"Never," he shouted, covering his whole face with his hands.

Daisy leaned over, lifted his chin with her finger and looked right into his eyes.

"Remember, sunshine. In this relationship, *I* wear the trousers. *Me*. Not you. So no more bossiness or slagging out of you, OK? Got it?"

Eddie playfully got down on his knees and hugged Daisy's legs tight.

"Got it. Totally."

"Now what were you saying about my dressing gown?"

"The dressing gown comes to Killshannon. Long live the dressing gown. I'd wear it myself if you asked, and I will love you forever and ever more."

"A week," she said, unclasping his arms from around her calves. "I'll pretend to love you for a week. And then we're finished. Forever. In the meantime, get up off that sofa. You're coming with me to Deane's for dinner. It's not every day my best friend comes to town."

Chapter 2

You Can't Bury Love...

If this were a movie, there would be slow, pulsating, romantic music playing softly in the background, thought Jonathan Eastwood as he watched his best friend Christian Devine wave off the love of his life at the terminal of George Best Belfast City Airport. *Yes, a big, soppy love song that would tear the heart from a stone should be belting out over the sound system right now.*

Nobody else seemed to notice Christian's torment and Jonathan found it so out of character that he didn't know whether to laugh or cry for his buddy.

Holiday-makers brushed and pushed past them, the smell of stale tobacco mixed with sun-tan lotion and a hazy mixture of different perfumes and colognes filled the stuffy June air.

"She'll turn around," said Jonathan, knowing what Christian was hoping for.

They waited for Anna to turn around and blow Christian a last farewell kiss as she reached the boarding gate. They watched closely, Jonathan hoping now as desperately as his friend was, as her dark curly hair bobbed further and further into the distance. Even a quick wave would do, but an air kiss would be spot on.

"Let's go, mate," said Jonathan. "Come on. We'll go."

"God, I am missing her already," whispered Christian. "How is this possible? You guys are right. I am turning into a sop."

"She isn't going to turn around," said Jonathan. "She's gone."

They walked away and Christian continued to mumble, craning his neck so he wouldn't miss it when she turned to wave one last goodbye.

But she didn't wave. Or blow a kiss.

Anna Harrison disappeared out of his life as quickly and as easily as she had come into it eight weeks ago. Now she was gone for six whole months without the blink of an eye or the shed of a solitary tear.

What a bitch.

What a totally gorgeous, funny, intelligent, bitch she was.

Two months was as good as a lifelong commitment in the Christian Devine relationship record books, and after all his good behaviour and fine efforts, he hadn't even been granted a last glance before she'd boarded the plane to Copenhagen. She wouldn't be home for six months at least.

"What goes around comes around," sniggered Jonathan Eastwood later that evening as the two friends jointly drowned their sorrows at The Chocolate Bar in Donegal. "And one thing's for sure, Mr Devine, you have certainly *come* around this town in style."

The Chocolate Bar was Donegal's latest effort at keeping up with tourists' demands and it was a far cry from the traditional smoky village pubs the boys had been brought up beside. The smell of fresh leather and alcohol gave an enticing mix, and a delicious waft of fried steak and onions spilled from the grill bar. Here in the midst of all the after-work revellers, Christian sat miserably, demented as to how he was to fill the next six months until Anna came home.

Jonathan was demented too. How was he going to listen to Christian for six more minutes, never mind six months?

"How can you say that? You know I'm mad about Anna," said

15

Christian in disgust, almost choking on his pint.

"Ha!" spat Jonathan. "Just because you have suddenly decided to ditch the Casanova lifestyle, doesn't mean the first woman you're serious about should fall hopelessly at your feet."

Christian mulled over this comment. It was always going to be the same between him and Jonathan. It always reverted back to the stupid High School dance story.

What goes around comes around. Jonathan had told him that back then and now he was finally enjoying Christian's pain.

"I cannot believe you are still living so much in the past, Jon." There, thought Christian. He'd said it. This would open a crazy can of worms. "It's about time you got over that rubbish. We were kids for goodness sake."

Jonathan ignored his friend. He wasn't in the mood for a row.

"I was talking about how you've wined, dined and done whatever else to every woman you set your lusting eyes on, then left them hanging out to dry while you moved on to your next conquest. Now that Anna isn't playing ball and has left you for six months, you don't know what to do with yourself. The tables have turned, like I always said they would."

Christian twisted a beer mat into a cone shape. He would kill now to be able to light up a cigarette. He was stressed out and upset, for God's sake. He needed a smoke.

"Fair enough. I get your point. It's just, when the shoe is on the other foot, it's not so easy to deal with. And I know how much you are enjoying your little 'I told you so' moment. But she didn't even look back. Surely if she cared, she would have looked back. I read somewhere that if someone doesn't look back after a goodbye, they don't really give a toss."

Jonathan wondered how long this anguish would last with Christian. Probably another day or two, and then the weekend would come and he'd be out on the prowl again. Christian *had* changed though. He had changed a lot over the past few months since he'd met Anna Harrison in this very same bar in Donegal town. Maybe he was being too harsh on his friend.

"Tell me this, Christian," he said gently, trying to reach some closure on the subject. "If you'd known from the start that Anna was planning on jetting off for six months, would you still have continued seeing her for so long?"

Christian took an imaginary puff from his rolled-up beer mat. Part of his on-off smoking habit was purely psychological and surprisingly this was working a treat. Maybe he should invest in one of those electronic fake cigarettes. Or maybe not. They looked a bit geeky. Christian Devine didn't do geeky.

"Yes. Absolutely, I would!"

"There you go."

"What?"

Jonathan was going to allow the moping a maximum of ten more minutes' airtime and then he was going to talk about horse racing or darts or cricket. Anything to take Christian's mind off his newfound heartbreak.

"Anna only dropped this bombshell on you last week. Maybe she was afraid to tell you earlier in case you backed off on her. She'll be home in no time. So, stick it out, Christian. Keep yourself busy. Play squash. Go to bingo."

"Yeah, right."

"Learn how to play the guitar. Or the spoons. There are lots of things you can do to put the time in until Anna comes home."

"Yeah. Lots of things. You're right, Jonathan. I knew you'd cheer me up. That bingo idea has definitely got me excited already."

Jonathan nudged Christian's arm so that he spilled some of his drink.

"You know what I mean. There is one thing I bet you *can't* do till she comes home, though."

"Oh, no way. Not another bet," laughed Christian. "You always lose at this! Haven't you learned your sorry lesson by now?"

Jonathan *had* learned the hard way, but he couldn't resist throwing this little challenge onto his friend's lap. This was a cert. A real winner for him.

"I bet...are you ready?"

"Go for it."

"Nah, it doesn't matter. You're right, I always lose..."

"You started so you'll finish. Place your bet. Go on."

"OK, then." Jonathan pulled his bar stool closer to the table. "I bet you a hundred euros that you can't stay faithful to Anna until she comes home."

Christian went to protest but Jonathan continued.

"Ah-ah! Six long months. Twenty-four weeks. One hundred and eighty-something days without a leg over. Can you do it, Christian? Can you?"

Christian slammed his empty glass on the table and took another puff on his imaginary cigarette. He would rise to this challenge, not that it would be a challenge at all. He really liked Anna. He definitely did and he would wait until she came home, just like he'd told her at the airport, even though she hadn't heard him.

"Not even a problem, my friend. The bet is on. Now, I do believe it's your round. I'm going outside for a well-deserved cigarette. I'm already four hours into my task, with a hundred percent success rate so far. A walk in the park."

Jonathan laughed and made his way to the bar. No doubt Christian would spot a few eligible ladies on his way. He'd be twiddling his thumbs, fidgeting with his cigarette and eyeing up every woman who walked past the pub. It was summertime now, and that meant tourists. Lots and lots of tourists from all over the world would descend on Donegal town and its surrounding seaside villages over the next few weeks. With the slightest glimpse of sunshine, girls would strip down to short skirts and tight tops and the heat would bring out an overpowering lust from Irish men. If Christian thought he would escape all of this, he was kidding himself.

"Two pints of the black stuff please, Gerry," said Jonathan with a smug smile. This was going to be so easy.

"Coming up," said Gerry, the barman whose family was from the same fishing village; a place where everyone knew everyone else's business at broadband speed. At almost fifty-two years old, Gerry O'Donnell had a quick way with words and a slick eye for business. He had transformed The Chocolate Bar into a haven for young executives who had grown tired of the clubbing scene. "Tell me this, how's your mum? I just heard the news."

"Not so good, Gerry. Not so good at all."

Gerry tutted and shook his head. "You boys have had a tough time over the years. Your dad would be very proud of you both."

"Yeah, he would," said Jonathan. His enthusiasm over his bet with Christian now seemed utterly futile and childish. Cheers, Gerry, he thought. But he knew the man meant well.

"Young Eddie's doing well for himself, too, isn't he? I was speaking to him in here this morning. He's a good-looking lad. The spittin' image of your mum."

Jonathan noticed Gerry's trademark smirk and did a double take.

"Eddie was in here this morning? I didn't know that," he said with a frown. Killshannon was a good forty-minute drive from Donegal town.

Gerry wondered whether he had said the wrong thing. There was something edgy about Jonathan, and Eddie had been in the same sort of mood earlier.

"Em, he just mentioned that he was off to Belfast to pick up his girlfriend?"

Jonathan did a double take.

"His *girlfriend*? Are you sure it was our Eddie?"

"Of course I'm sure. He was telling me all about San Francisco, about coming home for your birthday and your mother's terrible news with the big C. Then he said he was off to Belfast to pick up his girlfriend. Funny, that, eh?" Gerry tittered to himself and wiped the shiny counter with a damp cloth. "I always got the impression that young Ed preferred the boys."

19

Jonathan paid for the drinks and nodded in acknowledgement to Gerry the know-it-all-and-the-price-of-it barman. He must have got it wrong. Eddie was here today on his way to Belfast? To pick up a woman? Belfast wasn't exactly around the corner. Eddie wasn't exactly straight. This was strange and Jonathan couldn't wait to find out what was going on.

He made his way over to Christian, who was now seated back at the table, full of energy, following his nicotine fix and drumming his fingers in anticipation of another pint.

"It's so great to be off work for eight whole weeks," said Christian, eyeing up the drinks. "A teacher's life is for me. And you can set that pint down in front of me whenever you're ready. My mouth is as dry as the Sahara."

"Christian. There's something really weird going on here."

"My God, I was just trying to be more positive. A bit of fresh air around my lungs mixed with a bit of nicotine has given me a new lease of life. I thought you'd be delighted."

"I'm not talking about you. It's Eddie."

Christian could normally read Jonathan's facial expressions like a book. Better than a book, sometimes, despite both of them being English teachers at the same high school. This time, however, he was baffled. He didn't know whether to expect good news or bad news, such was the confusion on Jonathan's face.

"What about Eddie? I was talking to him yesterday and he seemed fine to me. Bronzed, blond and still walking like a girl. What's up?"

"According to Gerry, he's gone to Belfast to pick up his, wait for it...*girlfriend*?"

Christian spurted a mouthful of Guinness around himself in shock.

"Jesus Jonathan, as if Eddie has a woman! He's as gay as a maypole!"

Jonathan sipped his pint and then licked the creamy white froth from his upper lip. Christian was right. None of it added up.

20

He'd have to phone Eddie and find out what he was playing at.

"Maybe it's just a friend. A female friend, as opposed to a girl-friend, eh?" he said hopefully.

"I suppose. Most of his friends *are* fag hags," agreed Christian. "It's probably some American chick who wants to use his visit over here as an excuse for a free holiday. It almost happened to me when I first came home from Australia. You think you're escaping from the place and the next minute everyone and their granny wants to follow you here to trace imaginary Irish roots that probably went down with the Titanic."

Jonathan nodded. That sounded likely enough. But it was hardly good timing for an influx of extras around the Eastwood kitchen table, though.

"Nah, I'd doubt it. Eddie's way too gutted over Mum's bad news. If he'd invited a guest from the States, he would have cancelled once he heard Mum's news. I'm sure Gerry's made a mistake."

"Probably."

They supped their pints in a comfortable silence. The subject was closed. Jonathan tried desperately to think of a soccer conundrum to throw Christian's way. It was the perfect conversation stirrer after the third pint. Then he remembered his bet.

"So, any word from Anna, then?"

Christian sat his glass down on the table and raised an eyebrow.

"Very funny. She wouldn't even have arrived yet, you smart-ass. So much for trying to take my mind off her. It did work for a while. Good one with the Eddie story. I fell for it hook, line and sinker. Eddie with a girlfriend. As if!"

"No, no, I was serious about that. It's what Gerry told me. I swear."

"Gerry's a liar. He makes up stories to make his life sound more exotic than it really is. He once told me that this place used to be a secret brothel in the seventies and that's where he met his ex-wife. I mean, a brothel in Donegal? Gerry with a wife? Now if you believe that, you'd believe anything," said Christian with a smug grin.

Jonathan squinted and looked at his friend for a second. Then he leaned forward and whispered.

"That *was* true, actually. Da told me that a few weeks before he died. Gerry's wife was a Spanish prostitute and he met her here in 1977. They have a daughter too."

"Swear!"

Jonathan held up his hand. "On my life."

Christian stared back at him in disbelief. Gerry had a wife? And this place used to be an illegal whorehouse? He didn't think he could handle any more excitement in one day.

"Cheers," said Jonathan with a smile, raising his glass. "To Gerry, the liar, who seems to tell the truth after all?"

Christian shook his head. This was turning into an eventful day. If every day was to be like this, the six months till Anna came home would go by in a flash.

"And to that old dark horse, Eddie," he said, clinking his pint with his friend's. "Cheers to the bold Eddie who, despite all the rumours and all his absolutely fabulous ways, has gone and bagged himself a woman!"

Chapter 3

Girls Rush In Where Women Fear to Tread

"So how do you find modern day Killshannon compared to the bright lights of California, Eddie?" roared Daisy over the drone of the car's vibrating engine. Eddie had insisted on getting his money's worth from the hire company by pushing the convertible car roof back at every given opportunity, even in gale-force winds. "Is it much different to before?"

"Much the same, I'd say," he shouted back. "Not as smelly, though, thank goodness."

"It's the weather! Wait till it warms up a bit and we'll all be holding our noses again."

Daisy pressed the button to put the roof back on. There was a time and a place to pose in a convertible, and now wasn't it. Her hair resembled a garden hedge and her nipples were almost touching the dashboard with the cold. The car was so small that her knees were almost at her ears, and not in a good way.

"Not that I go back to Killshannon so often now," she said, thankful for a bit of warm air around her face from the car heater. "Nothing to do with the smell of fish, though."

"Why don't you?" asked Eddie. "Doesn't your mum make you? I know mine would if I lived anywhere in this country."

Daisy fell silent and Eddie waffled on quickly.

"Jonathan thinks he's doing well having escaped to Donegal Town, but he still has to show his face at least once a week, and always turns up for Mass and Sunday dinner, hangover or no hangover."

Daisy turned up the radio when she heard the sounds of Snow Patrol's latest song. Plus, she didn't want to hear about Jonathan. Not yet.

"Mum comes to stay with me quite a lot in Belfast," she said, to divert the conversation. "She loves Stranmillis because it's like a little village within the city, and then we go for long walks along the river, into Cutter's Wharf for a glass of wine and make a full Sunday lunch in my apartment, just like the old days at home."

Leaning her head back, she closed her eyes and drifted back to those childhood Sundays when she and her brother had played out in the back garden with Jonathan and Eddie until they'd been called in for dinner. Jonathan had always thrown spiders down her good dress. Every bloody week. Even then he had been a pervy bastard. She sat up straight in the seat of the car and unstuck her legs from the leather upholstery. That was the end of that blissful memory.

"So what's Jonathan up to these days?" she asked in a slightly sour tone. "I ask out of polite, mature conversation, not out of interest."

"What do you care about how Jonathan is or what he's up to?" Eddie replied with a casual smirk and changed the Mini into fifth gear as they approached the straight road into Donegal town.

"I don't really give a shit, actually. Don't tell me anything about him. I don't want to know *anything*."

Daisy turned her head against the window and watched the green fields race by. She hadn't been home in three months – since her brother Richard's wedding. On that particular occasion she'd been sure to make a swift exit as soon as the toasts were over.

"Does he have a girlfriend?"

"Who?"

"Jack the flippin' Ripper. Who do you think? *Jonathan*."

"Nah. Not that I know of. At least I hope he doesn't."

Good, thought Daisy.

"He has a wife, though."

"Piss off, a what? A wife?"

Eddie sat up straight and kept a forward gaze, his mouth pursed into a pout. This was fun. Then he gave in.

"Not exactly," he said. Daisy raised a fist playfully. "No, don't hit me when I'm driving! Ow!"

Daisy shook her hand. If she could kill Eddie now she would, for taunting her like this.

"Jonathan doesn't have a girlfriend, Daisy. He has a fiancée. *That*, I'm not joking about. But again, what do you care? You never see him anymore."

Daisy's stomach did a cartwheel. It must be the sea air, she thought.

"Since when?"

"Since forever."

"Since when does he have a fiancée? Not, since when do I never see him anymore."

Daisy's reaction told Eddie to break the news gently.

"They got engaged at the weekend. I think they originally planned to announce it on his birthday but brought it forward to give Mum a lift. Didn't your mum say?"

"Actually, no," said Daisy in bewilderment. She felt a sudden pang of hunger. Or was it nausea? "But then I'm supposed to be in Spain, aren't I?"

"Mmm," said Eddie, waiting on her to prompt for more.

She did.

"Go on…"

"He's getting married in six weeks," he said. "Rushing bull-ignorant into the whole thing if you ask me."

"Oh," said Daisy, her heart sinking unexpectedly. She looked out at the cows in the fields again. Flashes of black and white mixed

25

with green whirred by, and she got a strange sense of longing to turn back the clock to her younger days, when she really hadn't had a care in the world. No men you hate to make your tummy go swishy, no internet holidays that could crash at the last minute, no friends with rich boyfriends when you'd happily settle for a pauper. Well, not quite. Not yet.

"Woooh. Someone's gone all quiet. Don't you want to hear all the gory details about Jonathan's wedding plans?" asked Eddie eventually. Gosh, she was taking this even worse than he'd expected.

"Strangely, that would be a *no*."

"You're on the guest list."

"Like hell I am." Daisy didn't dream it for a second. "Am I really? I don't really think I'd want to be there. Actually, I so don't want to be there."

Eddie decided to quit while he was ahead.

"Sorry that was totally made up. I haven't seen the guest list. In fact they probably haven't even drawn it up yet, but it's all happening so fast."

"Six weeks? Huh, they certainly don't waste any time." Daisy's hunger turned into a dead, sickening feeling. She hadn't thought of Jonathan Eastwood for ages. Well, not in the past six months or so. Occasionally he would pop into her mind as she stared out of the window of Super Shoes onto the hustle and bustle of Cornmarket and she'd shake her head to get his face out of her memory. There was no point wasting time on what could have been.

History was history.

As the yellow Mini zoomed along Donegal's windy, stone-lined walls, Daisy closed her eyes and tried not to imagine Jonathan in a morning suit and his bride in a tight-fitting corset and a full skirt with a tiny waist and big, beautiful doe eyes, looking deeply into his as they shared their first dance.

"I bet she's blond with massive tits," she said, as they turned a sharp corner. Eddie faked a cough and Daisy reached across to turn down the radio again.

"She is, isn't she? I bet she's gorgeous," she said bitterly.

Eddie turned the radio back up.

"Actually … now that you say it, and not that I would normally notice such things, but yes, she is. She is blond and I suppose she is quite well-endowed in the breast department."

He let go of the steering wheel and made a big-boob gesture with his hands. Daisy threw her eyes up towards the heavens, or at least the roof of the car, but the effect was lost.

"I knew it," she said in a higher pitch than she intended.

"Boy, you do have good intuition. I wish I'd inherited that particular feminine quality when God decided to make me gay. She's very intelligent too. A teacher, like Jonathan. A science teacher at St Benedict's."

"Does *she* have a name?" Probably Sophie or Susannah or Samantha, thought Daisy, going by her description so far.

"Shannon."

"I knew it again."

Why was she talking like she'd inhaled a balloon full of helium? She couldn't help it.

"How?"

"I knew she was an 'S'. He always goes for girls with 'S' names. So bloody predictable."

Eddie thought for a minute. Actually, now that he thought about it, Daisy was right. His brother *did* seem to have a thing about girls with names beginning with S.

"Do you remember Sinead from Strabane?" she spat.

"How could I forget?" Eddie laughed out loud at the memory of his mother's face when she caught Jonathan snogging Sinead from Strabane on the new living room sofa with her skinny ankles wrapped around his waist.

"I thought he would never live that down," said Daisy. "Or what about Sarah, the slapper? Do you remember the time you took a garden trowel to her make-up and then rubbed it onto your own face when no one was looking? And when your mother caught

27

you, you said it was for me."

"You wanted some too."

"Just because I wasn't allowed any of my own. I was thirteen, after all. I was supposed to do those things growing up. You, on the other hand…"

"Shut it, girlfriend."

Eddie indicated left at the sign for Killshannon, its lettering almost hidden in the overgrown bushes so that it read 'Kill Shannon'. Daisy hadn't even met Jonathan's girl but she was tempted, for some reason, to do exactly what it said on the tin, or steel, or wood, or whatever the sign was made of.

Kill Shannon. Slowly.

"I'm sure she's lovely," she said, as if she was spitting out nails. "Really lovely."

She managed a faint smile when they drove past the poky, ivy-clad post office of her home village. Rebellious schoolgirls with skirts that could have passed for belts skipped past, celebrating the last day of the term by drawing over each other's polyester shirts with permanent marker. Old Jackie still stood in the shelter waiting for the bus that seldom came, and the smell of freshly baked soda bread smothered the car's interior, making Daisy's stomach growl for some home cooking.

"Right," said Eddie, slowing the car into a crawl and then pulling the handbrake firmly when they finally reached the entrance to Ivy Cottages. "Here we are in the grand old hamlet of Killshannon. We have driven approximately one hundred and thirty miles and hardly shut up the whole way. However we still haven't figured out how to tell people how we miraculously became involved after not seeing each other for four years."

"Three and a half."

"Whatever. You're missing the point."

Eddie was starting to fear his abilities as an actor and was merely seeking reassurance from the more experienced Daisy.

"Oh, so now you're starting to panic, Mr I've-got-a-great

idea-but-haven't-thought-it-through.' Don't start trying to come up with a plan now. We're here and it's too late to stage anything."

Eddie gasped and clasped a tanned hand over his mouth in despair.

"Who or what rattled *your* cage? Don't you dare back out on me now, Daisy." He dramatically ran his fingers through his hair and Daisy was astounded they didn't break off midway in a battle with all the wax and gel.

"I'm just saying, it's way too late. If you hadn't bored me to tears all the way home with tales of your pathetic love triangle with a Hollywood screen writer and his juvenile son, I might have been able to think of something. You snooze, you lose."

Eddie bit his lip. If this backfired he would eventually have to tell his mother the truth, but the only problem was that she didn't believe there was any other meaning to the word 'gay' than 'happy'. It would kill her quicker than the cancer would.

"For the record, the son – Brad was his name – was not a juvenile. He was twenty-one years old," said Eddie with an ever-so-slight American accent.

"Brad. Of course. I should have remembered that one."

"Perfectly legal. So there. And if *I* recall properly, a lot of the conversation was dominated by Jonathan's love life. Not that that you care one tiny bit, of course."

Why was he taunting her like this? If anything he should be complimenting her and trying to win her over. He wasn't doing himself any favours at all.

"Well, anyway," said Daisy, reaching for the door handle. "Thanks for the free ride home. Good to see you again and all that. I'll be over later to see your mother."

"Daisy, don't be like that!"

She stuck her nose in the air, knowing she was acting like a six-year-old. She didn't care. The whole idea was bloody ridiculous anyway.

"I'll just pop across and see *my* Mum, say hi to *your* Mum and

29

then it'll be back to Belfast for me. You come up with some other crazy scheme to convince your poor mother that marriage and babies are on the horizon…"

"But Daisy, we can still do this. Please. I'm begging."

"Maybe sexy Shannon has a sister called Simone or Sorcha who would play along with you. That really *would* be keeping it in the family."

Daisy opened the car door and stormed out, stomping across the cobbled road of her childhood. She then turned on her heels back to the car where Eddie was sitting with his mouth open, catching flies.

"Did, er, did you change your mind, Daisy?"

He reminded himself of Bambi. Pathetic, weak and unable to stand on his own two feet.

"Not a hope," said Daisy, reaching into her car. "I just forgot my bloody shoes."

She slipped on her new pink flip-flops, which felt horrible and squidgy under her feet that were wet from the rain and marched towards her mother's house with an air of vengeance. She could hear the engine running in Eddie's car and the wipers beginning to squeal as the rain subsided. She looked a mess. Her make-up was running, her feet were soaked and she looked rough from the two-hour drive, but she didn't care.

She didn't care one bit how she looked…until she glanced up at the house on the end of the row and saw Jonathan Eastwood staring at her from his old bedroom window as if he'd seen a ghost. Her heart hit the floor. Now she really did care how she looked. A lot.

Chapter 4

Hell Knows No Fury Like A Woman With Runny Make-Up

Even from the steamy windows of the Mini and the giant splodges of rain that bounced, seconds apart on the windscreen, Eddie could see the shock on his brother's face. In the middle of the street, Daisy also stood like a pillar, frozen to the spot.

She couldn't believe he was at home. If only it wasn't raining. If only they had stopped the car up the road to freshen up. Maybe then she could have fixed her hair that had looked so glorious this morning and touched up her make-up. A spray of perfume wouldn't have gone amiss either. She'd kill for a generous spray of the stuff now. She had a massive bottle of it in her suitcase but that wasn't much use. Anyway, it was too late to be thinking of dolling herself up now, she thought. Jonathan had already seen her and there was nothing she could do about it.

With her head spinning, Daisy turned on her heel and marched back towards the car. Eddie turned down the automatic window, fearful as she came bounding towards him, all wild, wet hair and streaky make-up. This wasn't what he'd planned at all.

"You didn't tell me he would be here," she hissed, and without giving him time to answer, she stuck her head straight into Eddie's, and planted the fullest, most passionate kiss right on his lips.

Eddie couldn't breathe. Daisy's lips were like pneumatic tyres, pressing on top of him. He raised his hands for mercy, but like a woman possessed, she grabbed his wrists and clasped them round her neck, twisting and turning her face as if in the throes of passion. All of her best drama school workshops were being put to the test now. In her mind she was kissing Johnny Depp, but sadly, in reality, she was stuck to the face of a Graham Norton wannabe. She opened one eye and tried to sneak a peek up at the window to see if Jonathan was still there.

The firm tap of her damp shoulder confirmed he wasn't.

"Am I seeing things? What on earth is going on here?" asked Jonathan in disgust.

"What does it look like?" Daisy stood up straight and tucked a strand of wet hair behind her ear. Inside she was shaking. Could she really pull off this ridiculous stunt? Jonathan looked more handsome than she could ever remember. She couldn't believe she was face to face with him after all these years. Snap out of it, Daisy, she chided herself. The past was in the past now.

"Daisy and I are engaged to be married," piped Eddie from the driver's seat of the car, now able to breathe again.

"No, we are *not*," said Daisy, pushing Eddie's head back into the car and enjoying the look of sheer confusion written all over Jonathan's perfect face. "Not *yet*, I mean. I still have to pick my ring, don't I, honey?"

She opened the car door and Eddie stiffly climbed out, his legs about to sing with joy after being cramped up to his chest for nearly two hours.

"So this is the *girlfriend* you left to collect this morning? *Daisy* is your girlfriend?" Jonathan looked into his brother's eyes and Eddie saw a bewilderment he had never seen before. At least he seemed to be buying their happy-couple story, though. That was a great sign. After all, if they could convince Jonathan that he and Daisy were a couple, then telling his ailing mum would be a doddle.

"Fiancée, Jonathan. We plan to announce our engagement later

32

in the week." Eddie was so confident now that he had almost convinced himself he was a future groom. All he needed now was a deep voice that Sean Connery would be proud of.

Jonathan glanced at Daisy, who was nodding profusely.

"Friday, actually. We'll be announcing it on Friday," she said. She was beginning to enjoy this in an odd sort of way. Although, perhaps just seeing Jonathan again was making her delusional.

Eddie threw his arm around Daisy's shoulders and crossed his ankles but Daisy gave him an indiscreet nudge so he stood up straight, flicked his golden hair and flashed his bleached white teeth in a bid to show he really was in the flushes of true love.

"Aren't you going to say anything, Jonathan? I squealed with delight when you and Shannon got engaged. You could at least say *something*."

"Actually, Ed, there's quite a lot I could say right now to both of you, but I think I'll bite my tongue."

Daisy felt like she'd eaten a whole pack of Skittles. She hadn't felt such a rush of energy since she thought she spotted Vanessa Feltz in a pet shop in Monaghan last November. At the time she'd only gone in to treat her flatmate Lorna to a new tarantula.

"Ah, Jonathan. It's not like you to be so shy," she said, ever so sweetly, even though her heart was thumping.

Jonathan looked at the unlikely twosome and was stunned at how his brother could be so flippant and selfish. Eddie only knew half the truth of Jonathan's torrid history with Daisy, but he knew how long he'd taken to get over her. It was cruel to bring her back into their lives again, and back into their family. A tidal wave of emotions raced through his veins. Guilt, anger, hurt, memories. Memories he would rather forget. Eddie was playing some sort of stupid game and he wouldn't stand for it.

"Actually I have just thought of a word to sum all this up…'

"Go on, then," said Eddie with an edgy smile. "What is it? Congratulations?"

"No. Bullshit," whispered Jonathan. "That's what I think.

33

Bull fuckin' shit. This has got to be a big fat joke." He sauntered away, back through the shiny red door of his mother's house, with his hands stuffed in his pockets and his head hung low.

Eddie and Daisy stood together in silence, watching as Jonathan entered the cottage and closed the heavy door with a thud, so hard that Daisy was sure the whole house shook. She gripped her arm tighter around Eddie's waist and leaned her head under his arm, wondering how she'd let herself get into such a state. It was amazing how long you could avoid meeting someone if you really wanted to. You never really forgot your first love, did you? Or was it first hate? First heartache? Was there a difference?

"Well, that was an all-round success," she said. "Our little plan got off to a fine start. Not. Eddie, this is all a bit too much. Are you up to something else? Something you are not telling me?"

She wiped the rain from her face with a tissue and looked down in horror at the mess it made. It was black from the mascara that had dripped onto her cheeks. Great.

"Don't worry about Jonathan, Daisy," said Eddie. "He's just really uptight lately with Mum's bad news, and to tell you the truth, Shannon is piling on the pressure by insisting they bring the wedding forward even more in case the inevitable happens. Poor Jonathan can't even think that far ahead. Getting married is the least of his worries at the minute."

"I can imagine." Daisy leaned against the bonnet of the car. It was drenched but then, so was she. "Gosh, I wish I hadn't given him such a hard time. Both of you must be going through hell right now. I'm so selfish."

Eddie nodded and kicked an invisible stone across the street. His eyes had started to fill up again and he bit his lip hard, then stretched his arms high above his head to fight back the tears.

"He'll be fine. We'll all be fine," he whispered.

"Listen," said Daisy. "Why don't you go in and have a chat with him, and I'll go and see my mum. She'll get the shock of her life when she sees me on the doorstep, what with me looking so gorgeous and all that. And I'll call over to see your mum later, when the coast is clear. We can give an Oscar-winning performance then. I'll even practise snogging on the back of my hand. It's been a long time for me, you know."

Eddie laughed and gave Daisy a quick peck on the cheek. There was no way he was risking another snog-a-thon. "Good idea. I think I've quite a bit of work to do to convince my big brother. Anyway, Mum will be so delighted to see you."

"Well, I'll see you later then. Give your mum my best wishes. I always did love Isobel. And good luck."

"I think I'll need it," he sighed, giving her another hug just in case Jonathan was still peering out at them from somewhere. "My confidence in my acting skills has taken a bit of a dent after the hisses and boos of the first audience. The next scene will have to be straight out of a Hollywood blockbuster."

Daisy smiled. "You bet. Oh, and Eddie?"

"Yes?"

"Maybe we should just tone it down a bit. Don't mention the engagement story. In fact, leave it out entirely from now on if you can. After all, we haven't seen each other in quite a while."

"True, true."

"Emails, phone calls, love letters and now the start of a blossoming relationship between childhood friends. Much, much more convincing. What do you think?"

Eddie flashed a generous grin in agreement. Yes, that sounded much easier.

"You're totally right," he said. "Maybe I was trying too hard to impress Jonathan. I'll tell him the engagement was just a heated moment of excitement between star-crossed lovers. OK, Daisy?"

Eddie walked towards his house and Daisy skipped towards hers. They were both smiling and thinking the same thing. How could they have let their friendship lapse for so long? Of course, they both led totally different lives, in totally different cities, yet the bond they'd formed as children was still as tangible as ever. Only the uncomfortable issue of Jonathan stood between them now, like a hurdle waiting to be jumped over.

"Daisy! Wait a minute. One more question," shouted Eddie, running back to her like a schoolgirl and dodging puddles in case he splashed his Armani jeans.

"What? Remember, Ed. We're supposed to be keeping it simple."

"I know, I know. But I just need to know this one last thing." He drew a breath and flicked his eyelashes upwards. "Have we *done* it yet?"

"Done what?"

"You and me. You know, *it*," he said, gyrating his hips and glancing up and down towards his manhood.

"Oh." Daisy thought carefully "*Oh*. Good question. Yes. Yes, we have. And you can stop that loin-grinding. It's doing nothing for me at all. We made passionate love this morning when you came to see me in Belfast and it was wonderful, remember? Earth-shattering. Raw." Daisy gave an animal roar.

"Pure, animal lust. Yes, that's right, I remember now," laughed Ed. "Mmm…how could I forget? It's just in case Jonathan asks. I need to know what I'm talking about," he said and walked away with a new spring in his step.

"Don't tell your mother that, for goodness sake," said Daisy as the most horrible thought of Isobel imagining them having sex flashed into her mind.

"I won't," promised Eddie and waved his hand in the air. "It's *men* talk after all. I'll have to do a bit of bragging about how far I've got with you. I'll tell him I slipped the hand on you years ago during hide and seek in our bedroom cupboard when he wasn't looking and it all took off from there."

He ran back towards the pillar-box door of his mother's house and inwardly practised manly back-slapping and dirty talk in his head, reminding himself not to get carried away with talk of marriages or engagements.

But, he thought, as he turned the key in the front door, if it meant making his mother happy, he would get married to Daisy in the morning. He would go through it all. Meringue dresses, bridesmaids, tantrums, tiaras and the works. And then they'd be divorced, of course. Very, very soon afterwards, he thought, remembering how annoying Daisy could be when she was drunk. He let out a shiver, stuck out his chest and entered the hallway in a brave attempt to face the music like a man.

Chapter 5

Home Is Where The Hurt Is

Daisy wasn't sure whether to use her front-door key and walk on in unannounced, or knock on the green door of number 9, Ivy Cottages. She lifted the huge brassy doorknob and then set it back down easily so that it didn't make a sound.

Knocking on the front door of her childhood home seemed a bit over the top, but the last thing she needed was her mother collapsing from the unexpected sight of her standing soaked in the hallway. Especially as she bore an uncanny resemblance to the Bride of Frankenstein right now. As she stood on the doorstep collecting her thoughts, she remembered fondly back to the time when she couldn't reach the doorknob herself and would have to shout through the letterbox to announce her arrival home from school. She remembered when her dad would lift her up to let her knock it, even though he had a key. It was still hard coming home, knowing that he was no longer around. Daisy shook herself. She was determined not to get all mopey on this visit. She took a deep breath, knocked on the door twice and then turned the key.

"Mum," she called. "Mum, it's me. Are you in?"

The house smelled fresh and clean, with Maggie's incense hanging in the air. Once a hippy, always a hippy, laughed Daisy

38

and inhaled the familiar scent of her childhood.

"Daisy, is that you love?" Her mother's shrill voice came from the converted second floor of the cottage. Daisy was sure she was hanging upside down from the rafters from the way her voice sounded. "This *is* a pleasant surprise. Is everything OK?"

"Yes, it's me and I'm fine. Where are you? Are you doing hand-stands up there?" asked Daisy, running her hand along the pine dado rail and then wiping the fine layer of dust onto the leg of her wet jeans.

A huge thud came from the first floor and Daisy shuddered.

"Sort of," answered Maggie. "I'll be with you after I finish my mantra. Nearly done."

Yoga. That's right. How could Daisy forget? Her mother had lately developed an inexplicable obsession with Madonna. Anything the pop star could do, Maggie could do better. Daisy had vowed that she would address the issue once and for all if she ever saw her mum sporting a red stringy band around her wrist, bagging a toy boy and snogging women. Yoga was one thing, but changing her religion or messing with her sexuality to keep up with her idol would be taking things a step too far.

"Take your time, Mum. I'm not going anywhere."

Daisy grabbed a towel from the hot press and dried off her sodden hair so that it frizzed up even more. Then she sank into the soft, brown leather armchair that faced out onto the small herb garden. It was like a mini jungle, full of lush countryside greenery, with huge flowered bobbles of pink and baby blue swaying in the light breeze. The patio doors were splashed with summer raindrops and a white metal summer seat sat on the patio waiting for the real summertime to come. Nothing quite beat lazy Sundays for fun-filled barbeques or quiet reads.

Outside, the faint smell of the sea was a reminder that the ocean was near, and when the sun came out, the sound of fishing boats mixed with the scent of flowers in full bloom meant that the family home was a little haven away from the world. The cottage was quieter now that she and her brother, Richard, had flown the nest, but there was still a delightful atmosphere you could almost touch.

Daisy thought of poor Isobel Eastwood, who had helped to plant the garden with her mother many years ago. Isobel had initially sniffed at Maggie's choice of wild, overgrown shrubbery but soldiered on, adding minimal water features and decking.

She and Maggie were still great companions, which was perfectly understandable considering the circumstances that had gelled their friendship. However, two more opposite souls could never have met. While Maggie Anderson owned her own mobile phone, iPod and drove a black Volkswagen Beetle, Isobel Eastwood's dearest accessory was her rosary beads. Jonathan and Eddie's mother's idea of a good night out would probably be a Missionary Mass followed by the Credit Union tea dance.

Despite such vastly differing tastes, the women propped each other up like two bookends and knew exactly when the other needed a time to laugh, a time to grieve or a time to shout out obscenities. But neither friend blamed the other for what happened that warm, tragic July night nearly eight years ago.

The two gardens, separated by a narrow brook, which led into the Atlantic Ocean on the mouth of Donegal's finest fishing port, illustrated their differences perfectly. Isobel's landscaped setting was immaculately groomed, while the Anderson household's colourful blooms reflected the colour and life that bounded from Maggie and Daisy's bubbly personalities.

"Hey, Dad. What do you think of all this?" whispered Daisy to the large portrait of her father that commanded the entire room. "Say a prayer for poor Isobel and her boys, won't you?" Danny Anderson's smiling eyes twinkled back at his daughter from above the high mahogany mantelpiece. Even now, Daisy could still hear his laughter in this very room. His smell still filled the air, diluted ever so slightly by a faint aroma of furniture polish. Very faint. Her mother wasn't exactly known for being a domestic goddess.

But Daisy was sure that if she listened hard enough, she would hear her dad mumbling to himself like he used to when he was trying to work out a cryptic crossword clue.

Could it really be eight years since the accident had happened? She remembered it like it was five minutes ago. She missed her father so much, as if she hadn't seen him in eighty years. So why then had she came back to Killshannon on such a whim? Under normal circumstances, it would have taken a herd of highland cattle to drag her there. Funnily enough, something had urged to her follow Eddie's crazy path back to the village this time. A village where she'd locked away all of her earlier memories, and in her mind, had virtually thrown away the key.

A drama course at Queen's University in Belfast had supposedly been her ticket to freedom and she'd left vowing never to form a bond with Killshannon again. There was too much pain involved. Now, as she daydreamed, she realised her hand was automatically resting on her stomach as the memories flooded back. Her mother's footsteps entering the cosy room interrupted her silent musings.

"Hello, my love," said Maggie in a lively voice, her arms spread-eagled. Her face was make-up free and women ten years younger would have envied her complexion. "This really is a lovely surprise," she added, beaming from ear to ear.

Daisy stopped staring at the painting of her Dad, dragged herself from the depths of the armchair and hugged her mother tight.

"Hi, Mum. How are things in this little neck of the woods?"

"Oh, Daisy, you're damp right through,' she fussed, handing her daughter a second towel. "I was going to phone you this evening. I'm afraid I have bad news about Isobel."

"I know, Mum. I heard. Eddie told me…"

"Have you seen him? The poor boy thought he was coming home for Jonathan's birthday party but walked into all of this. I can't imagine what those poor lads are going through. How was he when you spoke to him?"

Maggie sat down and curled her feet under her legs. Her yoga

41

session had reduced her tension slightly but the shock of Isobel's illness was etched like a scar on her mind.

"Well, he was very emotional at first, but he's come round a bit," said Daisy, munching on a handful of nuts that she'd found in a bowl on the coffee table. She spat them back into her hand when she realised they had been sitting there so long they'd almost grown a beard. "He picked me up in Belfast this morning, so we had a good long chat on the journey here. Jonathan seems in bad form, though."

"Yeah, he is. You do know he got engaged at the weekend."

"I heard." Daisy's head dropped but she shook herself and gave a weak smile.

"That's another piece of news I've been putting off telling you, love. Shannon's her name. I've only seen her once but she seems a nice girl. A little outspoken for Jonathan, but pretty, and they're getting married really soon. I wasn't sure how you'd react. After all, at one stage we all thought it would have been you..." said Maggie shaking her head slightly. She could still remember her daughter posing nervously with Jonathan on the night of her debs ball. "It could have been, you know."

"Anyway, whatever." Daisy felt a childish rant coming on but she couldn't control herself. The reason she had come home wasn't to talk about Jonathan and she'd no intention of doing so. "I'm sure you would rather want to know what brought me *here* when I should be in Spain. Lorna should be with me, but she's not because she's sitting in a jacuzzi drinking posh mineral water and being treated like a princess!"

Maggie considered the subject closed. She reminded herself not to mention Shannon's name again. It was for the best, obviously.

"What a terrible disappointment that your holiday collapsed." Maggie commented to her only daughter. "What's up with you anyway? I hope it's nothing more than a bit of man trouble. I could have come to stay with you for a few days up in Belfast if I'd known you were lonely."

Maggie was delighted at Daisy's unexpected arrival. However she wondered what was behind the surprise visit. She stood up and straightened her yellow t-shirt. It said "The Virgin Tour 1985" across the front.

Daisy made a mental note to hide the Madonna t-shirt or dump it before she went home. She could always recycle it and use it as a polishing rag if she was stuck, although Lorna would die of shock if Daisy suddenly started taking an interest in housework! Her flatmate had a strange fetish for micro-fibre cloths and could spend hours pondering over lotions and potions at the super-market while Daisy headed straight for the pizza aisle or towards the special offers on red wine.

"I think I'll put the kettle on," muttered Maggie. "Sod my detox plans; I have a feeling I'll need a caffeine fix before I hear the end of all your news."

Daisy followed her mother closely through the narrow hallway, chattering non-stop into the cosy kitchen and almost treading on Maggie's heels when she stopped at the fridge to take out some milk.

"Mum," she said, having finally used up all her small talk on the weather and the smell of fish outside. "Does Isobel know that Eddie is gay?"

Maggie swung around and looked her daughter in the eye.

"Of course she does. Well, at least I assume so," she shrugged and poured some milk into a jug. "Yes, of course, she has to know."

Daisy paused. "But he said he's never told her."

"Does he really need to? Isn't it obvious?"

"Mmm," said Daisy. "You have a point. It's just, if she does know, my whole life will be so much easier."

When the kettle finally whistled, Maggie made two cappuccinos and sat them on the chequered table. Daisy scraped her chair along the floor and sat down, hugging the cup in her hands. Please let Isobel know the score, she prayed to herself. Please, please let all this monkey business be totally unnecessary.

"Well, it's hardly something we've ever sat down and discussed," said Maggie, wondering where on earth all of this could be leading. "Isobel, as you know, would hardly speak of such things, so she has never really said so. However even a blind man could see that Eddie is gay. Since he was a child, his destiny has been so unbelievably obvious. His passion for Barbie dolls, *clothed* Barbie dolls, gave the game away when he was about ten years old."

"But she hasn't actually *said* it, has she? Has she even hinted?"

"How do you mean?"

"Like, does she ever mention how Eddie is living in the gay capital of the world, or that he perhaps has a very special friend called Brad, or that he has shirts in multiple shades of pink, as well as posters of his icon, Ellen DeGeneres, on his wall, just beside his altar to Cher?"

Maggie thought for a few seconds while dunking a Kit Kat Chunky into her cup of froth.

"No."

"No?"

"I'm afraid not. Anyhow, what's the big deal? I'm sure Isobel *has* realised it by now. But even if she hasn't, what has it got to do with you?"

Daisy fidgeted with the edge of the tablecloth.

"This is going to sound crazy," she said. "Because it *is* crazy. Pure mental, actually."

Her mother frowned. "OK, just spit it out, for crying out loud."

Daisy coughed quietly and shifted in her chair. She could sense her mother's patience was wearing thin.

"Eddie wants me to pretend we're an item."

Maggie seemed startled but then started to laugh.

Daisy ignored her. "Eddie wants me to pretend we're an item so that Isobel's last few months are content in the knowledge that her son's a heterosexual." She paused for breath. "He wants his mother to think he's just a run-of-the-mill lad's lad whose main ambition is to settle down here in Donegal and have two point

44

four children."

There, she'd said it. And it was beginning to sound more stupid every time.

"Wow," said Maggie. She loved that word. It really was so effective when she couldn't think of anything else to say.

"Silly, isn't it? And I'm even worse for agreeing to go along with it," said Daisy.

Maggie opened another Kit Kat and handed half of it across the table.

"I see," she whispered. "And have you thought of Jonathan's feelings at all?"

"Oh, he'll be fine," said Daisy dismissively, licking the melted chocolate from the side of the biscuit in a ritual that mirrored her mother's.

"Will he? Look, don't you think Eddie would be better just to tell Isobel he's gay? I know she's a Holy Joe but she does live in the twenty-first century," Maggie pointed out. This all sounded a bit over the top, ridiculous even. "I'm sure she knows in her heart anyway."

"He just doesn't want to put her under any more stress. It would be nice for her to think that Eddie was planning to follow in his older brother's footsteps...in more ways than one. Oh it doesn't feel right at all."

Daisy couldn't even bring herself to mention Jonathan's name again.

Maggie shrugged her shoulders and sipped her cappuccino, trying to take it all in. Daisy's home visits were normally to escape from work frustration, or to moan about the lack of good men. Pretending to go out with a gay guy she was practically reared alongside was definitely a first.

"Well, I don't really think there's any need for this, Daisy, but if it takes Eddie's mind off the bigger picture, then why not just run with it for his sake? For a while anyway. Isobel didn't come up the river in a bubble. She will know from the outset it's his wee way of coping, so if it makes him feel better, go along with it knowing that the rest of us all know it's as unlikely as…well, it's just not even logical in the first place."

Daisy shrugged and then nodded. "I said I'd give him a week. In the meantime, I'll try to convince him to *come out* with it gracefully, sooner rather than later. He would feel much better for it."

"Good idea. And if all this settles his mind for a short time, it won't do either of you any harm. It's Jonathan I'd be more concerned about. You two haven't been in touch in years."

Maggie thought carefully before she broached the next subject. "By the way, guess who I saw today? With Jonathan?"

"Oh, don't tell me you're another Sexy Shannon fan? I've heard enough about her today already, thanks very much."

"I wasn't talking about Shannon. Three letters," she said with a bright smile.

Daisy's cheeks went a deep shade of pink and her eyes widened. "TLC? No. Way. With Jonathan?"

"*Way*." That was Maggie's second-favourite response. She'd overheard it from a teenager standing in the express aisle at Asda.

"Where was he?" Daisy's face lit up. Suddenly she felt like doing a chant or a dance on the kitchen floor.

"At Isobel's. Briefly. He and Jonathan are teaching in the same school in Donegal. They're big buddies, apparently."

"What? *Really*? Oh, Mum, I'd love to have been here. Did you get a good, long look at him? Did he see you?"

Maggie raised an eyebrow. "Ah, Daisy, I wasn't staring. You should know me better than that. I was in the front garden tidying the flowerbeds and he pulled up with Jonathan in a taxi. They must have been coming from the pub, and he didn't hang around, but yes, I took in every last detail for you. And I have three words."

"I can guess."

"Drop. Dead. Gorgeous."

Daisy bit her lip with excitement. TLC, or The Lovely Christian, to give him his full title, had once been the lust of Daisy's life.

Well, the lust of half the village's life, to be more accurate. Young married women mostly, but Daisy strongly believed that there was something about Christian Devine that would make a nun weak at the knees. Devine by name, divine from top to toe. If he was around town again, this little unexpected visit home might not be so bad after all.

"Right," Daisy brightened. "Hit me with all the details. Long hair? Short hair? Yummy scale one-to-ten?"

"Short...*ish*. And a bit messy, but nice messy if you know what I mean. Yummy scale is a huge ten out of ten. No, eleven."

"Tanned skin, pale skin?" Daisy wanted a full description. Christian couldn't be long home from his worldly travels. The last she'd heard of him, he'd been trekking across Australia.

"Tanned as always. *Deeply* tanned. Black t-shirt, faded jeans, very hunky...in a rugged, arrogant sort of way that only Christian Devine could get away with."

Daisy swooned.

"Single or attached? This is the most important bit."

Maggie thought for a moment. How could she let her daughter down gently? She scrunched up her face and then told the truth.

"*Heartbroken*, actually. Yes, heartbroken is definitely the word that Isobel had overheard. His latest girlfriend has left him for six months to do some travelling and apparently he's gutted."

Daisy gulped. "Heartbroken and gutted? That's not good..."

Heartbroken was better than single, but worse than attached. How do you ensnare somebody who is heartbroken? It would be like competing with a ghost, thought Daisy. A living ghost, if there was such a thing.

"How heartbroken can he possibly be? I didn't think Christian Devine even *had* a heart. I can't believe Eddie failed to tell me all of this." Daisy shook her head in a haze of excitement and disbelief. "I mean, this is high-quality need-to-know information, and I, of all people, have a real need to know. He is the biggest eye totty ever to come out of this backwater! He is like the Killshannon version of Colin Farrell. Phwoarr!"

She reached for the kettle and poured a second cup of cappuccino.

"I'm sure the tracking of TLC's love life is at the very bottom of Eddie's 'to-do' list at the moment," said Maggie. "Anyhow," she continued, "that's as far as my research has gone. The rest, I'm afraid, will be up to you."

Daisy was very impressed with her mum's work to date. Most mothers would have locked up their daughters at the sight of someone like Christian Devine. His reputation had left bleeding hearts all over Killshannon when he was a teenager, but he had been born with charm and a reputation as his own father had been a serial womaniser too. Maggie knew all about that from her own single days growing up around the village. Besides, the looks and charm of a movie star could get you further than most in a small town, and Christian, like his father, had certainly made the best of his finest assets over the years.

"Ah well," sighed Daisy. "He's probably caught some terrible, nasty STD on his travels." There was no hope competing with an absent girlfriend, so she figured she'd try and dwell on the negatives.

Maggie looked at her in horror. "Daisy! Christian is a school-teacher now. Don't be so quick to judge people. Didn't I always preach that to you?"

"So, what? He's a teacher. Big deal. A leopard never changes his spots and if *he's* heartbroken, I'm the Virgin Mary."

Maggie straightened her Like a Virgin t-shirt and Daisy started to laugh.

"I'll really have to update your retro wardrobe some of these days, Mum. That yellow is wild and mothers aren't supposed to dress in t-shirts from the eighties."

"If that's what you think," said Maggie with a nod. "Mothers shouldn't really dress like their daughters, but some do. English teachers aren't supposed to be sexy. But some are." She cleared the table and made her way over to the tiny pantry. "Now, what would you like for tea?"

Daisy's stomach grumbled. Why had she left it so long to come home? This was better than Spain, she thought. Well, almost. So far, Killshannon was showing fantastic potential for a week of fun. All she needed now was for the sun to come out, for Eddie to come out, and she would happily reignite her friendship with her miserable suitcase and suntan lotions once and for all.

Chapter 6

Anything That Can Go Ring, Will Go Wrong

Jonathan wiped his face with a towel and stared closely at his reflection in the mirror. To shave or not to shave, he thought, rubbing an even patch of fair stubble across the bottom of his chin. Shannon would be here soon with a "to do list" that was the length of her pretty legs, but Jonathan just couldn't get his head around guest names or menus or anything remotely wedding-orientated at the moment.

He had sincerely been looking forward to the whole occasion, which they had originally planned for the following year. But then Jonathan's entire world had turned on its axis a few days ago and Shannon had insisted that the big event be catapulted into the very near future.

His mother had cried the entire way home from the hospital on Friday. Having learned that her cancer had spread was a huge shock and poor Isobel had been diagnosed with a worst-case scenario – liver cancer and no option of surgery or treatment; just a very short space of time to suffer dreadfully in full view of her friends and family.

Thank God Eddie was home, he thought, even if he *was* pulling some sort of silly stunt by bringing Daisy into the equation with their stupid tale of a made-up love affair. Even the dogs on the street knew Eddie was gay. Why did he feel he had to pretend? And why Daisy of all people? He was playing with fire by bringing her so closely back into their lives. Jonathan fished a disposable razor from his holdall and squirted some shaving foam onto his chin. Just because the walls were caving in around him didn't mean he had to turn into a scruff, and Shannon was bringing her mother along today so there would be hell to pay if he didn't look the part.

He pulled on a pair of navy tracksuit bottoms and a cool white polo shirt that complemented the tan he'd picked up on a quick weekend in the South of France with Shannon and her parents. Despite the heavy rain, the air in Killshannon was muggy and if the weatherman were telling the truth, they were in for a heat wave over the next few days.

On his way through the hallway, Jonathan could hear laughter spilling from the kitchen. He could hear the words "girlfriend" and "Daisy" in the same sentence and he shook his head. When was his baby brother going to grow up? And what did Daisy think she was playing at? This was nonsense and if Eddie kept this up he'd have to have a firm word in his ear. He and Daisy were history…a very hurtful history at that, so this was unfair on everyone and he would soon be telling them so.

The front doorbell rang and caught him unawares so he tidied himself quickly and sprayed on a dot of aftershave in a last-minute dash to look respectable. Shannon was early as usual and he wasn't half-prepared for her arrival. He ruffled his hands through his hair, pulled on a pair of trainers and went to answer the door.

"Hi. Er, I had no idea you would still be here, I swear. Sorry."

Jonathan squinted in the evening light and took a step backwards. It wasn't Shannon. It was Daisy and, like himself, she looked a lot fresher than she had done earlier. Her fair hair was tied back into a loose ponytail and she was dressed in a white t-shirt and comfy track bottoms. She looked gorgeous. He stared at her and couldn't even manage an answer.

51

"Snap," she said with a strained smile, taking in his attire from top to bottom and he was glad of the twilight to hide his shock at seeing her again so soon. He glanced down. Their outfits were almost identical, and he managed an equally forced smile, before composing himself again.

"If it isn't the Sunflake Girl," he replied. "Your boyfriend's in the kitchen. Come on through."

Daisy didn't know if she was more stunned that Jonathan was still in Isobel's house or that he'd remembered that she had appeared in a long-running cereal bar commercial years ago. He turned and led the way through to the kitchen, where Eddie was cracking open a bottle of wine at the table.

"Daisy, my darling. It's so great to see you," chirped Isobel, in the liveliest voice she could muster. "Eddie has been filling me in. This is so wonderful. It's been months since you've been in Killshannon and years since we've all been together."

Daisy glanced at Eddie, who had already developed black lips from the red wine and was giving her the thumbs up behind his mother's back when she stood up to welcome her visitor.

"Oh, Isobel. It's so good to see you too." Daisy wrapped her arms around her frail shoulders, afraid she might break them. The tears welled up in her eyes. "How do you feel?"

Isobel sat weakly back onto her chair and nestled her stemmed glass of sparkling water between her tiny fingers.

"Oh, you know," she said with a look that shouted "shit happens." "But I'm just having a wee drink with my baby boy to celebrate his homecoming. I can't tell you how happy this has made me, Daisy. I always knew you'd end up with one of my boys."

Isobel winked at Daisy when the boys weren't looking and Daisy realised straight away that, just as her own mum had predicted, Isobel was happy to play along for now. Jonathan met Daisy's eye and then quickly turned away.

"Any word from Shanny yet, Mum? She's normally really punctual," he asked sternly.

Daisy rolled her eyes. *Shanny*. How sad. It rhymed with a certain part of the female anatomy and didn't sound very endearing at all.

"Who?" asked Isobel. "Oh, Shannon? Of course. You know, with all this news from Eddie, I almost forgot that Shannon and Mrs Cassidy were coming over this evening. Isn't this great? We'll all be together for the first time."

"Mum, you know Mrs Cassidy prefers to be called by her first name," said Jonathan and then realised he had opened a can of worms. This could only add to his misery and discomfort.

"I know, love, but I just can't bring myself to say it," giggled Isobel. "I mean, who in their right mind would want to be known as Fanny nowadays?"

Daisy looked at Eddie whose eyes widened with delight. He could have fun with this one. He and Daisy specialised in toilet humour and this was right up their street.

"I'm sure she will be thrilled to see us all," said Daisy with a newly found confidence. "And I can't wait to meet Fanny face to face myself. There's a first time for everything."

Eddie thought he was going to explode, but the look on his brother's face warned him not to.

"So am I. I've never seen Fanny face to face either," he roared.

"Oh, here we go. How very mature," muttered Jonathan, "and how very, very true." He reached for a wine glass from the top cupboard of the kitchen and poured some wine, then remembering his manners, he turned to Daisy.

"Red or white, Daisy? Or maybe you'd prefer some champagne? We have some on reserve for the run-up to the wedding, but maybe the marvellous news of yours and Eddie's, er, *relationship* deserves an extra celebration?"

"Ha ha," mimed Daisy towards him with an outward smile, hoping that Isobel didn't see her. "Champagne would be wonderful, please Jonathan," she said cheerily. "That's only if you're sure there's enough left for Shanny and Fanny. We wouldn't want to leave them *dry*."

53

Eddie couldn't hold it in any longer. He'd tried his best but he just had to give way to an almighty explosion of laughter from the corner of the room.

Jonathan ignored his brother's reaction and handed Daisy a glass of champagne with a forced grin. His mobile phone sang a funky ring tone from the worktop and he grabbed it quickly, praying it wasn't Shannon phoning to cancel their plans. As much as he hated the thought of wedding chat, he really needed Shannon and her mother here right now to relieve the tension between him and Daisy. Having her back in his family home reminded her too much of the past. Right now, he felt suffocated and outnumbered.

The caller display showed it was Christian, and Jonathan breathed a sigh of relief as he made his way out of the kitchen to take the call.

"Hey Christian, what's the craic?"

"The craic's good, Jonathan, the craic's good," said Christian's familiar husky voice from the other end. He always sounded as though he had gravel in his throat and could easily have made a fortune on radio or audio versions of bonk-buster novels. "I couldn't be better. Top of the world."

"So the heartache is finally over. Congratulations. You've suffered for approximately, er, six hours and fifty-seven minutes. I pity you. Truly, I do," laughed Jonathan, shaking his head.

"No, no. You're getting me all wrong, Jonathan. I've just heard from Anna. She's arrived safe and sound in Copenhagen and is missing me terribly. Not that I should be surprised, of course. She's wondering if she has done the right thing, parting company at such a blooming stage of our relationship. I'm on a high after hearing from her, that's all."

Jonathan considered himself well and truly corrected. He had pictured his friend in a town-centre bar, eyeing up each and every skirt that walked past and frothing at the mouth with thirst. It might have been only six hours, but Jonathan was proud of Christian's commitment to Anna so far.

"So, what's up then? What can I do for you?" asked Jonathan. Surely Christian hadn't rung him to tell him he'd got a phone call from his girlfriend. If that was the case, the pair of them would be on the phone constantly.

"You'll never guess what I've just heard. This is going to crack you up, big time," said Christian.

"Go for it."

"Remember Gerry whatshisface – the smart-ass barman from The Chocolate Bar earlier today?"

"Yeah, Gerry O'Donnell. What about him?"

"Well, I just met him in the video store and he had the latest episode of your brother's love life all wrapped up in a nutshell. You're right about old Gerry – he has all the best contacts for gossip but this is pure mental."

"Christian, please just get on with it."

His friend paused. This was going to sting.

"He reckons your Eddie is shagging Daisy Anderson. *Your* Daisy Anderson."

Jonathan didn't warm to Christian's way with words and couldn't hide it.

"He's not *shagging* her, as such. Honestly, Christian, you and your filthy mind. And she's not *my* Daisy. Not anymore." Eddie shagging Daisy? Gross, he thought, as pictures flashed through his mind. No, that would be a giant step too far.

"What? So it's true he's at least seeing her, then? Excuse me while I just pick myself up off the floor. And here was me expecting he had hooked up with some weird American transsexual."

Jonathan felt irritated by Christian's gloating where his brother and childhood girlfriend were concerned.

"Christian, it's really no big deal. Daisy and Eddie have been good friends forever. We *all* were until…" He halted before saying something he might regret. "Anyhow, I think you're getting a wee bit over-excited about something that probably won't last a second. Eddie's just upset over Mum and needs some reassurance

55

from someone he knows. He trusts Daisy. That doesn't mean for a second that he's shagging her, so for God's sake don't ever say that again. It's a scheme he has dreamed up, thinking he is pulling the wool over Mum's eyes, but we all know the score. I'm going to have a good chat with him when I can. Daisy is just playing along to give him the reassurance he needs."

Christian gave out a dirty cackle. "I wouldn't mind getting a bit of reassurance from Crazy Daisy myself if it's up for the taking."

"Don't say that. She's not crazy."

"She was at one time, in a nice way. Is she still? Come on, just because you're getting married soon doesn't mean you've lost the power of your eyes. Or your heart."

"You are one messed up mother…"

"Don't worry, I've no intention of hitting on her behind your back. I've eyes for only one woman myself but I'm still curious. Is she still hot?"

At that, Daisy came into the hallway, brushing past Jonathan on her way to the bathroom. The hallway in the houses of Ivy Cottages were extremely narrow and Jonathan's manly frame took up most of the space as he leaned with one arm against the wall. Daisy looked at the floor the entire time, breathing in so that their bodies wouldn't accidentally touch.

Jonathan waited until she turned left through the pine door and locked it from the inside before answering. He rubbed his forehead and took a breath.

"Not really hot. Sort of lukewarm, I'd say."

In truth, he felt like he was in a sauna. He was burning up from how hot Daisy looked right now.

"Lying bastard. Don't lie to me. How does she look?"

Jonathan was getting really peeved. Just because Christian was bored without Anna didn't mean he had to stand here all evening and listen to him talking shit.

"Christian, will you drop it for God's sake?" he whispered through gritted teeth. "She just walked past and you were drooling

56

down the phone like a bloody pervert. You might still think she's hot but I don't. Now give it a rest, will you? "

"Wait a minute. Daisy is *there*?" asked Christian. "In your mum's house? And Shannon is on her way over with her posh mummy-poos Fanny? I swear to God I would pay money to be a fly on the wall."

The lock of the bathroom door opened and Daisy walked back into the hallway. How women managed to pee so quickly when you didn't want them to was one of life's greatest mysteries, thought Jonathan. He glanced towards her and then darted his gaze away when their eyes met for a second.

"So, honey, I'll see you very soon," he said loudly to Christian so that Daisy could hear his every word.

Christian let out a stammer. "Is this Jonathan or Eddie? I'm not gay, Ed. It's time you faced the truth."

"I love you too, Shanny. Yeah, I know, I know. I'll see you real soon."

Jonathan continued to mumble sweet nothings to a bewildered Christian when the doorbell rang.

"You hang up."

"No you hang up," said Christian in a girly voice. He had finally caught on to the fact that this was all for Daisy's benefit.

"I'll get it," said Daisy, turning and making her way back towards the front door. "I'd hate to disturb such a romantic conversation."

"Yes, yes, I'll see you in a few minutes, pet. I can't wait either. Drive carefully," said Jonathan.

Daisy opened the door while Jonathan continued to mumble into the phone behind her and she was greeted by a colt-like girl with platinum hair in a neat bob and wearing a pale-blue trench coat. Her mother stood alongside her, lean and fair, equally as glamorous and grinning like a Cheshire cat.

"You must be Shannon and Fa…, I mean, Mrs *Cassidy*. How are you?" Daisy couldn't speak more enthusiastically if she tried, and managed to do so at ear-bursting volume. She extended her arm to shake hands with the pair on their way in through the shiny red door and shot Jonathan a smug glance with raised eyebrows. "I'm an old friend of the family – Daisy Anderson. I'm afraid Jonathan is just taking a *very* important phone call."

Daisy opened the door wide to let the visitors in and looked over at Jonathan, who had his mouth open and the phone still to his ear, knowing his act of cable romance had been well and truly discovered a farce.

"Lovely to meet you, Daisy," said Shannon. She appeared no more than sixteen but had a streetwise look in her eye and her coat had obviously cost an arm and a leg.

Daisy longed to touch it.

"It's John Rocha," said Shannon, noticing how Daisy was eyeing her coat up. "Ahem. I can't say Jonathan has ever mentioned you, but you know what men are like. I'm sure he would have told me about you sooner or later if you were important to him."

Daisy smirked and nodded towards Jonathan, who was making his way towards them. "Yes, I sure do know what men are like," she said. "Especially the Eastwood men, now that you come to mention it. I know them very, very well indeed."

Jonathan marched towards them before Daisy could say any more and took his visitors' coats.

"Daisy is Eddie's new girlfriend. My very *happy* brother, Eddie," he said smugly. That would put her right back in her place. "Come on through, ladies. Mum has opened a few bottles of wine to lighten the mood."

Jonathan was humiliated. Why had he felt the need to pretend he was talking to Shannon on the phone anyway? He knew she would be arriving on the doorstep any minute and he would have his chance then to show Daisy how happy and in love he was. If Christian hadn't been putting him under so much pressure he'd have been able to think straight. Now he had to pull himself together.

"Ah, Shannon, love. Mrs Cassidy. It's wonderful to see you both," said Isobel when they entered the kitchen. "This is my son, Eddie. I don't think you've all met before."

"Shannon and I met just yesterday," said Eddie. "We had a very worthwhile chat, but I've never met Mrs Cassidy before. It's a pleasure."

Eddie really wanted to use her first name but saying he had never met Fanny before would be just too close to the truth. He felt the laughter rise again. Think of a compliment, quickly.

"Lovely to meet you, Eddie, and Daisy of course," said Shannon's mother as she looked at the unlikely couple.

"Totally likewise," Eddie replied in a nervous stammer. "Jonathan has told us all about you and I can definitely see where Shannon gets her good looks from."

Eddie could feel Daisy's eyes burn through him like hot rods.

"What a charmer. Just like his big brother, eh?" said Mrs Cassidy. "Please, just call me Fanny."

Eddie had to turn towards the sink and pretend he had something stuck in his throat before he totally let himself down. He could see Daisy's glare turn into a smirk from the side of his eye and was getting hot under the collar from the urge to laugh every time he heard the woman's name.

"How about we put on some music, Isobel?" said Daisy, coming to the rescue.

"Good idea, darling," said Eddie with relief as he swallowed a mouthful of tap water. "What would you like to hear, Mum? Elvis? Tom Jones? I bet you're in a Cliff mood. You have that look in your eye." Eddie knew he had to try to be funny very quickly in order to release some of his pent-up laughter, so he smacked his teeth and danced around the kitchen mocking his mother's favourite singer. Isobel pretended to be embarrassed but inside she was glowing with pride.

"Oh, go on then. Cliff it is. You know me too well," she said, even though music had been the furthest thing from her mind over the past while. Perhaps it would do her good.

"I have the entire wedding guest list written out, but nobody told me about Daisy so I'll have to add her on alongside Eddie," said Shannon in a loud voice as she sat at the kitchen table and pulled out a ream of A4 paper from a folder marked "Our Wedding". "This is so exciting. I don't have any sisters to help me with my wedding plans. Do you, Daisy?"

"No. Just one brother, Richard. But I'm not getting married for a long time, so I really don't mind."

Shannon wrote down Daisy's name in her neatest handwriting and Daisy felt bile rising in her throat. A neat freak. How could Jonathan have settled for a neat freak?

"I don't know anyone else called Daisy," said Shannon as she wrote. "You don't look like a Daisy."

"You mean, she doesn't look like a yellow and white flower," said Eddie. "I think she does. So cute."

"No, you look more like…like a Mary or an Anne," said Shannon. "Something a bit plainer than Daisy."

Daisy felt her cheeks burn. She knew she was dressed very casually but "plain"? Oh dear…

"I'm sure Daisy would be only too delighted to come to our wedding," Jonathan said, with a touch of sarcasm.

"Yes, and maybe you can help Daisy when it comes to *our* turn to walk up the aisle, Shannon," said Eddie. "Daisy would be only too delighted to have you as her bridesmaid since you will be sisters-in-law after all."

Daisy kicked Eddie hard on the shin from under the table but he was too busy smiling at his mother, who was too engrossed in the happy scene to heed Daisy's anguish.

"Really, Eddie," said Daisy. "I'm sure Shannon would rather concentrate on her own wedding for now. It's hardly fair to start planning for ours just yet. We're not even engaged, *remember*?"

Jonathan noticed squinting and shrugging between Eddie and Daisy and when he saw Eddie reach under the table to rub his battered shin for the second time, he recognised a moment for triumph.

"Actually, we'd love to hear about your wedding plans. Go on, tell us all," he said with glee. "Am I the best man?"

Daisy gave him a hard stare. "That is entirely up to Eddie, not me, thank goodness."

"Oh, have you set a date yet?" asked Shannon, lifting a diary from her handbag in a matter of seconds. "I hope it's not on a school day, with so many teachers in the family. What do you work as, Daisy? You look like...let me guess..."

"Ahem, like I said, we haven't officially got engaged yet so this really is all a bit premature..." said Shannon. She would have loved to have told Shannon that she was a famous actress like that scene in Notting Hill where the guy didn't recognise Julia Roberts and watched her squirm, but she didn't get time to even answer...

"And will you start a family straight away?" asked Shannon. "I just know Jonathan is dying to be a daddy. Oh, do you hear me! Maybe you already have children, do you Daisy? You never know with modern couples these days. Most people have so much baggage. But not Jonathan and I, thankfully."

Daisy's heart beat as though she had just run a marathon. What was this – The Weakest Link with Shannon as quizmaster? Where the hell had that last question come from? What did she know? Her stomach felt sick.

"That's not exactly the immediate plan and...no, to your, um, second question."

She glanced at Jonathan, who swiftly looked away.

"But we *are* madly in love," piped Eddie. "It will all be announced soon, so dust off your frocks, folks and put the champers on ice. And yes, Jonathan, I suppose you can be my best man. I was trying to decide between you and my other five invisible brothers."

Daisy realised the keep-it-simple plan had now disintegrated entirely as Eddie was almost bouncing in his chair. He looked so gay that Shanny and Fanny would have to be dumb and dumber not to realise it. Poor Eddie was the only one who believed in his little game. Oh, and Shannon too, but so far she wasn't proving to be on the ball at all.

"Tell me all your ideas, *please*," squealed Shannon. "I'm *so* into weddings at the minute and I just love to swap stories with other brides-to-be…plus I want mine to be the best, of course, so I need to hear about the competition."

Daisy shuffled uneasily in her seat.

"How about a venue? We could recommend a few beautiful hotels," suggested Fanny, joining in with as much enthusiasm as her over-excited daughter. Dumb and dumber they were, then. "And we have all the latest bridal magazines so no need to buy any. You can have all of ours."

"I…I'm not quite sure if…" Daisy couldn't get a word in.

"Or a photographer?" added Jonathan. "Shannon has all the names and contact numbers on file. Why don't you meet up over the next few days and make a few provisional bookings? You don't want to waste any time."

Daisy's mouth tightened. She could see what Jonathan was doing and what a big a kick he was getting out of it all. Well, two could play that game.

"I suppose so," she said, and his face fell. "In fact, I'd love that. We should set a date as soon as possible, eh Eddie?"

Eddie looked over with glee at his mother, who to him was quietly enjoying all the buzz and fuss filling her house. This was worth all the pretence, he thought, worth all the little white lies if would give her a sense of contentment in her last few months.

"Of course. This is so exciting. What do you think, Mum?"

"Whatever makes you happy," she said. "That's all I want."

Eddie leaned forward and gave his mum a cuddle. This was working out a treat and Daisy was really finding her feet in her leading role. He'd have to praise her fine acting skills at a later stage. The girl was wasting her time in a city centre shoe store when she had such obvious talent. Thank goodness his little plan was beginning to take shape.

In fact, all Eddie needed now was to run into Christian Devine and everything would fall into place nicely.

Chapter 7

Absence Makes The Heart Go Wander

Christian walked onto the veranda of his apartment and squinted in the early evening sun. He held his mobile up to the sky. Yes, it did have a signal. The same way that it had a signal in the sitting room and in the kitchen, when he was boiling the kettle, and in the bathroom, when he was brushing his teeth and urging it to ring.

Maybe if he put the phone in the bedroom, under his pillow or somewhere else out of sight and went to pick up a takeaway for his tea, by the time he came back he might have some sort of message from Anna. It was twenty-two hours since she had phoned to say she'd arrived safe and sound in Copenhagen. She had found her apartment. It was clean and in a safe area and the man who had arranged her job didn't particularly look like a rapist or a mass murderer or a scary karate axe fiend.

So far, so good.

"This place is so amazing," she'd cooed in her delightful, soft Leitrim accent. "The food is nothing like I'd expected and the people are so friendly. I just know I'm going to love it."

Christian was excited for her. He just didn't know it yet, and was simply showing his excitement through other uncontrollable human feelings, such as rage and jealousy.

"What's your room-mate like? Is she Danish?" he'd asked, trying to sound enthused. At least if Anna was in good company, he wouldn't have to worry about her being burgled or mugged while she slept.

"Oh, he's so nice."

"*He*?"

"Yeah, he's called Brian and is such a sweetie. He's only twenty-two and has the strongest Scottish accent I've ever heard. He reminds me of a young, what's-his-name from the band Wet Wet Wet. I've warned him not to leave the toilet seat up," she laughed. "We're like an old married couple already."

Christian thought he was going to choke. He pretended he had a frog in his throat to disguise his terror and downed a mouthful of water, which he soon realised was raw vodka from the night before. Marti bloody Pellow. His own sister, Jess, had been mad about Marti Pellow since he'd first smiled and wished he was lucky in the 1980s. Now it sounded like Anna might fancy him too. *Shit!*

"I miss you," he blurted out in reply. That was it. She was going to think he was a desperate, needy saddo now but what could he do? He couldn't listen to any more of her gushing about cultural delights and arty theatres and smiley housemates. What was happening to his "love 'em and leave 'em" programming? His system needed tuning up, big time.

Anna didn't answer at first and Christian wondered if Marti Pellow had interrupted her for a quickie. Just the thought of another fellow being around his girlfriend was enough to make him sick.

"Ah, that's really sweet, Christian," she sighed eventually. "But you're going to have to find something else to amuse you for the next six months while I'm gone. It's so exciting here. To be honest I've hardly even thought of home since I got here. You've got to keep busy and I promise we'll pick up where we left off when I get home, okay?"

"Okay," he murmured like an obedient toddler. "And Anna?"

"Yes?"

"Nothing. It doesn't matter. Take care."

Anna was silent again and more sordid pictures flashed through Christian's mind.

Eventually she answered. "Chat soon, Christian. Bye."

****

Christian simply couldn't settle since he'd hung up the phone the night before. The idea of Anna sharing accommodation with a cute young Scottish man was driving him insane with jealousy. She could have lied. She could have at least pretended he was buck ugly with halitosis, a serious body-odour problem or a mysterious skin disease. He had hardly slept a wink all night and he had even got up to feed next-door's blind cat at the crack of dawn. The cat, which he had decided to call Buddy for the time being, had been a great listener.

"You know what, Buddy? This isn't like me at all," Christian had whined, hunkering down to confide in his new feline friend. The cat had cocked his head ever so slightly in between mouthfuls of cereal and milk. Some crazy people paid big money for counselling like this.

"Nobody believes me, but I really think this is the real thing for me. I am officially 'in like' and it's a bit frightening, to say the least. Bring back my one-channelled male emotions, or tell me how to find them again. This isn't good for the old rep, you know?"

Buddy purred, lapped the last of the milk and took with it a stray Cheerio from the bottom of the bowl.

"At least you're pretending to be interested," said Christian. "Even if I had to bribe you with my breakfast."

It was true, though. Only the cat seemed to be listening to him these days. When he had phoned Jonathan the previous evening, his friend had just been preoccupied with Shannon, the Wedding Psycho, and his old ex Daisy Anderson. He had then tried his mother, who couldn't talk to him either because she'd been engrossed in a repeat of the Late Late Show. And to top it all off, his sister hadn't answered her phone. That left nobody, but Buddy.

Christian wearily made his way upstairs and tucked his phone under his pillow. He would leave it there for at least half an hour, and when he returned there would surely be a message or at least a missed call from Anna. He rubbed his head. Is that the way things would be from now on? Didn't Anna miss him? Was it a case of "out of sight, out of mind?" Even his own mother didn't have any confidence in his ability to stay faithful. "Once a philanderer, always a philanderer," she would say, shaking her head. She thought he was just like his father and the rest of the Devine men before him. Mud stuck. He'd heard it all a hundred times before.

Christian lifted a navy sports jacket from the bottom of the bed and decided to go for a walk across town to clear his head.

He'd prove them wrong, he thought, as he marched out into the evening sunshine. The weatherman had been right for a change. Donegal's summer had finally begun. He skipped down the stairs from the first floor of the apartment block and waved at Gerry, the barman, who was serving drinks to revellers lapping up the sunshine outside The Chocolate Bar across the road.

"Hey Christian, how's the single life treating you so far?" Gerry bellowed as the sun reflected off his silver hair.

"I'll tell you when I *am* single, Gerry," he shouted back. "Maybe you could give me a bit of advice yourself since you seem to be a long-term expert?"

Pervy prostitute-lover, he thought, strolling past the bank with an impossibly long ATM queue, the butchers with sawdust on its floor and the post office with the oldest counter clerk in the world. At the bakery, which sold his second-most favourite sausage rolls, he became aware of a horrible, uncomfortable feeling that something was wrong in his apartment. He frowned wondering what it could be. He had definitely locked the door, he convinced himself. And he hadn't used the iron in at least a fortnight. The kettle could flick itself off, so it wasn't that. Nevertheless something was niggling at him. The immersion heater? The gas cooker? Something wasn't right.

Then he realised what it was. He was suffering from classic twenty-first century withdrawal symptoms, otherwise known as leaving the house with no mobile phone. It was similar to feeling like you'd lost a limb, or suddenly realising you'd left your toddler nephew home alone by accident.

"Sod this," he said and sprinted back past the bakery, the post office, the butchery and the bank. He signalled the middle finger across to Gerry at The Chocolate Bar, who responded by opening his mouth and then shutting it again like a goldfish. Breathless, he turned the key in the main door of the apartments and raced up the stairs like he was being chased for his life.

What if she's already phoned? What if she's phoned all the way from Copenhagen and I've missed her call? I am such an eejit, thinking I would last without my phone!

"Did you hear my phone ring, Buddy?" he asked the cat, while almost stumbling over him. The cat blinked back at him.

"Oh forget it. You're probably deaf as well as blind. "Thanks, mate."

Christian stormed into his bedroom and scrambled under the pillow and bedclothes until he found the smooth, welcoming feel of his phone – his sole lifeline to Anna. It was worrying, though. Six whole months of this nonsense could send him around the bend. With a deep breath, he turned to look at the screen. Yes! Two missed calls! It had worked and he'd only been gone about ten minutes. His heart took a leap and he lay down on the bed. He couldn't wait to hear Anna's voice again.

Chapter 8

Desperate Times Call For Desperate Pleasures

"He's not answering."

"Try again," said Eddie, almost doing a Riverdance on the floor with impatience. "He'll have to answer eventually. He's probably just bleaching his teeth or miming into a hairbrush in the mirror, the vain bastard. "

Jonathan handed Eddie the phone. "You try phoning him yourself," he said before walking into the kitchen, where Shannon was preparing a salad for the barbecue.

Eddie pressed redial and held the phone to his ear. Damn! Still no luck. Why wasn't he picking up, for God's sake?"

Eddie had just hung up when the phone rang, startling him so much that he fumbled to take the call.

"Here, quick, quick, it's him." He raced over to Jonathan, holding it at arm's length as if it was on fire.

"Talk to him yourself and for God's sake stop acting like a star-struck teenager. You are getting stranger by the day," hissed Jonathan back at his younger brother.

Eddie pressed the button and put the tiny phone to his ear.

"Hiya Christian."

"I just got two missed calls from you. I thought they might have been from Anna, so this better be worth my disappointment. And when did you start saying 'Hiya'?"

"This is Eddie, actually."

"Oh, well that kind of figures then," said Christian in his trademark rasp.

Eddie was trying his best to sound controlled and cool. Christian Devine was a bit of a hunk alright, and a ladies' man, but Eddie couldn't help but swoon.

"Hey Ed, what's up? How's the love life going?" said Christian's husky voice and Eddie almost fainted with delight. "I'd say it's a hundred times better than mine at the minute."

Eddie wondered for a second if Christian was trying to hit on him. Then he remembered how he was now a heterosexual himself, supposedly. He even had a girlfriend and a marriage proposal to prove it.

"Fab," he replied. Shit, how gay did that sound? He cleared his throat and deepened his voice. "Grand, I mean. Grand." Grand wasn't much better. He made a mental note to brush up on "tough guy" words.

"So, what can I do for you, Ed? Has Jonathan unstuck himself from Shannon yet? Is he finally allowed out to play with the boys?" asked Christian. If Anna wasn't going to phone soon, he may as well enjoy a night on the tear.

"Er…sort of," said Eddie, hiding his eyes as Shannon fed his brother cherry tomatoes in a pornographic manner in full view of a Sacred Heart picture in the kitchen. "As you've probably heard, we're all trying our best to keep Mum's spirits up and were just wondering if you'd like to join us all for a barbecue this evening. Here, in Killshannon. Jonathan's staying here for a few days."

"A barbecue? Em, I'm not sure…"

"Do you have something else on?"

"Actually, er…no." Christian glanced around his apartment and Buddy the cat gave him a glare. "All I have on is a pair of jeans. Nothing else."

"Stop that nonsense! I meant…"

"I know, I know, take a chill pill, Ed. Who else is going to be there?"

"Well, *me* obviously," he giggled and then cleared his throat again. Shit, he was losing his self control again. "And Jonathan and Shannon. And Daisy."

"Mmm…" said Christian. "Interesting."

Eddie fanned his flushed face with a telephone bill he'd found on the worktop. "Er, and I bought a swingball."

Crap, he thought. Another dead giveaway. Now Christian would definitely know he was as camp as a Bunsen burner.

"A swingball? Is that supposed to be, like, the ace up your sleeve?" laughed Christian. If Eddie Eastwood was straight, then Buddy, the deaf and blind cat, was a good watchdog. "Now that is an offer I cannot refuse. A game of swingball with Shannon and Daisy? I'll grab a few beers on the way. Give me an hour or so."

"Yes!" said Eddie, pressing the hang-up button on the phone with delight. They could all make fun if they wanted, but who could refuse the prospect of a game of swingball during Wimbledon season? He danced outside to where his big brother had finally torn himself from Shannon's clutches and was setting up the picnic table in the garden. Jonathan plus Christian plus Daisy plus lots of wine and beer thrown in for good measure equalled…well… he'd have to wait and see.

Jonathan, on the other hand, was only going through all of this pretence for his mother's sake. No matter how uncomfortable he felt in Daisy's presence, he was not going to ruin Isobel's evening. She was so looking forward to having her happy offspring and their friends around for dinner al fresco.

"So is he coming, then?" he asked Eddie.

"Who?" replied Eddie with raised eyebrows, holding out a pitch-fork at a dangerous angle. It was extremely important for him to at least try and play it cool.

"The Messiah. Christ Devine as you used to call him."

"He sure the hell is. Mind you, I still can't believe *you* can talk to him without wanting to scratch his eyes out." Eddie was almost dancing on his tiptoes with excitement.

Jonathan marched over to the barbecue and flipped a burger, trying to ignore his brother.

"I mean," continued Eddie regardless, "he used to beat you at *everything* and you couldn't stand it. Football, fishing, girls, eh… er… football and did I mention *girls*? I can't believe he's now your new best friend."

"Shut up, Ed," muted Jonathan. "You have no idea what you are talking about. People do grow up, you know. Why don't you try it yourself sometime?"

"I mean, don't get me wrong, I think it's great. Very mature. I don't know if *I'd* be so forgiving, that's all."

Jonathan threw the tongs onto the garden table in a bad temper. Eddie was pushing his luck, big time.

"Just who the hell do you think you are?" he asked, walking towards his brother.

"Eddie Eastwood," Eddie grinned. He took two steps back, however, knowing he had overstepped the mark. "And you're my big brother. Come on, Jonathan. I just don't like to see you being walked all over by everyone. Why not do what *you* want to do for a change, eh? Say what *you* want to say?"

Jonathan closed the patio doors tightly so that Shannon, who was enjoying a glass of wine in the kitchen and humming along to the radio, very out of tune, couldn't hear his reply.

"How exactly do you mean, Eddie? Do you think you can arrive back unannounced after running away and leaving me to pick up the pieces with Mum on my own? How do you think you can swan back into our lives with some foolish story that you've hooked up with Daisy? Mum's not stupid, you know. At least I'm not living a lie."

Eddie could see a faint line of sweat form across his brother's head. That was enough for now, he thought. This was a family get-together after all and he still had quite a bit of ground to cover as the evening progressed. Daisy and her mum were due in any minute so the night was young.

"Aren't you?" he asked, wincing at the realisation he was due a chop in the gob.

"No!" said Jonathan firmly.

They stood in silence for a few seconds, Jonathan staring into Eddie's eyes and Eddie holding his gaze for as long as he could.

"Whatever," he said. "If that's what you want to believe, then time will tell. Deal with it, bro."

Just then, Eddie heard Daisy and Maggie come into the house and he made a rush to greet them. Perfect timing; they'd just saved him from the gallows. He knew he had almost pushed his brother to the limit this time.

****

Eddie believed that if he had been born straight, Maggie Anderson would have been the most ideal mother-in-law in the world. They had so much in common and Eddie loved Maggie's glamour and unique sense of style. She looked quite reserved this evening but he knew her personality was as big as a house and she was sure to bring a smile to Isobel's face.

"Maggie, baby! How are you today?" he bellowed. "I have something nice for you in my suitcase."

Maggie was back in her old hippy gear, with a navy crinkled scarf around her hair and a long tie-dye skirt that reflected her individuality but was demure enough to show her middle age. Daisy stood beside her in short denim cut-offs and a spray tan, which she'd blissfully discovered at Killshannon's one and only beauty salon. Her face looked different too, but then Eddie realised she'd had her eyebrows plucked into a high arch. Very becoming.

"Oh, Eddie, how sweet!" said Maggie.

"Just let me go and get it. It's in the bedroom," said Eddie, running away like an excited teenager. "I just know this will be right up your street."

On hearing all the fuss coming from the hallway, Shannon turned her tiny frame from the chopping board and made her way towards Maggie and Daisy.

"This must be your mum, Daisy?" she cooed, turning on the charm. "I've heard so much about you, Mrs Anderson. Jonathan says you've been a real rock to Isobel all down the years. And you've had it so hard yourself. I'm so pleased to meet you."

She reached out to give a most polite and sophisticated hug.

Daisy nearly gagged. Sickly wasn't even the word for it. She could actually feel her teeth sticking together and ran her tongue along them in disgust.

"And you too, Shannon," said Maggie. "And look at that for a sparkler, Daisy. Isn't it absolutely stunning? Such good taste."

Shannon held out her hand to show off the platinum solitaire that almost matched her bleached hair. "Thanks, Mrs Anderson."

"And of course only a fine finger could get away with such a delicate piece of jewellery. It's magnificent."

Daisy shot her mother a quizzical glance. She couldn't stomach this mutual love fest for much longer. Didn't her mother realise that this culprit was engaged to her ex-boyfriend?

"Here we are, babes. Close your eyes!" Eddie bounded into the room with a tiny parcel, wrapped in an American flag and handed it to Maggie.

"Can I open it now?"

"Oh, please do. I can't wait to see your face. No, actually don't". He held up his hands, palms out, for her to stop unwrapping. "Wait till I get Mum in. She has to see all of this for herself."

When Isobel Eastwood shuffled into the kitchen Daisy's heart sank. She looked paler than the night before, and desperately tired. She was smiling, despite her pain.

"Ah now, would you look at this. All of my favourite girls here together," she whispered, settling into a chair with Eddie's help.

74

"Go on, Maggie, you can open it now," he said draping an arm around Daisy's shoulder.

The room fell silent as Maggie carefully peeled back the flag-style wrapper. Shannon "oohed" and "aahed" as each piece of tape was unfolded and even Daisy found herself doing the same.

"Food's up," roared Jonathan through the doorway and everyone shushed him.

"Sorry," he whispered.

"Eddie has bought Daisy's mum a present," said Shannon. "Bless!"

"What is it?" Maggie quizzed.

"A new Madonna t-shirt, signed by the lady herself," Eddie beamed. "My friend Brad managed to nab it at one of her gigs. He gave it to me but I knew it had to be yours when Daisy told me you were such a huge fan."

"I am? I mean, I *am*. I don't believe this. Oh, thank you, Eddie."

Daisy noticed how much effort her mother was making. Shannon, on the other hand, looked like she'd walked into a scene of the Rocky Horror Show. The look on her face was priceless.

Daisy stood in a smiley daze as everyone fussed around her. And then she saw it. The vision! All rugged and handsome with a six pack of beer in one hand and a bunch of garage flowers in the other.

TLC. The Lovely Christian Devine stood no more than two feet in front of her. His sexy dark hair was ruffled, and a faint, dark stubble lined his chin.

"Christ!" she gasped, a little louder than she'd intended.

"Daisy Anderson!" he grinned, making his way past everyone and straight over to her. "How are you, stranger?"

He leaned across to give her a lingering kiss on the cheek and she inhaled his delicious, manly scent, closing her eyes to savour the moment. God, he smelt *so* good.

"I'm wonderful," she smiled demurely.

"Isobel, these are for you," he said gently, handing over the

75

mixed bouquet.

The room fell silent.

"Ah, Christian, how kind of you," said Isobel. "Any word from Anna yet, love?"

Daisy's ears also pricked up. She also wanted an update on Christian's famous love life.

"So far, she's having a great time," he said with confidence as Daisy shifted uneasily from foot to foot. 'I miss her of course, but she keeps in regular touch.

At that moment, Daisy decided she didn't particularly feel like standing in a poky kitchen in Killshannon waiting on a burger from a barbecue, listening to Christian ramble on about his true love. She wanted true love too, and feeling Jonathan Eastwood stare at her wasn't doing her any good at all.

Chapter 9

It's Not The Size Of The Ball, But The Motion In The Potion

Eddie's Super Swingball tournament had begun in earnest. He'd cleared back the patio furniture so that everyone could eat at the far end of the garden.

"What's the prize?" asked Shannon as the game heated up, showing her competitive streak rise to the surface as she practised her swing. "I am so going to win. I always win."

"Me," said Christian.

Jonathan shook his head. "Hands off, Devine," he growled, draping his arms around his fiancée's waist. "You're worth a close watching. The prize is the last spicy chicken kebab, split between the winners."

Shannon tightened Jonathan's grasp around her slender waist and caught Daisy's eye while doing so. "I already have my prize," she cooed, and turned to peck Jonathan on the cheek for full benefit.

"Okay," said Eddie, tapping the table with tongs to get everyone's attention. "The teams are as follows: Jonathan, Maggie and Shannon on one team, and Christian, and myself, and Daisy on the other. Mum will referee. Good luck, everyone."

Eddie was in his element, issuing scores to his mother, who marked them on an old chalkboard that had been retrieved from the attic. As the game progressed, Jonathan's team were kicking ass, and Daisy became nervous.

"I'll never beat him," she whispered to Eddie as Jonathan prepared his serve. "Can't I change to play against Shannon?"

"Are you kidding?" said Christian, rubbing her shoulders in preparation for the game. "Shannon is an ex-school tennis champ, whereas Jonathan's only sporting claim to fame is a county medal for Gaelic football. Go on, you can do it."

Daisy wrestled from beneath his manly grasp. As much as she would have liked to have stayed under it forever and a day, this was a game she simply had to win.

She lifted the red, plastic racquet, struck a Venus Williams-style pose and asked Isobel to call a start to the game. The atmosphere was electric, with all contestants eyeballing each other like gladiator and lion in a Roman coliseum.

"Come on Daisy, love. Do it for me, darling," shouted Eddie, remembering whose side he was on. He seriously wondered whether a real boyfriend would let someone like Christian Devine be so near his girlfriend.

"Remember, the prize is only a chicken kebab. There's no need to take this all so seriously, and I am the tennis champion after all," Shannon warned the pair of them.

Daisy flashed her a reassuring smile, even though her insides were on fire. The chicken kebab was the last thing on her mind right now and she had heartburn even thinking about it. Poor Shannon didn't have a clue. Nobody had, except, perhaps, Jonathan.

"Is someone going to start? Whose turn is it to serve first?" asked Isobel, who was taking her job *very* seriously indeed. Refereeing for a chicken kebab between her son and her best friend's daughter was trying, to say the least. "Let's get a move on. It's almost dark."

Daisy lifted the ball, and charged it forehand in Jonathan's direction with such force that he had to duck. The ball swung unmercifully through the air, around the pole twice, before he had a chance to return her shot. He whacked the ball back hard and high, so that it looped over Daisy's head, totally out of reach and then wrapped itself around the steel pole again.

"Sorry," he muttered, unravelling it and handing it back to her to serve for the second time.

"Atta girl, Daisy. You're psyching him out. He's putty in your hands," said Christian from behind her, patting her shoulder to boost her confidence.

"Right, that's it, Devine," snarled Eddie. "Touch her again and it's you and me; bare-chested in the garden, man on man, alright?"

Christian looked down incredulously at Eddie who was staring back at him, chest puffed out. He couldn't help but laugh.

Christian then watched Jonathan's face tighten with concentration as he waited for Daisy to serve the ball. What the hell was going on between them, he wondered? Whatever their problem, they should just sort it for the sake of everybody else.

Daisy lifted the ball and tried to poise herself, but her concentration levels were faltering under the pressure. She had never intended coming face to face with Jonathan like this and no matter how she tried, she couldn't play happy families with him. Not now, not ever. Her eyes were beginning to sting and her head felt fuzzy. She shouldn't have had that fourth glass of wine.

"Do we really have to do this?" she asked.

"Yes," said her mother defiantly. "It's only a bit of fun. Don't be a party pooper."

"I'm with Daisy. This is all a bit pointless," argued Jonathan. "I mean, at this stage all I want to do is chill with a cold beer. Whose daft idea was this in the first place?"

"Eddie's," said Christian. "It certainly won me over."

Daisy leaned forward with a sigh and caught contact with Jonathan's blue eyes. Sensing her discomfort, he shrugged at her and then nodded for her to continue the game, if only to shut everyone else up. But suddenly something in Daisy snapped. She couldn't pretend any longer. Dropping the ball from her hand, she handed her racquet to Eddie, who was still too busy scowling at

Christian to notice her aggravation, and raced into the warmth of the house.

This shouldn't be happening, she thought, pounding through the kitchen as steaming tears ran through her make-up. Why was she letting the past haunt her so much? Why now?

"She never really was a good sport," concluded Maggie, reaching eagerly for the solitary kebab on the barbecue. "Every sports day at primary school I had to write a sick note for her teacher."

"Maybe, she's had too much to drink," said Jonathan, dropping his own racquet on the patio and reaching for a beer.

His face was sullen. If it wasn't for his mother's illness, he wouldn't be here at all. He was uncomfortable around Daisy and Eddie and their stupid games.

"Yeah, she didn't have a good colour. Should one of you go after her?" said Isobel with concern.

"Yes, I'd better go," said Maggie. "I'm her mother."

"Oh, don't worry," said Eddie in a panic. "Finish your wine. I'll go. I'm her betrothed."

Eddie made a face at Christian, who just shook his head in amusement as he watched Eddie skip in through the patio doors after his "girlfriend." This was entertainment at its best.

"Daisy. Daisy will you let me in?" Eddie tapped furiously on the bathroom door. "Daisy! Even if you don't want to tell me what's wrong, at least just open the door 'cos everyone is wondering what's going on!"

The lock eventually turned and Eddie gasped when he saw the state of his supposed 'girlfriend.'

"Where's your make-up bag, Miss Anderson? Your face looks like a mini war zone."

Daisy sniffled and wiped her nose with a tissue, then tried to clean around her eyes.

"It's in my bedroom across the road," she sniffed. "Be a pet and go and get it. If I leave it will only draw more attention. I need some time to compose myself."

80

"Okay, then," said Eddie. "Let's get you tidied up, and you can tell me exactly what all this is about, once and for all."

Daisy closed the bathroom door, put down the toilet seat and sat down for a good cry. The flashbacks were hurting her brain and she felt like a dam of emotion had crumbled after all these years of holding back feelings of regret, fear and of what might have been. She had never expected to react like this. Not in a million years.

On top of all that, this was so downright embarrassing. What was Christian thinking? That she was an out and out basket case probably. And as for Eddie? Well, she would have to think quickly of a good excuse for her pretend boyfriend. After all, he and Maggie would probably be faced with the Spanish Inquisition once she left for home.

There was a knock at the door again and Daisy straightened her clothes, threw a third sodden tissue down the toilet and tucked her hair behind her ears. She could always say she had PMT. No man, woman or beast would ever be fool enough to question that if they knew what was good for them.

She took a deep breath and unlocked the door. A bit of fresh make-up would work wonders. Maybe she could say she had a headache as well as PMT. She could also say she'd got soap in her eyes, or was that just taking things a step too far? All in all, it had been a bad day. She put her hand around the door, not wanting even Eddie to witness her progressively worsening appearance.

"Just hand it over quickly, Ed. I can hear everyone whispering. The longer I stay in here, the worse this will all seem."

Daisy grasped the purple silk purse that held her most worldly possessions and felt better already. She leaned on the door to close it but it wouldn't budge.

"Eddie, would you let go of the door? I'll only be two more minutes."

"Daisy, it's me," whispered a voice on the other side of the door. "We need to talk. Please."

Tentatively she opened the door, her heart leaping when she

81

saw Jonathan. He was leaning with one hand on the doorframe, his face crumpled and sore.

"No," she gulped, avoiding his gaze. "I can't talk about it."

The tears started to sting again and she bit her lip so hard it almost bled. She felt like a toddler with absolutely no control over her emotions, and she also felt drained.

"But if it helps? We both need to talk about it. I know I do…"

Daisy tucked her make-up bag under her arm and squeezed out of the bathroom past Jonathan. "I'm sorry."

He grabbed her arm but she shrugged him off.

"Don't, Jonathan. I said I don't want to talk about it. With anyone. And especially not with you."

Daisy walked purposefully towards the kitchen where Christian and Shannon had taken over the game of swingball in a bid to win the chicken kebab. Her mother and Isobel were engaged in a deep conversation and Daisy knew that their casual reminiscing would lead to emotional trips down memory lane. They always did. She looked back down the corridor at Jonathan who was still leaning on the bathroom doorframe, with his head tucked into his arm.

"I'm going to say goodnight to everyone now," she said back to him, searching frantically for inner strength. "I don't think this is doing any of us any good."

Jonathan looked up. His hair was ruffled and Daisy noticed his eyes watering, but she couldn't afford to acknowledge it. No going back.

"You're right," he said with a sniffle. "You run on home now, and when you come back tomorrow to continue this stupid game with Eddie, I for sure won't be around to witness it. If this is all for my benefit you're wasting your time, Daisy."

Daisy felt her blood boil. How downright arrogant was that? She marched towards him, all her sorrow and regret now turned to anger.

"Don't fucking flatter yourself, Jonathan! Can't you stand to see your own brother happy for once? Or do you always have to be one step ahead of him in everything?"

Jonathan looked at Daisy's tear-stained eyes. She looked so young and vulnerable that she could have been eighteen again. How she'd cried in his arms back then for nights on end. How their world had come crashing down around them. How often did he wish he could turn back time and make things different?

He couldn't help himself. He knew it was wrong but he had to touch her. His hands shaking, he lifted them and placed them gently on her slight shoulders. Then he reached out and cupped her cheeks, leaning in to kiss her. For a second he was sure she was going to respond, her lips opened and her eyes closed.

But then her hands met his and she turned away.

"No," she whispered. "No, Jonathan. This isn't right."

"Can't we at least talk about this, Daisy? We have to face up to it sometime." His heart was pounding with an overwhelming urge to make right all his wrongs of years gone by.

"This is hardly the time or the place to discuss things…"

"But when *will* be a good time? I need to know what you're thinking. We have a history we haven't got over yet. *Please.*"

His eyes were sorry. She had never remembered Jonathan like this. Daisy opened her mouth to reply when she was interrupted by somebody pointedly clearing their throat.

"Oh, excuse me. Am I interrupting something?"

Chapter 10

Close Encounters of the Second Kind

"Exactly, just *how* long have you been standing there, Eddie? You scared the *shit* out of me."

It took Daisy around three seconds to realise that Jonathan's hand was still frozen on her shoulder.

"That's irrelevant," Eddie snapped. "I've seen enough. This whole scenario has the strangest sense of déjà vu. Carry on, children. I'd hate to be the one to disturb love's young dream."

"Should I go after him?" Jonathan asked, leaning his head on the wall of the hallway. "I don't know what to think. Is he really upset or is this all part of the planned 'Daisy and Eddie' saga? This is all just Eddie's way pleasing Mum? Isn't it? Even though she knows and I know that?"

Daisy exhaled. She was weary now, her mind a muddled-up mess.

"Give it up and count your blessings, Jonathan. At least it wasn't Shannon who caught us."

Jonathan put his hand back onto her shoulder. He didn't care who saw them now. He just wanted to be close to Daisy. He lifted her chin again until their eyes met.

"I don't mind if she catches us, to be honest."

"Stop it. Stop it now. You *don't* mean any of this." Daisy pulled away from him for the second time. "Go back to your fiancée and forget all about me, Jonathan. It would never work. Never."

She marched away and Jonathan stood alone, cursing his emotions. They were out of control. He rubbed his temples and watched Daisy from beneath blurred eyes as she walked away from him. He was confused. Why had she come back into his life? Damn Eddie and his silly games. Didn't he realise just how much unfinished business existed between them? He had enough on his mind lately without all this added stress. It was time to get away for a while to sort his head out, he decided, once and for all.

****

Maggie unravelled her crinkled navy scarf and carefully removed her earrings in front of her dressing table mirror. Then she wiped the make-up from her face in the same skilful routine, which she'd practised since she was a teenager. She loved make-up. It had helped her disguise the pain she had suffered over the past few years.

Maggie wasn't ready to give into the years just yet, though. At fifty-six she was still sprightly and young at heart. Tragically she had been widowed young, but now, eight years later, she felt it was time to start enjoying herself again. Seeing Isobel stare death in the face had made her think differently about life.

She picked up her new Madonna t-shirt from the bed and placed it into her bottom drawer, tucking it safely beneath her winter cardigans and woolly jumpers. Her old faithful yellow version lay strewn over a chair in the corner of the room. She lifted it and held it to her face, inhaling its scent so deeply she could bring herself back to the day she'd first spotted it. Now she let her thoughts drift back to the man who had sold it to her from a market stall in Donegal.

It was funny. Everyone thought because the Virgin t-shirt was a genuine article from the archives that she must have developed a fanatic interest in Madonna, but the truth was that Maggie didn't even remember Madonna's Virgin Tour of 1985. Back then she had been a busy mother to her first-born child. However, because she'd recently taken up yoga and worn the t-shirt around the house a little too often, Daisy and her friends had come up with the notion that she was the singer's number-one fan.

Maggie had bought the t-shirt from an attractive bohemian-like artist. The man sold all sorts of trinkets from the back of his van – a feast of hidden delights and pure heaven for a hoarder like Maggie. Her favourite pastime was browsing through his collections of paintings, vinyl records and music memorabilia.

A widower of six years, his real job brought him to the most exotic corners of the world, painting landscapes and modern beauty. However buying and selling little novelties, and seeing a happy look on his regular customers' faces gave him great pleasure. Joining in at the flea market every other Friday was a pleasant hobby and chatting and bargaining with Maggie had made it even more worthwhile.

"Just tell me when you're ready and I'll treat you to a slap-up meal, no strings attached," he'd announced one day as he re-arranged seventies collectables on his small table.

"I'll hold you to that," Maggie had laughed, the twinkle in his eye making her own dance with joy at this virtual stranger's attention.

The Madonna t-shirt had been the last thing she had bought from him three months ago. She'd felt like a naughty schoolgirl when she realised how flirtatious their conversations had become. Still, Maggie sensed the chance of a new start, of some excitement in her small-town, often lonely, existence. Her easy chats with the marker vendor were far from the grief that seeped through the walls of her family home. Her outer confidence was, alas, only a delicate shell that hid the true hurt and loneliness she felt each night when she climbed into bed. Alone.

With the guilt of betraying Danny's memory looming over like an ever-present cloud, she'd nevertheless convinced herself to go out for her first dinner date with her new friend. Maggie had confided in her eldest child for some reassurance. Her son, Richard, almost always took her side, whereas Daisy had been the quintessential daddy's girl since day one. If she could only get the nod from Richard, it would give her the confidence to warm her daughter to the idea of her dating again. But to her surprise and disappointment, Richard had turned his nose up at the very suggestion of his mother being seen around town with a stranger. Thus the date had been cancelled. Now, she wished she hadn't listened to her son.

A knock on her bedroom door brought Maggie abruptly back to the present. Quickly she stuffed the t-shirt under her duvet, realising how much the definition of the parent-child role had become blurred with time. She shouldn't be hiding her feelings from Daisy, but after Richard's sharp reaction, she was afraid to mention going on a date again to anyone.

"Come on in, love. Is everything okay?" she shouted.

Daisy's tanned legs looked lankier than normal in her short nightshirt. Her blond hair bounced around her shoulders but there was a vulnerability in her eyes, despite her beauty and outer confidence. Maggie's two children had grown up as far apart as the ten years that separated their birthdays, and Daisy's confidence far exceeded that of her first-born. She definitely got that trait from her father, thought Maggie, glancing across towards the bed to make sure there was no glimpse of the yellow t-shirt winking from underneath the covers.

"I can't sleep, Mum. What the hell happened to me tonight?"

Maggie lay down on the bed and patted the spare pillow for her daughter to join her, just like in the old days. Daisy lay back and let her head rest into the squeak of her mother's marital bed.

"You're being very strange around Jonathan." Maggie rubbed her daughter's forehead like she used to when she was a child. "Do you still have feelings for him? Tell me the truth."

Daisy sat up and rubbed her legs, letting out an involuntary sigh. If only her mother knew just how complicated her memories of Jonathan were.

"I only wish I knew," she sighed. "I haven't seen him in so long and yet he seems to know me better than anyone else." She rubbed the duvet cover between her thumb and forefinger. "Christian hasn't changed a bit down the years. He'll always be a Jack the lad, but I can't read Jonathan at all anymore. Yet he still *knows* me. It's hard to explain."

Maggie wrapped her floral covers around Daisy's shoulders and looked into her sad brown eyes. Despite how carefree she tried to pretend she was, her mother could sense her distress.

"Perhaps part of your trouble is your reluctance to discuss the accident with him?"

"Mum, please don't…"

"But you'd both had such a row that day…" said Maggie softly. "It wasn't easy for him being plunged into the spotlight like that…" she said, trailing off mid-sentence.

"Has Richard called recently?" she asked.

"Richard? Oh, yes", said Maggie with pride. "He and Jennifer were here for dinner on Sunday past. You know your brother, Daisy. He may be stuck in his own ways but his heart's in the right place."

Indeed. In his mother's eyes, there was always an excuse for Richard's selfish ways, thought Daisy.

"Well, his heart might be in the right place, but the rest of him never seems to be in the right place at the right time. It's a wonder he comes around here at all since he hates the Eastwoods so much."

Maggie leaned away from her daughter and reached for a glass of water from the bedside locker. "I think *hate* may be too strong a word to use. He just finds it hard to accept what happened. It's different for him because he wasn't here on the night of the accident."

"Exactly," said Daisy, a little louder than intended. "He wasn't *here*. He was never *here*. For you, for me or for Dad. In fact, he was cruising around Monaco with his rich girlfriend when Dad died."

Maggie sat up in the bed. She could sense where this conversation was leading.

"Look, love, you can't fault Richard for wanting to spread his wings and see the world. It wasn't his fault he wasn't here at the time. I know I can't stop either of you from making lives of your own away from Killshannon."

Daisy knew her mother was right. Who was she to fault anyone for fleeing the nest? She, herself, had avoided her home town like the plague since her dad died. However she still had a stack of reasons and old wounds that just wouldn't heal.

"I know, Mum. But it just irritates me that since Richard has settled down and married his posh wife, he thinks he can throw his opinion around Killshannon like he's king of the castle. When we needed him he wasn't here. And the way he speaks of the Eastwoods! Does he forget that Jonathan and Eddie lost their own father that night?"

Maggie sighed. It was hard playing referee all the time.

"He's probably mad at himself for not being here, love, and he needs someone to blame…"

"No, Mum, this has got to stop. The court ruled that Jonathan was not at fault. Nobody was. And it was eight years ago. We all have to move on."

Maggie glanced at the picture of Danny on her bedside table while Daisy closed her eyes and let the nightmare of July 7th unfold once again. She remembered the apologetic policeman on the doorstep. She could still hear him mention the names of the two victims. She could still vividly recall the questions being asked about boy with no licence who was driving the car that killed Danny Anderson and Brendan Eastwood. Why had the two male victims been arguing in the back seat? Why? Why?

Daisy had her own precious secret memories. Nobody knew about them, except Jonathan of course, and the two men who went to heaven that day.

"Richard's wrong, Mum, so wrong. And even if I do still have feelings for Jonathan, I know we can never be the same again."

Maggie didn't respond so Daisy continued. "There's the minor detail of his fiancée for a start."

She turned to face her mother and her eyes were filled with tears.

"Oh, love. Just be careful, eh?" said Maggie. "I don't want you to get hurt all over again."

"You're right," she sniffed. "I don't know why I was stupid enough to agree to help Eddie in the first place. This isn't fair on Jonathan, me or Shannon. This isn't a game anymore. It's gone too far and I've had enough. I'm going back to Belfast tomorrow."

Chapter 11

It Never Pains But It Pours

Eddie awoke to the tick-tock of his mother's Grandfather clock which was coming from the narrow hallway of the cottage. Apart from its loud clicking sound, Killshannon was deadly quiet. As a child, if he listened hard enough on a windy day, Eddie could have heard the waves crashing from the nearby rugged shoreline. But this morning, the sun was splitting the trees and a hangover was splitting his head. He was not capable of concentrating on any noise whatsoever, and the clock's ticking felt like a family of woodpeckers nesting on his forehead.

He sat up to check on his brother, who lay peacefully sprawled across the single bed at the opposite side of the room. Isobel had never re-decorated their teenage bedroom and the boys' different tastes were still apparent by the opposing music icons that adorned the walls on either side.

Eddie's posters of Take That and Boyzone had moustaches and warts drawn over them by Jonathan. He was embarrassed by his brother's girly taste, preferring instead to build a shrine to Oasis and Blur on his side of the room. By way of revenge, Eddie had got his own back by colouring Liam Gallagher's lips pink and drawing huge eyelashes on Damon Albarn.

"Hey, Judas," he hissed when he sensed movement from beneath Jonathan's covers on the other side. "On a scale of one to ten, how much does your head hurt this morning? I'm sort of hoping for a ten plus."

"Huh?" mumbled Jonathan. "You talk too much, Ed. Give it a rest."

"Well, *my* head is banging and I'm still hearing Christian's rock god impressions from last night in my brain. How's yours? Go on, one to ten, with ten being excruciating and one being a fresh cool spring morning?"

"Em…," said his brother, rolling around in his half-sleep. "So far about four but I sense a creeper. I think it's going to be a killer of a day."

Jonathan turned in the bed and battled to open his eyes, knowing that because Eddie was wide awake, he would have to wake up too, otherwise he wouldn't have a minute of peace. He rubbed his forehead and shuddered when he recalled how he had promised Shannon he would go and look for wedding suits today. *Shit.*

"You know, Daisy and I once compiled a list of the top ten reasons not to drink alcohol," said Eddie. "It was called The Cringe Factor and it turned into a top thirty list instead. Very deep and meaningful, I might add…"

"Oh, shit no!" Jonathan shot up in the bed when he heard Daisy's name. His stomach flinched when he remembered about their encounter in the hallway and how close they had been to getting caught. He had even tried to kiss her.

"Right now, I could actually add quite a few of my own reasons to that list of yours," he groaned as the cringe factor kicked in.

"Mmm," said Eddie. "I could add a few on your behalf too. Let me see. 1, Alcohol makes you mess with your brother's girlfriend. 2, Alcohol makes you think you're a teenager again. 3, Alcohol makes you forget you are getting married in six weeks…Will I continue?"

"Please don't," said Jonathan, lying back and pulling a pillow over his head. "What the hell was I thinking? If Shannon had walked in on us, there would have been blood on the floor. She would have freaked. Oh holy *fuck*."

Eddie smiled to himself, then sprang up straight and pulled the duvet over his chest to cover his bronzed modesty.

"*Shannon* would have freaked? What about poor *Eddie*? Did *Eddie* not walk around the corner to see his brother and his own girlfriend locked in an embrace and looking all sorrowful and romantic? *Huh*? Does *Eddie* not have feelings too? Is *Jonathan* forgetting something? That Eddie *did* catch you two out?"

Jonathan's face broke into a wide grin at the sight of his brother as he gripped the bedclothes tight around his middle. His own bedclothes were strewn around his waist, and he was naked underneath while Eddie's pyjama bottoms were tucked under his pillow each morning in preparation for the night ahead.

"Look, Eddie," he whispered. "Please don't feel you have to keep up this act with me. I know you mean well, but Mum is a big girl now and I really think she can cope with the fact that you're gay. You don't even have to say anything to her. Just stop pretending you're something you're not. Leave Daisy out of it."

Eddie was about to open his mouth to protest when he realised he was just wasting his time. Jonathan didn't believe his efforts for a second. He decided he may as well come clean.

"The thing is, Jonathan, that I *so* want to tell Mum. I swear I do. But I can't. I'm so afraid of letting her down."

"Oh come on, Eddie..."

"It's alright for *you*. Mum thinks you're the bees' knees – an English teacher at St Benedict's, settled and marrying into an affluent family like Shannon's. What am I to her? Only an LA bum waiter who hangs out with Hollywood wannabes."

"Hang on, Eddie. Do you think I have all the answers in my life? I am so, so fucking confused right now."

"*Hardly.*"

"I am. What I did last night with Daisy, or tried to do, only proves how much so. I am scared shitless of what lies ahead for our family in the near future. Mum may only have months, weeks even, and all Shannon wants to do is talk about weddings and honeymoons. My head is astray. I haven't a clue if I'm coming or going."

Eddie sat up straight and let out a sniffle.

"Well then *tell* her so. Tell Shanny and her Fanny to slow down with the wedding plans, if that's really how you feel. You have to make sure you're doing the right thing. Till death us do part is a big commitment. *Huge*. And you mightn't even die for another forty years."

Eddie pushed back the navy cotton curtains of the bedroom and saw a car pull into the driveway.

Jonathan frowned. "Shannon would be devastated if I postponed everything. She would marry me today if I could get it arranged. I don't want to let her down."

"But you've only known her five minutes! I just want you to do what is right for you, and from what I saw last night, I'm not sure if getting married is what you want or need right now."

Jonathan took a deep breath and sat on the edge of his brother's bed.

"Do you honestly think I could possibly stall the wedding planners from hell? I don't fancy my chances…"

"We could always have you kidnapped by gypsies or pirates or something. Leave it with me. I'll come up with something."

"Eddie, can you be serious for once in your life?" Jonathan said in exasperation, shaking his head at his brother's reluctance to face up to reality. "I am not going to cancel the wedding just because you want me to, so get off your high horse and admit that you have a bit of facing up to do yourself."

"*Alright*, then," sighed Eddie. "I'll try to tell Mum my own truths soon. Do you have any idea how hard it has been for me, growing up in the fear that I will some day let my mother down for being different?"

"Eddie, Mum adores you."

"But what if this changed things? I can be who I am in San Francisco. I can stand up and be proud of who I am and I can be myself, but when I come here and I look at Mum and her traditional views on marriage and children I think of how much it would break her heart if I wasn't the person she wanted me to be. I'm so scared, Jonathan. I'm so scared of letting her down."

"I think you are underestimating her, big time," said Jonathan. He hated to see his brother put himself through such unnecessary pain. Eddie was his mother's blue-eyed boy, just the way he was, but he would hopefully learn that before it was too late.

"Maybe I am," said Eddie, "but in the meantime, please play along with what I've asked Daisy to do for me. Just to buy me some time to get my life sorted out. *Please*. And I'll try and do the same for you."

****

A few doors down, Daisy knocked back a handful of painkillers while her mother prepared a full Irish breakfast.

"Can you please leave out the eggs, Mum? The very look of them is turning my stomach."

Maggie ignored her and clicked on the frying pan.

"So, what are your plans for today?" she asked.

"My plan is to race back to Belfast as quickly as I can and crawl into a hole after last night…"

"Ah, Daisy you don't have to leave yet, do you? Things aren't that bad. What about your promise to Eddie?"

Daisy winced. If it wasn't for Eddie and his wild idea, she wouldn't be in this situation at all.

"I don't know if I can keep up with his efforts. They're so forced. Oh, Mum, what will I do? You're supposed to have all the answers."

Maggie lined up some streaky rashers in the sizzling frying pan.

"I am? I say you should do what you think is best for yourself.

You know your own mind by now, Daisy."

Daisy sighed and stared out the window across the cul-de-sac to where the Eastwoods' house stood.

"The problem is that I can't really think straight at all at the moment, which is why I feel like running right back to Belfast."

Daisy noticed a new sadness in her mother's eyes that tugged at her heart when she mentioned leaving Killshannon. She walked towards her and gave her an impromptu cuddle. Maggie took a deep breath and pushed Daisy's hair from her eyes.

"Why would you want to go back to an empty city apartment when you can get some fresh sea air here?"

Daisy felt torn but she couldn't deny the beseeching look on her mother's face. She seemed almost lonely.

"I suppose I *could* stick it out for another day or so, but please make sure I stay out of Jonathan's way. I don't want to be labelled a marriage-wrecker."

Maggie brightened immediately.

"How about you and I go for a nice walk around town?" she asked, delighted that she'd convinced her daughter to stay a bit longer. "We can go into Donegal and have a browse around the shops. It always works for me when I can't think straight. It'd be nice for us to share a few girly hours together on our own."

Ow. That went right to Daisy's heart. She hadn't spent a day alone with her mother in so long. The last time had been in Belfast on her mum's last birthday. They'd had a lovely time browsing in boutiques on the Lisburn Road and relaxing over a coffee afterwards in Randals Coffee House. Maggie loved pretending to be a trendy city lady and even though Daisy was not the shopping type, browsing with her mum was always fun.

"Shopping? Are you sure?" she asked. "But I thought you'd planned a day in the garden with a good book? I don't want to disturb your routine."

"I can have my routine any day of the week when you aren't here. The sun and the book can wait. We could go to the Blueberry

Teahouse for scones and have a look around the craft village. That will take your mind off the Eastwood boys for a few hours."

"Good idea," said Daisy, giving her mum a tight squeeze. "And I can only hope and pray that Eddie hasn't planned any more get-togethers in the near future. You know me, I can't bear all this happy family nonsense."

Maggie reached for milk from the fridge, then whisked four eggs in a glass bowl before adding them to the frying pan.

"Speaking of which," she paused, "I told Richard we'd meet him for lunch before you go back to Belfast."

Daisy plonked down on the cane chair in the corner of the kitchen. This was all she needed to add to the pain of her hangover. A lunch date with her pompous older brother? Fantastic, not.

"Oh, shall we go to the Ritz? Or have brunch with Donegal's answer to Posh 'n' Becks on the in-law's yacht?"

"Don't be rude now. He just wants to treat us to a nice meal, that's all."

Daisy grunted. "Is Her Royal Highness going to be there?"

"I take it you mean Jennifer? Yes, I'd imagine so," said Maggie, spooning the scrambled eggs onto a plate of mushrooms, sausages and bacon. The very smell was turning Daisy's stomach.

"Super. I can hardly wait to hear how Precious, the prize poodle is doing. I've been worried about her matted left paw for *so* long now."

Maggie couldn't help but laugh. She knew Jennifer could be hard work sometimes, but she was family now, so they just had to accept her.

"You haven't even seen their wedding album yet. You'll at least pretend you are interested, won't you, love?"

Daisy swung her legs under the chair like a disgruntled teenager.

"Yeah, yeah, I suppose. But if I'm asked by either of them about my five-year career plan, or when I'm going back to college to get a real degree, I'll tell them where to go."

Maggie tutted.

"Well, today they're eating with their solicitor friends," she said, "but I'm hoping we could arrange something sooner rather than later."

Daisy stuck her fingers into her mouth pretending she was going to be sick, but then decided she didn't want to push her luck with the vomit monster. It was starting to rear its ugly head after last night's antics.

"Why do all their friends have to fit into groups?" she asked in frustration. "Why is everyone referred to as 'solicitor' friends, or 'brain surgeon' friends? I must remember the next time Lorna and I are going out on the razz to tell the girls in Super Shoes that I'm going out with my 'hairdresser' friend, or that I just popped home to see Eddie, my 'waiter' friend. They'd be so impressed."

Maggie smirked. Daisy had a point.

"And what about Daisy the 'actress' friend? Does she still exist? I hope she does."

Daisy's head dropped.

"Oh come on, Mum. What's the point? It's in my heart to act, it really is, but I need some way of paying the bills."

"And working in Super Shoes does?"

"It's better than nothing. For now anyway."

Maggie sighed.

"But you were the Sunflake Girl," she said with pride.

Daisy's eyes widened. She was glad she'd never told her mum about the condom advert she'd filmed for a Germany in her early twenties.

"I see one of the support nurses has arrived to see Isobel," Maggie said, staring out the window in concern. "Today is Wednesday so it's probably just her routine check. I'm not going to rush over to investigate, now that the boys are home."

The kitchen fell silent apart from the scraping of Daisy's knife and fork as she played with her food, unable now to stomach any of it. She glanced at her mother and knew immediately that she too had lost her appetite.

"Right, come on you," she said. "Eat up your breakfast and we'll get away from it all for a day, just you, me and our credit cards."

****

Jonathan walked towards his mother's bedroom at the far end of the cottage first floor.

"You get the door, Ed, and I'll peep in at Mum and let her know the nurse is here," he said, pulling on a fresh t-shirt as he walked.

"No you go, please!" said Eddie. "I'm not even dressed! I wouldn't want to give the nurse the wrong idea…"

Eddie went back into the bedroom and shut the door tight. He fanned his nose when he smelt a waft of stale alcohol in the room and opened all the windows.

"Good morning," said the middle-aged lady at the door. "I'm here to see Isobel."

"Hi. Mum's in bed but I'll let her know you're here."

The nurse followed Jonathan through the narrow hallway and he gestured for her to have a seat in the small living room. Jonathan glanced out through the patio doors and saw the remnants of last night's get-together in the normally immaculate back garden. The swing ball swayed in the light breeze, a few empty wine bottles stood on the patio table, which had been pushed far back from its usual central position, and its wooden chairs were scattered in a haphazard fashion, so unlike Isobel's usual tidy disposition.

"Em, I'm sorry, I didn't get your name…" said Jonathan, peeping his head around the doorframe a few minutes later.

"It's Julia," replied the nurse. "Is everything okay? Would your mum like me to come and see her in her bedroom?"

Jonathan thought for a second. "Actually, I think that would be a great idea. She's seems very weak this morning. We had visitors last night. Maybe it was all a bit too much for her…"

The nurse shuffled behind him as he led the way upstairs. Jonathan could hear Eddie still rummaging about in his bedroom.

99

He felt like shaking him.

"It's quite normal for your mother to have an off day at this stage of her illness," said the nurse kindly. "I'll have a chat to her about pain relief and her feelings in general. We'll take it from there and I'll keep you informed."

Jonathan opened the door and let the nurse in to where his mother lay. A tiny figure in her huge marital bed, her eyes were becoming more and more sunken by the day and her skin was almost as pale as the sheets she lay on. She gave the nurse a weak smile and nodded a thank you to her son, who felt a wave of emotion seep right through his bones. His poor mother had been through so much down the years, but the way things now looked, a new bout of suffering was only beginning.

"Jonathan, your mobile is ringing," shouted Eddie from the bedroom. "I think it's your morning call from Miss Tippy-Toes."

Jonathan sighed at his brother's tactless timing and Shannon's too. He glanced back in at his mother, closed the door gently and reluctantly left to talk wedding plans with his fiancée.

Chapter 12

The Best Things In Life Are Freebies

Being cooped up in a small village for two whole days had given Daisy a sense of cabin fever. She was now only too glad to be going to the hubbub of Donegal town to give her a taste of the city life. The journey was pleasant, with the gentle hum of Highland Radio in the background as they passed through familiar colourful towns such as Milltown and Mountcharles.

The county town itself was heaving with shoppers and tourists and Daisy was eager to get stuck in as she eyed up tiny independent fashion boutiques, hotels and brightly painted cafés and restaurants, which sat under the watchful eye of the magnificent town centre castle.

Her mother expertly pulled the Volkswagen Beetle into a space in the Diamond and let out a sigh of relief when she stretched her legs out in the intensifying heat. The forty-minute drive from Killshannon was crucifying in hot sunshine and they both longed for a long cool drink before hitting the shops.

"Now, Mum. I was just going to ask if you'd like to have a manicure while I browse around the shops."

Maggie halted in amazement and examined her nails.

"That would be lovely, pet. But what are you going to get up

101

to yourself?"

"I'll keep myself busy. Don't worry."

The first thing on Daisy's "to do" list was to find a post office or bank where she could change all her now-useless travellers' cheques from her non-holiday in Spain. Lodging some of the money back into her account was something she'd just have to force herself to do. But she intended spending some of it today.

"This place looks quite posh," she said, spotting the bright-red door of Beauty Principles, a chic new salon right in the town centre, which offered top-to-toe beautifying without an appointment. "I'm sure you could while away a few hours in here, Mum?"

"I think I could. This is a lovely surprise, Daisy. I'm looking forward to a bit of pampering."

The door chimed on entry and the two women were greeted instantly by a cheery, middle-aged therapist who ran through all of the treatments available. She also outlined a special offer of the day, which included a mini facial, followed by a neck and shoulder massage.

Daisy saw Maggie's eyes light up at the sound of it all. The stress of dealing with Isobel's horrific news was beginning to take its toll on her weary mind and this offer seemed just what the doctor ordered.

"She'll have the special, please," chirped Daisy firmly.

The lady asked Maggie to have a seat in the pan-piped waiting room, where another young girl in the same white uniform was rearranging a stack of up-to-date glossy magazines.

"Really, Daisy, you don't have to go to any expense."

"Trust me, I'm feeling rich today. That doesn't happen very often."

With her mother settled in, Daisy set off to clear her own head and have a good long think about what Jonathan had done and said the night before. She found a corner shop and bought an ice-lolly, then spied a bench in the shade outside one of the town's newer hotels. Good. She could sit there and people-watch, while cooling down from the blistering heat. Then she'd definitely find a post office.

Donegal was a thriving town. In the summer it was a pleasure to watch the different cultures and nationalities mingle through its streets. Even tiny fishing villages like Killshannon attracted its fair share of tourists now, while the more remote parts of the county were known to appeal to worldwide celebrities. Donegal now had a small taste of the cosmopolitan life that Belfast enjoyed. With on-street café bars, scattered market stalls and a string of spanking new hotels, it was a very different town to the one she remembered as a child. Back then, there had been no craft village, no tourism push and the town had been much quieter.

As she absorbed the atmosphere of the busy streets, she found herself wondering where Jonathan lived, where he taught and how he and Shannon had first got together.

With her mind still in a muddle, Daisy took a stroll further into the town centre where several market stalls were set up in a haphazard fashion. They drew in her attention like a magnet.

One stall was decked out in Irish tricolours, leprechauns and lucky four-leaf clovers, much to Daisy's disappointment. However to the left of that tacky stall was another one where a fifty-some-thing man wearing denims and a cool grey t-shirt, was struggling with a life-size portrait of a 1970s model with big hair and an even bigger grin. Intrigued, Daisy made her way over.

"Did all models in the seventies try to look like Farrah Fawcett?" she asked the man.

"Oh, hi there. I'm not sure. You'd need to ask someone who was born then", he said with a smile, wiping beads of sweat from his brow with a handkerchief. "But before you comment any further, be careful. I know the photographer personally."

As soon as he turned around, Daisy noticed how the man's eyes seemed to sparkle in the sunshine. They were the brightest colour of blue and she couldn't help but stare. This was a man with an interesting story to tell, she reckoned.

"I missed the seventies myself," she chuckled. "I can proudly claim to be an eighties child. I make sure to remind my older brother at every opportunity. He's ten years older."

The older man leaned on the edge of a table as Daisy browsed around his stall. She could feel his eyes follow her as she lifted and admired much of his stock. Many items were probably worth a small fortune. This man must be off his rocker, she thought. Why was he wasting his time? He could flog this lot in one go if he played his cards right.

"OK, eighties child, let me give you my sales pitch," he said eventually. "Everything here is a one hundred percent authentic collectable from the past thirty years. If you see something you like, let me know and we can barter. Don't worry – I'm a big softie behind my steely exterior."

Daisy glanced at the man and looked away again when she realised how intense his stare was. It was almost as if he recognised her from somewhere.

"I believe you," she replied, lifting up and then setting down pieces of memorabilia and treasures from days gone by. "Excuse me for being rude, but haven't you ever thought of selling all of this on eBay? You'd make a fortune."

The man laughed and walked around to the other side of the stall. He leaned his strong, brown arms on the table and thought carefully before replying.

"The internet is a wonderful tool, but if I had a penny, or a sale, from everyone who made the same suggestion as yourself, I could donate more to charity than I currently do. I suppose you could call me old-fashioned…"

"You look quite trendy to me," said Daisy quickly, taking in the men's designer label on his jeans.

"My clothes? My teenage daughter dresses me. She doesn't want her old man joining the pipes-and-slipper brigade just yet. And besides," he said, tapping his chest, "being out and about like this keeps the old ticker healthy."

"But could somebody make a good living out of this?" she quizzed, curiosity getting the better of her. She quite fancied herself taking on a similar project. If she set up a stall it would be a good way to meet lots of interesting people.

"No, this is more a hobby than a job and I'm normally only here the odd Friday. However earlier on today I heard that a huge European business delegation is staying at the Lough Eske Castle Hotel up the road. I thought I'd practise my linguistic skills on them this afternoon."

Before he could say anything else, a familiar voice greeted Daisy from behind.

"Well, fancy meeting you here, Crazy Daisy."

She turned around swiftly to see Christian Devine walk towards her with a newspaper tucked under one arm and a tiny one-eyed cat following him.

"If it isn't Christ Devine! And what the hell is *that*?" she squealed. "Are you now going to tell me you're an animal lover as well as having found a heart somewhere along the line?"

Christian nodded in acknowledgement at the stallholder.

"Hi, Geoff," he said. "Is my good friend just talking the leg off you or has she actually got around to buying something yet?"

"Do you two know each other?" asked Daisy in confusion.

"We do indeed. Christian teaches my youngest girl at college. I'm trying to deny the fact that each and every one of her classmates has a blatant crush on him," laughed Geoff. "The cat, however, is as new to me as it is to you, young lady. Only a strapping stud could get away with it."

"It looks a wee bit strange to say the least," said Daisy.

Christian shrugged his shoulders. "Every man needs a companion, and deaf old Buddy here has been listening intently to me for the past few days."

Geoff threw his eyes up and whispered across to Daisy. "That guy knows he has a host of female buddies he could call upon any time. Just who does he think he's fooling?"

105

Daisy was just about to agree when she saw the look on Christian's face.

"My girlfriend, Anna, is on a six-month trip to Copenhagen," he said defensively. "She's teaching English as a foreign language."

Geoff shrugged. "I suppose we all have to settle down one day. Fair play to you, Christian. I hope it all works out for the best."

Daisy picked up a black and white Brigitte Bardot photo. "How much for this?" she asked Geoff, who was wiping his brow again from the glare of the sun.

"For you, my dear, it's on the house."

"What? No bargaining?"

"Nah, take it. I enjoyed the chat," said Geoff. "Maybe you'll come back another day."

"I most certainly will," said Daisy.

Geoff winked at her in appreciation and slid the small picture into a brown paper bag. Then he bade farewell as Christian and Daisy made their way back into the main shopping thoroughfare.

"Will I dump old Buddy back to my place so we can grab a coffee?" asked Christian as they neared the street that led to his apartment. "On me, of course, seeing as it's your day for bagging freebies."

Daisy checked her watch. "I have about thirty minutes. "How far away do you live from here?"

"Only a stone's throw. Come on, I'll show you."

The pair of them trotted off down a narrow street, which was lined with bars and restaurants of all shapes and sizes.

"This is a nice place. Very central," said Daisy, taking in the hustle and bustle of the various street cafés. She thought she recognised a bar waiter at one of the pubs they passed en route. He was serving some backpackers cool pints of Guinness at an outdoor picnic table. Suddenly he looked up and greeted Christian, who made a rude gesture in return.

Daisy was astounded. "Did I just see you give somebody the middle finger?"

"You absolutely did. Gerry's his name. He's one of the Killshannon O' Donnells and he thinks he knows it all and the price of it. That was just a bit of a joke between us. He knows the score."

"Ah, yes. I thought he looked familiar."

They carried on down the street with Daisy shaking her head in bewilderment as she followed Christian and Buddy up a narrow, concrete staircase to his apartment. Very much a bachelor pad, his place was bright and airy, decorated impeccably in soft coffee and creams. Christian flicked on the kettle. Daisy wondered why he hadn't treated her to the trendy espresso bar across the road.

"Are you getting stingy in your old age, Mr Devine? "Next thing, you'll be complaining about being paid a full salary all summer when you are mind-numbingly bored at home with only Buddy for company."

"I know, I know. The cruelty of it all. It sometimes is so tough being me," he laughed back. "So tell me, what on earth happened between you and Jonathan last night? You could have cut the atmosphere with a knife."

Daisy drew a sharp breath. "Look, Christian, both Jonathan *and* Eddie have a lot on their minds at the minute. I'm here to help Eddie out with something, but I'm *certainly* not here to interfere in Jonathan's relationship with Shannon."

Christian opened the window and lit up a cigarette. "That girl absolutely worships Jonathan to the point of obsession almost, but if he has strong feelings for you he shouldn't deny them."

Daisy almost did a double take. "And when did you become so philosophical? Aren't you the very man who is renowned for having one woman on your arm and another waiting in the wings?"

Christian didn't answer but took a deep draw on his cigarette instead.

"Ow, touchy subject. I'm sorry," she said, trying to retract the sting of her comment.

"I've changed, Daisy. Believe me, I have. I've spent four years away from this country, touring the world and seeing more than most people witness in an entire lifetime. Sure, I still flirt and give the odd stranger in the street the eye for the craic. But I've got a steady girlfriend now and nobody is taking it seriously."

Silence hung in the air as Daisy scrabbled to think of a reply. "Is Buddy blind *and* deaf?" she asked, hoping to lighten the mood, "because if so, then he's the lucky one. That sad, moping face of yours would turn anyone off their cornflakes."

Christian managed to laugh at Daisy's ability to bring him back into the land of the living with her humour. She'd always made him smile. Ever since the night he'd stolen a kiss from her back at the high school ball. He was still paying for that one, mind. She'd accompanied Jonathan to the dance so she should have been off-limits, but back in those days a bet was a bet was a bet.

"I'm more a Cheerios man, actually. But do go easy on Jonathan, Daisy," he muttered softly. "Everyone deserves a second chance, if that's what he wants."

Daisy raised an eyebrow. "Is that your new-found guilty conscience kicking in, Devine?"

"No, not at all. You two have a lot of history between you."

Daisy put her cup in the sink. "I know, that's the problem," she said. "I'm afraid to take any risks the way I'm feeling at the moment."

She looked up and their eyes locked for a moment longer than either of them felt comfortable with. Her heart started beating a little faster than normal when Christian pulled his chair closer.

"So, Sunflake Girl," he said gently. "Eddie was boasting last night about your fantastic acting talents and I was really impressed. How's that going?"

Daisy felt her face flush. "Oh, it's not as grand as he makes it out to be," she said, recalling her string of failed auditions and lack of agent. "I'm taking a bit of a break, to be honest. I'm trying my hand in the retail sector."

"Oh. So what type of acting do you normally do?"

She drew a breath and rhymed off her usual answer.

"Mostly theatre productions, the odd TV commercial – anything that will pay the bills, to be honest. I've had bit parts on movie sets. Remember the one shot in Belfast a few years back with Brad Pitt?"

"Yeah, I remember. The one where he'd the dodgy Northern Irish accent?" said Christian. He was sitting very close to her now and she was finding it hard to concentrate.

"That's the one. Well, I was skulking in the background in one of the scenes. You can see my shoulder if you squint really hard at the bottom right of the screen."

"Impressive," laughed Christian. "Now I can tell my friends I know someone who knows Brad Pitt."

"Well, my shoulder knows him quite intimately."

Christian laughed and their eyes met again.

"Listen, Christian. It's been great seeing you again but I'd better be off…" said Daisy, standing up swiftly.

"Yeah, of course."

Another uncomfortable silence hung in the air as she stood in the doorway.

"No, I didn't mean it like that. I mean, I know your mum is waiting…" he said quickly.

"I know."

"Look, it's been really great catching up with you like this. Maybe we can do so again before you disappear back to your new city life?"

Daisy felt her tummy give a stranger flutter. "Yeah, why not? It could be fun…"

Christian smiled and ran his fingers through his hair.

"And you must admit, my coffee is *much* better value than that overpriced nonsense across the way."

"Yip. That's the best instant coffee I've had in a long time. How on earth do you make it taste so good?" she laughed.

Christian led Daisy down the narrow side steps and shooed Buddy back inside.

"I'll tell you what. The next time I'm visiting my sister in Belfast you can return the favour. Here, take my mobile number and we can keep in touch," he said, handing her a torn piece of paper.

"Perhaps I'll see you before then," she said. "I have another few days of complicated acting left to do in Killshannon."

"You can do it. Break a leg, as always, Daisy," said Christian and he leaned forward to kiss her cheek. His lips were hot and she felt his soft stubble rub against her face. Hold yourself together now, she thought as her tummy did a somersault.

"I'll see you soon," she said quickly and walked away in confusion.

Christian watched Daisy make her way down the steps, then gave Gerry the barman another middle finger sign when he noticed him staring from across the road. He made his way back into his apartment with a strange glow in his heart because Crazy Daisy Anderson was back in his life and he had a funny feeling she was going to stay for a while.

****

When Daisy reached Beauty Principles she was glowing as much as her mother who had just finished her luxurious treatment. She'd enjoyed spending some time with Christian.

"You look like the cat that got the cream," said Maggie as they strolled towards the car. "Forget beauty therapy, you are a walking advertisement for retail therapy. What on earth did you buy? Where are all your shopping bags?"

Daisy squeezed into the front seat of the car and sat her handbag on her knee.

"You should know by now how much I hate shopping, Mum. It bores me to tears. But I did come across the most amazing little market stall, where I was given an authentic photograph of a young Brigitte Bardot. Look, it's signed on the back by the photographer, who is a personal friend of Geoff's, the really cool

110

guy who runs the stall."

Maggie turned the key in the ignition and her heart skipped a beat. Had she heard her daughter correctly?

"And, then who did I bump into, Mum? Only TLC! I had coffee with him in his apartment and he was so sweet, but I have to say, he is very, very settled now and in love with Anna. However, I did get a kiss on the cheek. Yum!"

"Uh huh," mumbled Maggie as she forced herself to concentrate on her reverse out of the parking space.

"Oh, am I rambling? Sorry, how did your treatment go? I was too distracted to ask."

Maggie straightened the steering wheel and drove under the barriers of the pay-and-display car park.

"That photo you bought," she said. "Did you check the photographer's name on the back of it?"

Daisy scrambled in her handbag again for the picture, then turned it over to make out the signature.

"It says Geoff something or other and it was taken in 1976. I can't make out the surname…"

"Gallagher? Does it say Gallagher?" asked Maggie.

"Yes, that's it. Geoff Gallagher. Geoff on the stall is the photographer! Wow! He never said. Do you know him?"

Maggie put her foot down on the accelerator. "Sort of," she smirked. "I sort of know him. Now, why don't you tell me all about your encounter with Christian Devine?"

Chapter 13

You Can Shoo Your Friends, But You Can't Shoo Your Relatives

"SOS. Earth to Daisy!"

Eddie pulled a single hair from the side of Daisy's head and tweaked it in a bid to wake her up.

"Jesus. That was sore," she said, rubbing her head and sitting up straight on the sofa in her mum's living room. "What way is that to wake anyone?"

Eddie lifted her ankles and sat underneath them at the far end of the couch.

"What age are you, anyway?" asked Eddie in defence. "One hundred? Imagine having to take a nap at this time of the evening. What a fader!"

Daisy gave him a playful kick and he grabbed her bare foot and threatened to tickle it.

"Please, please, no tickles. By the way, have you seen my mum?"

Eddie let go of Daisy's foot and winced. "She's over with mine," he whispered. "The nurse called earlier this morning. She's very low, Daisy. It's so, so hard to watch. I had to get out for a while..."

"Oh, Ed. Things are happening so fast and there's nothing you can do. I really feel for you."

"Yeah. Of course, Jonathan did all the talking to the nurse while

I hid like the cowardly lion in the bedroom the whole time she was there. I am totally useless. I'm a big baby and I know Jonathan is about to blow a fuse if I don't start acting like an adult throughout all of this. But I just can't face the truth. I mean, I can't even bear to ask any questions about how long she has left, or what her pain levels are. I just keep thinking this is all a bad dream and that she's going to get better. But she's not, is she?"

Daisy stood up and reached out her hand to Eddie's. "Come on. Let's go into the kitchen and make a nice hot cuppa and then we'll go over together and have a bit of a chat with her. What do you say?"

Eddie lifted himself off the couch and slung an arm around Daisy's shoulders, ruffling her hair amicably.

"I'd say you are turning into a proper little old Killshannon housewife – a hot cup of tea will change the world," he laughed. "If only tea was as powerful as we Irish believe it to be."

Daisy led Eddie into the kitchen and turned on the kettle. It hissed from the modern Rayburn cooker as Daisy grabbed two mugs from the cupboard. "So what's on the agenda tonight, then? A romantic meal for two, a cosy cinema date, a stroll in the park… go on, surprise me."

"Okay, your mission, if you choose to accept it, is to help me entertain my eccentric old aunts, Delilah and Dolores, over tea and triangular sandwiches. They're driving from Sligo to see Mum and the thought of facing them on my own is too much to bear."

"Oh, please!" Daisy could sense a disaster looming ahead. "Isn't Jonathan going to be there? This is all becoming very complicated."

"Er, no. After last night's little scene he has decided to keep a low profile. He's spending the evening in Donegal with Christian. He says he needs some male bonding to help him sort his head out, but I'm not supposed to tell you that. Woops, I just did! Besides, I think Christian got some bad news from Denmark."

Daisy accidentally poured boiling water onto the worktop at the news.

"Oh no. What's wrong? Did something happen to what's-her-name? Anna?"

"Not at all. I believe his little Anna is fine and having a whale of a time with her new-found foreign friends. On the other hand, Mr Devine, the serial philanderer of Killshannon, has for once been given a taste of his own medicine. He's been, if you like to say, he's been…well…"

****

"Dumped? Sorry, Anna. Did I just hear what you said correctly? Maybe, it's a bad line…"

Christian had heard his phone ring faintly in the background when he'd been chatting to Daisy at the bottom of the stairs of his apartment. After he'd said goodbye, he'd raced back upstairs and re-dialled immediately when he saw the missed call.

"I didn't say it quite as abruptly as that, Christian. All I'm asking is for a bit of space to enjoy myself. I'm meeting lots of new people here and I'm only twenty-five years old. You've been there, and done that, so you can't blame me for wanting some fun."

Christian was stunned. Didn't she realise what she was doing to him? He had pledged to stay faithful to her for six months while she couldn't even last three days! He had to think fast.

"Look, Anna, flying your kite around is not all it's cracked up to be, believe me. Yes, I'm a couple of years older but we're hardly Michael Douglas and Catherine Zeta Jones!"

Anna gave what sounded like an irritated sigh. "I'm really sorry, Christian, but I don't want to waste your time. I could sit here and promise you the world and then go out tonight and behind your back…"

"Enough. I think I get the picture," he mumbled, rubbing his forehead with frustration.

"I just don't want to hurt you by keeping you hanging on. After Copenhagen I might try Australia for a year. I've got a lot

114

of living to do before I settle down, and I get the feeling you're looking for 'the one.'"

Christian couldn't bear to listen to her any more. He felt like he had been stabbed all over and didn't know which part of him hurt the most. He'd made such a fool of himself, declaring his love for Anna at every turnaround and to anyone and everyone who would listen.

"Of course you have, and I shouldn't have presumed otherwise," he said with a lump in his throat the size of a golf ball. "Enjoy yourself, Anna, and be good. And if you can't be good be careful…"

"And if you can't be careful, buy a pram," she replied. "I think you told me that one before. Take care, Christian. You're a good guy."

"Yeah, yeah. Bye Anna."

Christian stared at the screen on his phone for at least ten minutes before he could decide what to do with himself. He lit up a cigarette, then stubbed it out again after two puffs. Right now, what he needed was a stiff drink or something stronger. He looked through the window to The Chocolate Bar across the road, where the lunchtime rush had subsided. Gerry had obviously left for his hard-earned break. Grabbing his phone and keys, he skirted down the steps of the apartment, dodging traffic across the road and darting into the cool shade of the bar, where he ordered a neat brandy to ease his pain.

****

Jonathan found Christian Devine sitting in a dark corner booth in The Chocolate Bar feeling very sorry for himself.

"Of all the corners in the world, you just had to walk into mine," said Christian with an ever-so-slight slur. "Thanks for coming over, mate. I know you have a lot going on at home. I really appreciate it."

Jonathan pulled out a small stool from beneath the table and sat down. "Ah, Chris, things are really going downhill now with

115

Mum. It's almost unbearable. Truthfully I'm glad to be here for a few hours just to have a sense of normality."

Christian signalled to the bar for another drink.

"So, how's the form anyhow?" continued Jonathan. "I am sorry to hear about your break-up, honestly."

"You win some, you lose some, I suppose. Anna Harrison wasn't the girl for me, after all. I got it so wrong. What a stupid dick I am," he mustered, shaking his dark hair with a tight smile. "How could I have been so bloody stupid?"

"You weren't stupid. That's a bit harsh. You may be thick-headed from time to time, but I wouldn't call you stupid."

A clean-cut boy, barely over the age of eighteen, served the men their pints and took Christian's money.

"Hey, do you have a girlfriend, young lad?" asked Chris when he returned with his change.

The youngster shook his head. "Not at the minute, but I'm open to offers. Have you someone in mind?"

"Nah, nah. Stay single forever 'cos women do nothing but screw up your head. Take advice from an expert who knows exactly what he's talking about."

The waiter scurried back behind the bar after looking at Christian like he'd lost the plot.

"You have turned into a right old cynic in the space of a few hours," accused Jonathan. "It was only a couple of days ago that you were love's number one fan and now you've turned into a grump. What will you be tomorrow? A celibate priest? Mind you, that *would* be a surprise."

"Actually, I quite fancy being a Shaolin Monk and shaving my head. I've wanted to do that ever since I first watched The Matrix."

Jonathan slurped his pint and smacked his lips without responding.

"Did you just hear a word I said?" asked Christian.

"About what?"

"About my ambition to be a Shaolin Monk? I was kind of

serious…"

"Oh…no, sorry I was miles away. You sort of lost me after giving that young lad relationship advice. That's rich coming from you. I bet you have your next victim lined up as we speak."

"Have not," said Christian as an image of Daisy popped into his head. He blinked hard and tried to erase her out of his mind but she stayed there. Her image was becoming stronger as the seconds passed. Shit. To make matters worse, Jonathan was staring at him as if he was looking into a crystal ball.

"It's Daisy, isn't it?" he picked up immediately. "You have your wandering eye on Daisy Anderson. Boy, but you are sick."

Christian tried to protest but he knew he had guilt written all over his face.

"I don't have my eye on Daisy, I promise. She was always your girl. It would be like going out with, well, your sister if you had one. It'd be weird shit."

Jonathan stood up and Christian saw strain in his eyes. "Daisy is *not* my girl. She hasn't been mine in a long, long time and in case you forgot, I'm getting married in a few weeks' time. To Shannon, remember?"

He walked away, leaving Christian feeling guilty for something he hadn't even done or even consciously intended to do.

"Well, what's the problem then? Wait a minute, Jonathan. Where are you going?"

Jonathan stopped in his tracks and then turned to face Christian. "I'm only going to get some crisps from the bar for God's sake. I'm sure that bartender doesn't want to get the quiz show treatment again from you."

Christian let out a sigh of relief and sank back down into his seat again. What on earth had made Jonathan think he was planning to hit on Daisy? And if Jonathan was in love with Shannon, as he was supposed to be, why should he bloody well care?

"Listen, I'm sorry about that little outburst," said Jonathan when he returned with two packets of salt and vinegar. "I've had

117

a tough day and I'm taking my frustration over mum's illness out on Daisy and Eddie."

"Oh, yeah, I forgot about their big romance. How's that going?" laughed Christian.

Jonathan chuckled too as he remembered some of his brother's antics of late.

"It's actually quite hilarious, come to think of it. He's really pulling out all the stops. He puts on a husky voice and watches violent movies when he knows Mum's within earshot. It's mental, but if it makes him feel better..."

"And what's the craic with the Bridezilla-mum? Is she still giving you lists and tick boxes to fill out? Next thing, Fanny will be giving you Performance Indicators to meet, just like they do to us in school."

"Don't even start. I swear, if she puts another raw silk cravat under my chin to see if the colour matches my complexion I'll box her lights out," said Jonathan, raising a hand to acknowledge Gerry, who had just arrived to take up his late shift. "What am I letting myself in for?"

"It's called marriage," laughed Christian. "Tell me to butt out if you want, but is this the best time for you and your family to be planning a wedding? You should be concentrating on your own mum's needs, not the desires of the mother-in-law from hell."

Jonathan rubbed his temples. "I know, I know. I wasn't exactly planning on it happening so fast either, but as annoying as Fanny can be, her pushy wedding plans are in a strange way providing some light relief from the depression at home."

Both men looked at each other and then laughed when they realised the double entendre.

"'Annoying' and 'fanny'. I've never heard those words said in the same sentence before," said Christian, almost doubled over. "Just proves there's a first time for everything!"

"Well," said Gerry the barman, as he reached over the booth to lift the boys' empties. "If it isn't Teachers 'R' Us? I only wish I'd listened to my wise mother who warned me to stay on at school. I too could be enjoying my summer holidays, instead of slaving after you two for weeks on end. Huh, it's alright for some people. His wee girlfriend only left the country a few days ago and the dirty tinker still managed to pull another one this afternoon. Young Anna has barely touched down in Denmark and her side of the bed is already being warmed by another lass."

"Bullshit," said Christian like lightning.

"Go on, tell me more, Gerry," said Jonathan. "Christian has obviously kept this particular little daytime rendezvous to himself. But I have a right to know as I have a substantial *financial* interest in his love affairs…"

"He's taking the piss, Jonathan. I have never two-timed Anna. What are you on about, Gerry? Or should I say, what are you *on*?" Gerry folded his arms.

"Well, maybe I shouldn't be talking out of school, pardon the pun, but I could have sworn I saw a certain young lady from Killshannon leave your apartment today with a broad smile on her face."

"What?" spat Jonathan as Christian's eyes widened.

"Daisy was here but it wasn't like that!"

"It looked like it to me," said Gerry with a chuckle.

"Shut up, you nosy—"

"You cheating bastard," said Jonathan and he sprang up, almost knocking the table over in bad temper.

"It's not what you think," said Christian, but Jonathan had already marched towards the door and slammed it hard on his way out.

"Did I say something wrong?" asked Gerry. "Oh wait a minute… isn't Daisy supposed to be going out with Jonathan's brother, Eddie? No wonder he's annoyed!"

"Shut your face, Gerry, you shit-stirrer," Christian snapped before running out after Jonathan to try and explain.

Jonathan was already a good ten steps ahead. He took a sharp turn into the street, leading to the apartment he normally unofficially shared with Shannon. Christian stormed after him, almost tripping over himself with haste and too much alcohol.

"You've got it all wrong, Jonathan. Please wait."

Jonathan turned back and traipsed towards Christian, bursting with anger. "My brother was right all along. You haven't changed a bit, Devine, and I was a fool to believe you had."

"Please let me explain," pleaded Christian. "It's not like that, I swear…"

"Stuff your stinking explanation. I should never have let you back near anything that is mine, and by the way, you owe me a hundred euros."

Christian lifted his hands to protest his innocence but Jonathan was gone.

"You seem to be forgetting something, Jonathan," he called after him. "Just like you said earlier, Daisy Anderson isn't *yours* any more. Do you hear that? She isn't *yours*!"

Chapter 14

Jump When You Are More Afraid Than Excited

Thursday delivered another scorcher. Daisy was in a sunny mood anyway, having impressed Eddie's sullen aunts no end the evening before. The episode had gone without a hiccup, despite the fact that one aunt kept insisting that Jonathan was much more eligible than Eddie. Daisy had just grinned vacantly back, giving her best performance to date.

She was now vacuuming the interior of her mother's car. Suddenly her mobile rang from her pocket. She pressed the hand-held dust buster button off and fished her phone out in quick desperation. She was thrilled to hear Lorna's voice on the other end.

"How was your shagfest in County Down, you lucky sod?"

"Not that lucky. I'm single, *again*. Can you believe it? But don't feel sorry for me, honestly. I couldn't give a toss. Thank God you're alive anyway!" Lorna rattled on. "I was just about to call the cops when I came home and realised the vodka I left for you to drink was only a quarter empty. That's just not like you. You nearly gave me a heart attack!"

Daisy pushed the passenger seat of the Beetle back as far as it could go and reclined the seat. It was good to hear from Lorna again. "I'm in Costa del Killshannon and the weather is glorious this morning," she said as the sun streamed through the car's windscreen. "Are you jealous as hell?"

"Are you off your rocker?" squealed Lorna. "Did the herd of Friesians drag you there when I wasn't available to babysit you?"

Daisy shuffled in the tiny front of the car, desperately trying to find a way to stretch her legs and get comfortable. It had never been this difficult when she was a nimble teenager.

"Er, not exactly. I was, sort of, erm, challenged?"

"Challenged? This sounds good. Do tell all…"

"Well," Daisy wasn't quite sure where to start. "Keep up with this if you can. You see, I'm supposed to be going out with Eddie, whose mum is dying from cancer. I have a shitty history with his brother, Jonathan, so things have been really awkward. Plus, his friend is really hot, but I haven't a hope of turning his pretty, heartbroken head. Savvy?"

Silence.

"Yeah, whatever. That sounds way too much for me to take in at the minute. I am just in through the door and have a ripping hangover from last night. Wait a minute, did you say Eddie? Isn't he the gay one who lives in San Francisco?"

Daisy got a strange sense of pleasure in messing with someone's muddled hungover brain when her own was as clear as a bell for a change.

"Correct."

"Em, so how the hell did *you* straighten him out all the way from Killshannon? Girl, you are good!"

"I didn't. We're just pretending for his mother's sake."

"Wow, this does sound complicated," sighed Lorna. Her head was starting to spin.

"Believe me, it is," said Daisy. "It's a bit like reading upside down."

"I can imagine. How on earth do you manage to get yourself into these situations?"

"Well, I had nothing else to do after you deserted me, you lucky cow. But I only have another few days of this and then it's back to days in Super Shoes and nights in with you watching soaps and reality TV. I dread going back to that hellhole, though. It's stifling, but then at the same time I miss my walk to work across the embankment every morning, past the Lyric Theatre and dreaming of taking centre stage there one day. And I miss having drinks after work at Cutter's Wharf with you and the girls."

"Is the sea air getting to you, love?" asked Lorna with mock concern.

"I'm just thinking too much, that's all."

"I see you've left me with a bit of clearing up to do," Lorna sighed. "It's just as well I'm all Thalgo-treated and purified or I'd have to get angry and swear."

Daisy remembered the champagne flutes, the wine glasses and the rest she had left behind on her hasty departure.

"Yeah, yeah, bossy boots," she said. What were a few dishes between friends?

"So, getting back to your problems... tell me about Eddie's brother and his friend and the history bits that I don't know about. They sound intriguing."

Daisy wondered just how many details she should divulge. Despite being best friends for a few years now, Lorna knew virtually nothing about Jonathan Eastwood or Christian Devine, apart from the fact that Jonathan was the driver the night Daisy's father was killed.

"You see, I used to have a, well, a *thing* with Jonathan when I was about eighteen. I took him to my high school formal dance – classic boy-next-door stuff, really. Christian was there too with another girl and at the end of the night he made a move on me and I went with it. It was just a quick snog on the dance floor, but there was uproar between the two boys about it."

"Woo, you are a dark horse. So did you hook up with Christian then?"

"No, no, no. For months Jonathan and I continued on and off

123

but…well, then Dad and Brendan were killed and that was that. Things could never be the same again"

Lorna gasped. "Oh dear. You two do have a torrid past alright…"

"That's just the tip of the iceberg. Now Jonathan is getting married, he and Christian are good friends again, and the other night Jonathan made a move on me and we were caught by his brother."

"Eddie? The gay one you are pretending to be going out with?"

Daisy was impressed. "Correct. Gosh, for someone with a hangover you *are* on the ball! So what do you think? Messy or what?"

"Em, I think…I think you are treading on very dangerous territory, Daisy."

Daisy's head began to throb so she let Lorna continue with her party political broadcast.

"So, your ex, Jonathan, is getting married soon, and is all over the place with what's going on with his mum, right?"

"Right," said Daisy wearily.

"He sees you and suddenly wants to turn back the clock to a time when all was rosy and safe. In my opinion, the best thing to do is get back to your own life pretty quickly before you cause havoc."

Daisy fiddled with her necklace and bit her lip. For once Lorna's straight talking made perfect sense. The longer she hung around Killshannon, the deeper the trouble she was going to find herself in. She opened her mouth to answer but from her horizontal position in the car she could see a man's torso in the wing mirror storming towards the house.

"You're absolutely right, Lorna," she muttered into the phone, "I'd better go. Eddie is on his way over."

She hung up the phone and peeped outside again to see where Eddie had disappeared to but couldn't see him. Had she imagined it? Then she noticed to her amazement that there was a man standing at her front door ringing the bell. And it wasn't Eddie, but Jonathan.

In a panic, Daisy lay back down on the car seat and tried her best to stay still. Please, please don't let this be happening, she prayed. She knew Jonathan certainly wouldn't be calling for a social chat. He started clearly calling her name.

"Daisy, I know you're in there. Your mum told me you were at home. How could you do this? After everything I said to you the other night?" he shouted, totally oblivious to the volume of his voice.

Wait a minute, thought Daisy. How could she do what? She hadn't done anything.

Sitting up in the car, she beeped the horn so loudly that Jonathan almost fell off the step. He staggered a moment, and then marched towards the driver's side of the car. But before he could open it, Daisy jumped out of the passenger side and leaned on the bonnet, looking directly across at him.

"Do what, Jonathan? What the hell did I do now?"

Jonathan's mouth was tight with anger. "You just had to rub my nose in it, didn't you? Why Christian fuckin' Devine of all people? Again!"

Daisy was flabbergasted at how Jonathan had got it so wrong. "Where did this all come from? I did nothing with Christian Devine."

"How could you? How *could* you?" Jonathan's voice was crumbling.

Daisy could feel her temper rise. Who gave him the right to dictate what she did or didn't do in her own time?

"Even if I'd shagged Christian from here to eternity it still wouldn't be any of your goddamn business. You're the one who's engaged, not me. You don't see me smashing Shannon's door in, do you? It's about time you grew up and moved on!"

Jonathan sat down on the grass verge that separated the cottages and put his head in his hands.

"Let's go inside and have a chat, Jonathan," she said gently, noticing the confused and miserable look on his face. "I've a feeling we've a bit of ground to cover."

Daisy had no idea where he had got his information from, but was determined to find out. She reached out a hand to help him up and reluctantly he accepted it. Obediently he followed her around the back of the house, through Maggie's wild garden and into the sitting area through the patio doors. Glancing uncomfortably at Danny Anderson's photo, which hung prominently above the mantel, he sat down on the brown leather sofa. He had hardly slept a wink all night, tossing and turning and thinking of Daisy in Christian's arms, in his bed. It had brought back all of the hurt he felt years ago.

Even when Shannon phoned earlier from her mother's house on the other side of Donegal, he'd ignored her call, not feeling any urge to talk to her. Then, first thing in the morning he had sped all the way back to Killshannon, checked in on his mother and Eddie, and then seized the opportunity to talk to Daisy alone.

"This is a mess," he said, looking at his first love with sad eyes. "Don't you think so, or is it just me?"

Daisy sat down on the other edge of the sofa and kept her eyes on the floor, avoiding his question. She noticed Jonathan reach for the bowl of peanuts on the coffee table.

"Don't do it!"

"What?"

"The peanuts. They're about my age," she said, lifting the bowl and chucking its contents in the nearby bin. She'd been meaning to do that all week.

"First of all," she continued, "There is absolutely nothing going on between me and Christian Devine. We had a coffee and a bit of a chat, that's all. But what's it to you? What about Shannon?"

"I know, I know. I can't even think about Shannon right now. When I thought you'd been messing with Christian again I just flipped. I'm sorry."

Daisy felt the urge to move closer to him but common sense prevailed and she held back.

"At least you managed to hold your dignity during a game of

swing ball," she said with a smile and was pleased when she got one back in return. "Look, I think we both know there will always be something between us, Jonathan, but I'm not sure if it's enough to keep us together."

Jonathan edged closer and took her hand. "Says who? We never even really tried, did we? I could call off the wedding. You could come clean with Mum about this Eddie rubbish and we could give it a go. We've still got time."

Daisy shook her head sadly. "We have no time, Jonathan. We were never meant to be. You were always so settled, so mature, so straight down the line while I had to take the long way around for everything in my life – school, boys, my non-existent career. No matter how much I want to believe I've changed, I'll always be Crazy Daisy."

She felt her eyes well up knowing what was about to come up. "Do you ever think about him, Jonathan?"

Jonathan paused before answering and turned to look towards Daisy, who had fear written all over her face.

"Always," he said, locking her eyes with his. "I've tried to guess what he wants for his birthday, and every year I pick a present in my mind and wish it his way. I've already an imaginary eighth birthday gift chosen, stupid as it may seem. But I've nowhere to send it. What about you?"

"Always, too," answered Daisy softly. "I can't talk to anyone about giving up my baby like that Jonathan and it's so hard. So, so hard."

She couldn't hold it in any longer. Sobbing, she wept until she felt Jonathan's warm arm around her, strong and secure. She let her head rest on his broad shoulder. He rubbed it gently and let his own tears fall. Tears of guilt and sorrow, tears of regret and pride. Tears spilled onto his face that he couldn't blame Christian or Eddie or Daisy for. He could only blame himself.

"I'm so sorry, Daisy. I am so, so sorry for everything," he mumbled into the softness of her hair.

"No, Jonathan," she muffled. "You have got to stop blaming yourself. None of this is your fault. It never was." Her face was so close to his now. She could feel his breath on her face, weary and hot, and despite everything, she leaned closer still until their lips locked in a deep kiss that took them both back to the night they remembered so well.

Daisy's heart thumped in her chest as Jonathan's arms moved firmly up and down her back. His mouth reached her neck and she leaned back to let him taste her delicate skin.

This was so wrong; she knew it was. But she couldn't allow herself to stop. She followed his lead, gripping his t-shirt tightly and pulling him closer and closer until she could feel his chest press against hers. She opened her eyes and met his mouth again till they slowed down, both knowing the risk they were taking in Maggie's house.

Jonathan was first to pull back. He kept hold of Daisy's hands and looked into her eyes.

"Tell me this isn't right, Daisy and I'll go. I'll leave you in the past and try not to think about what we might have had together. Tell me…"

Daisy thought of Shannon and her wedding plans and her heart filled with guilt. Lorna's earlier words echoed in her head. She might leave a trail of destruction behind if she stayed around Killshannon any longer. She had to be very sure about this. She took a deep breath.

"Jonathan, I've seen how Shannon looks at you, at how you look at her, at how she looks at me, like she *knows*. What do you and I have? Memories and a whole lot of maybes? We can get over this. We've lasted this long without getting involved again."

"But I can't stop thinking about you. I never have." he said. "This isn't going to go away. Eddie is right. I panicked when I heard of mum's illness and jumped the gun with Shannon. And then you came back and now I know I was wrong to ask Shannon to marry me. No, not wrong, actually, just plain stupid."

Jonathan walked towards the door that led to the garden and stared outside, his hands stuffed in his pockets, while Daisy wiped her eyes.

"I think it's best if I go back to Belfast for a while and let you get your head around this, eh? And while I'm there I'll try to do the same." Daisy wondered where she was finding this common sense, but it seemed to have come from somewhere. She and Jonathan both needed to know this was right. "We can't afford to take this lightly. There are too many people involved."

****

Daisy looked around her bedroom. Her green case was all packed up again and after teatime Eddie stuffed it into the tiny boot of the Mini Cooper and closed it tight. Her urgency to attend an appointment in Belfast had been met with raised eyebrows all around, but she wasn't taking no for an answer.

"Do you really have to go? I was getting sort of used to having a girlfriend for the first time in my life and our week isn't even up yet," pleaded Eddie. "Can you not change your appointment for another time?"

Hiding the truth from Eddie and her mother hadn't been easy, but an unexpected slot at the doctor's concerning women's issues, had been her excuse.

"I'm sure you'll manage, Ed. You have a lot to be getting on with and I'm always on the phone if you need to talk. And besides, I'm a real bitch from hell at the minute."

Eddie felt a girly sniffle coming on. Or else it was a childish tantrum. He couldn't quite decide.

"I bet you're just itching to get back behind that shoe counter, aren't you? You've had enough of the fishy smell around here and you're longing to be surrounded by fashions in new leather and fresh suede. Go on, admit it."

"If only you knew how much the very thought of that turns

129

my stomach," said Daisy with a sigh. "Come on. Let's go before I change my mind."

****

As usual, the journey back to Belfast seemed quicker than the journey to Killshannon. Daisy remembered trying to figure out why, as a child, going on holidays always took ages, and coming back was like a flash. Her father's explanation had been that the longing you felt going to your new destination made the journey seem longer, and when you were coming back, the anti-climax made it go quicker.

Her mother had been disappointed that her family lunch with Richard and Jennifer had been called off, but that was the least of Daisy's worries. The prospect of ruining someone's marriage was too much a risk to take for the sake of a toasted panini with her brother and the sister-in-law from hell. Paninis were so over-rated anyhow. So were sisters-in-law as replacements for the real flesh and blood version. And anyway, she was looking forward to being herself again, back in the comfortable surroundings of her independent city lifestyle in leafy South Belfast.

"It doesn't seem like four days ago since you picked me up here, does it?" she asked when Eddie pulled the car into the small parking area of her apartment block almost two hours later.

"That makes you sound like a hooker. I like that," said Eddie. "But yeah, it seems like ages ago, doesn't it? And so much has happened since then. I bet you never thought you'd snog both me and my brother in the space of four days."

Daisy glanced warily at Eddie.

"Oh, come on, Daisy," he retorted, yanking the handbrake up hard. "You could have cut the atmosphere between you and Jonathan with a knife. It was scary. And then he sneaked over to see you this morning. What was all that about?"

Daisy gathered up her empty drinks can and crisp packets from the journey and racked her brains to see if she could possibly avoid this twist in the conversation. But Eddie's eyes were like lasers on the side of her cheek and she could feel her face start to burn.

"Alright, alright, if you must know, someone gave your brother extremely exaggerated information about me and Christian Devine, and the green-eyed monster from yester year came back and bit Jonathan on the bum. He jumped to conclusions. That's all."

"That's all? So…"

"So what?"

"So nothing happened between you two?" Eddie seemed to be enjoying this.

"No!"

"Do you think is it going to?"

"Eddie Eastwood! What sort of a best man are you going to make in a few weeks' time? You'd almost think you wanted me and Jonathan to rekindle our teenage fumblings."

Eddie didn't answer.

"Do you?" she squealed.

It was now Eddie's turn to want to divert the subject. He opened the car door and looked up towards the window of Daisy's apartment.

"I take it that's the infamous Lorna," he said, pointing upwards. "Is that her scarlet head bobbing up and down?"

"Yip, that's Lorna alright. She's a sucker for celebrity get-fit DVDs and does them every day. Come on in and I'll introduce you. This should be interesting."

131

Chapter 15

Enter At Your Own Risk

Christian tried to figure out how he should react to Jonathan's recent wobbler. Maybe it was best to stay out of his way for a while, but with all the commotion in Killshannon, an influx of tourists in Donegal town, and Buddy's strange disappearance of late, he knew there wasn't much to keep him amused for the next few days.

A few hours later, out of sheer boredom, Christian found himself agreeing to babysit his sister's two toddlers. He packed an overnight bag in preparation for the next morning and left out a bowl of Cheerios for Buddy, who had last been seen trailing a mouse that afternoon.

He changed into a pair of track bottoms and discarded the need for a t-shirt as it was still so humid in the early evening sun. With a large bowl of nachos resting on his tummy, he lay on the large couch, flicked on the television and fought the urge to phone Jonathan, whom he hoped, right now, was settling his differences with Daisy.

****

Jonathan was glad of a few hours' peace in Ivy Cottages. Since the news of Isobel's illness had become known, the house had been a constant hive of activity, with visitors arriving almost around the clock. He realised that he himself was as guilty of causing commotion as everyone else. His engagement announcement hadn't help curb the stream of house traffic. Now, however, he could see that all the activity was taking its toll on his mother. He badly he wished he could turn back the clock.

It was almost ten now, and Eddie should be home soon. That's if he turned in at all, he thought darkly. Usually when he and Daisy got together there were all sorts of parties and general excitement.

To her credit, though, Daisy had left Killshannon as quickly as she'd promised to and Jonathan felt more settled already. He needed space, some time to breathe, away from his heartfelt feelings and burning memories of Daisy and the pressure to make his mind up over his relationship with Shannon.

But he already missed her like crazy.

It had been hard watching having Daisy come and go so freely around the village, considering she had stayed away for so long. Daisy had spread her wings and hit the road soon after her world had come crashing down after her dad's death and the loss of their secret baby.

She had never been a follower anyway. Wild horses wouldn't have been able to keep Daisy in Killshannon. She wouldn't have stayed for anybody, including Jonathan. But there was still a pull between them now and he would have to sever that indefinitely before he could let her go for good.

"Are you going to bed already?" whispered Isobel when Jonathan suddenly got up from the sofa.

"I was just going to put the kettle on, Mum. Fancy a cuppa?"

"Oh, go on, then," she smiled, even though Jonathan knew her stomach was in knots from the mixture of painkillers she had been given earlier. She had been sick so many times today, more than ever. Jonathan had noticed how she really concentrated on her breathing now, as if she was becoming more and more aware of every intake of oxygen. He had read up about every symptom of her cancer, as well as spending hours on the internet, researching options for pain relief and care packages. Right now, he felt alone and helpless as he watched his beloved mother become a shadow of the woman she once was.

****

The Chocolate Bar was heaving with activity when Christian walked through its glass doors for a nightcap. He felt good about agreeing to do his sister such a good deed. Minding two toddlers, whose housekeeping rules read like playschool on speed, was a huge sacrifice for a single man of his age. And on a Friday night, too. He deserved a medal for agreeing to take on the challenge. Well, at the very least he deserved a drink.

A two-piece rock band played an eighties selection in the far corner of the room, and scattered groups of regulars and tourists mingled at the bar and across the tiny dance floor. There was something fresh about his local tonight – he barely recognised anyone he knew and the atmosphere was different. Not better, not worse, but different. In a nice, floaty, summery way.

Some of the bar staff were new too, he noticed. Good job. If he saw that mouthpiece Gerry O'Donnell any time soon he would stuff his throat with a knuckle sandwich.

A swarthy Italian student barman stood only feet away from him, shaking cocktails and showing off ridiculously, while a flock of scantily clad holidaymakers hung on to his every move. Some men have all the luck, thought Christian. At the minute, he could barely pull a pint let alone a group of good-looking female tourists.

Damn women. If Anna Harrison only knew how she'd ripped out his heart and stamped all over it, she would be crying into her Carlsberg or whatever Danish drink had become her new tipple over in Copenhagen. His self-esteem had gotten a fair old battering in the break up too. Maybe even more so than his heart.

"Any chance of a drink around here?" he eventually asked the new female member of staff when he'd had enough of observing the changes in his local and feeling sorry for himself. The girl stumbled at his somewhat abrupt request as she pushed by him, balancing a tray of empties on one hand, but Christian hadn't even looked into her face when he spoke. His eyes were fixated on her pert derrière, which was nicely squeezed into a pair of black, fitted trousers.

"Is that your way of asking a question, sir?" the girl asked in broken English. She sat her tray on the bar and started restacking the five or six glasses she'd almost dropped.

"I'm ever so sorry," he mustered a reply.

"Okay, you're forgiven, I suppose," she added when she noticed how handsome Christian was. "Maybe we could start again, if you ask me nicely…"

"Oh, alright then. A vodka and cola, *please*," Christian replied with a cheeky grin. "Now, can I chance asking you another little question…nicely of course?"

"Go ahead, sir," she said, fluttering her long eyelashes while resting her elbows on the bar.

"What's your name?"

"Eloise," she said swiftly. "Now, can I ask you the same question, *very, very,* nicely of course?"

Christian smiled and took her pale hand in his.

"Christian Devine," he whispered and could almost feel her shiver under his touch. Since Anna, he'd temporarily chosen to forget the sheer power he had over women and his ego had taken a firm punching. But now, he decided, it was nice to pick it up again. It was easy enough to do with a girl who radiated as much sex appeal as Eloise did. She was hot, *really* hot, and every man in the county would be flocking to The Chocolate Bar if they knew she was here.

He watched Eloise as she left his side, coyly making her way behind the bar. He took in her curvaceous young hips as she poured his vodka from the optic. In turn, she caught his eye in the mirror at the rear of the drinks section and blushed slightly. Then she set down his drink on the bar and waited for her payment, but Christian wasn't ready to let her go just yet. He gulped back his drink in one mouthful and slammed his glass on the bar.

"I'll have another, please."

"Already?" she asked as she gave him his change from the first drink. "That is very greedy."

"Maybe I'm a greedy boy. Why don't you join me?"

The young girl shook her head emphatically.

"No, I can't. I'd get the sack and then I'd be back to Denmark before my time."

Denmark? How ironic! A strange wave of pleasure engulfed him.

"But I'm finished in twenty minutes," she added, warily. "That is, if you can wait for me, Mr Devine."

"Oh, I can wait for you," said Christian, leaning in closer so that their lips almost met. "I'm sure I can wait at least twenty minutes for you, Eloise."

****

Jonathan gently stroked his mother's downy hair, which was still so fine since her previous stint of chemotherapy a few years ago. He also held a bowl under her chin, wondering how sore her pain could possibly be. It was killing him to watch her like this. She had been sick on and off for over an hour now, and the strain of it was taking its toll on her frail body.

"That's it, Mum. Better out than in," he whispered, repeating the words she used to say to him when as a small child he'd crouched over the toilet bowl suffering from a tummy bug. He noticed a light smile cross her lips, and realised how much the tables had turned. He was now the nurse, the carer.

"You shouldn't be doing this on the night before your big birthday, love. You should be out celebrating. It's not every day

136

you turn thirty," murmured Isobel. She wiped her mouth with a tissue and Jonathan noticed her begin to settle. His birthday was the furthest thing from his mind at the moment

"Think of how you felt this time thirty years ago," he recalled. "I bet that wasn't such a pleasant experience. I was huge. Didn't Dad say I should have been born with a schoolbag on my back?"

Jonathan knew that discussing the births of her children was one of his mother's favourite things to do. She loved people to wow at how such a fine-framed young woman like her could have managed to naturally deliver such big, healthy, strapping boys into the world, both weighing in at over nine pounds each. And each time, she had quickly regained her neat figure. It had been like a high mark of achievement in her simple, pleasant life.

"I'd say at around this time thirty years ago, your father was placing his bets down the pub as to whether or not you were going to make it into the world before midnight. Of course you arrived only a few minutes later, and he joked that you'd cost him a ten pound note before you'd even let out your first cry."

Jonathan's smile lessened and his eyes fell to the floor. "I was always late in his eyes, for everything, wasn't I?"

"Now, son." Isobel's tiny voice shook as she spoke. "How many times have I told you? Don't be so hard on yourself. You should have no regrets as far as your father is concerned. We both were always so proud of you boys. No matter what."

Jonathan wondered if this was his mother's way of saying she knew about Eddie's sexuality. Eddie's pretend relationship with Daisy was a no-go zone in his top ten conversation topics at the moment and he was determined to keep it that way. Things were complicated enough.

"Er, I know that, Mum. I know that." He leaned over and gave his mother a gentle peck on the cheek. "Sorry for being so petty."

The telephone rang and Isobel urged Jonathan to take the call, despite his initial reluctance. He had a feeling he knew who it might be. The last thing he wanted was a challenging conversation.

"Hi, honey. Happy birthday," cooed Shannon as soon as he lifted the phone. He looked at the clock. It was two minutes past midnight.

"Aw, thanks, Shanny," he whispered, running his hand through his hair. "You're such a sweetheart. It's exactly the time of my birth. Mum and I were just reminiscing. Well, Mum was. Obviously my memory of the occasion is pretty blurred."

Despite his initial dread, Shannon's voice was a surprisingly soothing distraction at first. But then, as usual lately, she began to irritate him.

"So, birthday boy. Just wait till you hear what I have planned for you tomorrow! I hope you haven't made promises to anyone else. I intend to have you all to myself."

Jonathan glanced in at his mother again, who was holding her chest and swallowing hard. She was trying so hard to fight the appalling nausea that had now become part and parcel of her everyday so-called life.

"To be honest, I'm not sure I feel like celebrating, Shanny. Mum's pretty low this evening and I'm not sure when Eddie is due home."

Shannon sighed dramatically. "Where the hell is _he_ off to now? Has he no sense of responsibility? It's your bloody birthday!"

Jonathan voice broke into a whisper. His mother didn't need to hear any arguments and he was sure this wasn't going to be a nice, pleasant conversation.

"Look, Eddie has just gone to drive Daisy back to Belfast. He might be home tonight, but then again, he might drive back in the morning. I'm not so sure yet, but one thing is certain, he hasn't fled the country and he will be back. I'm not his keeper."

"Well then, phone him and make sure he _is_ back first thing and let him take over so that you and I can celebrate. Or else get Maggie or some other do-good neighbour to let you off for a few hours. I need you too. I haven't seen you in two whole days. I miss you, Jonathan."

Jonathan's head throbbed when he thought of how far he had

come with Daisy recently and a ball of guilt settled in the pit of his stomach. He couldn't face Shannon in person with his head in such a muddle. Definitely not.

"Look love. I don't want to disappoint you but you aren't making things any easier here. Thank you so much for thinking of me but over the next few months, maybe even weeks, Mum has to be my main priority…"

"And Eddie's. Your mother has two sons, you know. And we have a wedding to plan. You do want your mother at your wedding, don't you? Isn't that the whole point of bringing the date forward?"

Shannon's voice was reaching higher by the second and Jonathan reckoned she was probably stomping her feet at the other end of the phone. He tried to remain calm, but a light sweat was already forming on his brow. Now was not the time for Shannon's petty demands.

"Please just leave it with me, okay? I can't promise anything. If Eddie doesn't show, I'll see if Maggie can take over for a few hours."

Shannon fell silent. She obviously wasn't expecting Jonathan to give in to her so quickly. He didn't normally.

"Oh. Oh, that's wonderful, Jonathan. You won't be disappointed, believe me. I'll phone you first thing in the morning and let you in on the agenda. You're going to have the best birthday ever."

Jonathan hung up and rubbed his head. He had no doubt that Shannon would phone him first thing in the morning. But would it really be his best birthday ever? Somehow he didn't think so.

****

Christian's apartment was too handy for The Chocolate Bar, he reckoned. He needed to play it cool with young Eloise. If she realised how near he lived to her workplace, it could become messy later if she turned out to be a pain in the arse.

"So, Christian," she said, playing with a straw along her lips. "Where are you taking me to? I've had a very long, busy day."

Christian leaned closer to Eloise's soft, peachy face across the table they were sharing in a cosy corner of the bar.

"Are you hungry?" he asked. He quite fancied a takeaway himself. Something cheap and cheerful.

"Starving. I've heard there's a really good pizza place just down the road from here. Do you like pizza?"

I like this girl, thought Christian as they strolled down the dimly lit street towards the pizza parlour. She had a quick sense of humour, was easy company and had a body to die for. What else could a newly found single man want on a Friday night?

"So," said Eloise, as they sat down at their table moments later. "Do you have a girlfriend waiting for you at home?"

"No," said Christian. "Nor do I have a wife, a child or anyone else waiting up for me. What about you? Do you have a boyfriend?"

"No, I only arrived in this country three days ago and my last boyfriend is at home in Denmark. You are the first Irish boy I have seen so far that I like."

Christian was tearing a second slice from the pizza box they shared in the makeshift dining area of the takeaway. Should he throw caution to the wind and invite her back to his apartment? He needed to weigh up his options carefully.

"Thank you. That's a real compliment coming from a pretty girl like you. So, who do you live with, then? And more to the point, would they mind a late-night visitor?"

Eloise shook her head demurely and continued to chew her food before answering.

"No, no. I share a room with my sister and she is asleep by now, so we can't go back to my place. Maybe some other time, yeah?"

To hell with this, thought Christian. I might as well be hung for a sheep as a lamb.

"Well, would you care to join me for a coffee back at mine? It's only a few minutes away and we can chat more then?"

"I would like that," said Eloise, smiling. "Yes, I'd like that very much."

140

Chapter 16

Careless What You Wish For

In her Stranmillis apartment, Daisy was becoming tired of playing referee between her two friends. Even a bottle of Australian red wine between them had miserably failed to oil their crevices and they were still bickering. In fact, to say Lorna and Eddie had failed to hit it off was putting it mildly. If they continued like this, Daisy was sure they'd eventually hit each other; such were their very different opinions on everything from celebrities to cellulite.

"Look, you two. How about a change of subject? I'm sure there are much more important things to talk about than my love life. It's really not that important," said Daisy as she poured the dregs of wine into Lorna's glass. With any luck it would send her to sleep.

"I'm sorry," said Lorna in a high-pitched squeal, "but I don't understand how you could be actually contemplating renewing relations with a man who is about to be married. I mean, you have barely mentioned the name Jonathan Eastwood to me in all the years I've known you. I just don't get it."

Daisy could tell Eddie's blood was reaching boiling point at Lorna's forceful opinions.

"I'm sure there are a lot of things Daisy hasn't told you," he hissed.

Daisy felt like standing between the two and doing a striptease or something equally gross, just to stop them referring to her in the third person.

"I'm not questioning that, but believe me, Mister, Daisy and I have had some very frank conversations around this kitchen table. And your brother has probably only ever received a maximum of twenty seconds' airtime. Now that hardly makes him the love of her life."

Daisy tried her best to intervene again but there was no stopping them now. She felt like a ping-pong ball, bouncing from one end of the table to the other.

"Did you ever stop to think that maybe there's a reason behind why Daisy hasn't spoken about Jonathan till now?"

"Hello! I am still here, you know," shouted Daisy. "Do I have any say in this conversation at all?"

"No," they said loudly in unison.

"Is there some other issue with Jonathan? Would someone please let me into the big secret?" asked Lorna, waving a cigarette in the air dramatically.

"I think Eddie is referring to the car accident in which our dads were killed, Lorna," said Daisy quietly.

"But I thought you said it was nobody's fault. Isn't that what the word 'accident' means?" said Lorna.

Tea, thought Daisy. Then she realised she really was morphing into Killshannon housewife mode again by thinking that a cup of tea could settle any row. There was way too much tension in the air for her liking.

"I'm going to get more wine," said Eddie, who was in no mood for tea. "I think we'll just agree to differ on this one, Lorna. I'm sure you know Daisy just as well as I do..."

"Better..."

"Oh, would you two please..."

Eddie stormed out through the front door of the girls' apartment and Daisy rushed to the window.

"Please don't take the car you idiot. You've been drinking," she muttered against the glass. To her relief Eddie strolled past the yellow Mini and made his way towards the main road.

"Does he even know where he is going?" asked Lorna, stamping out her ciggie. "The nearest off-licence is ten minutes away."

Daisy slumped onto the couch and set the precious remainder of her wine down on the floor beside her, while Lorna leaned over the slim counter that separated the apartment's living and kitchen areas.

"Oh, don't worry. Our Eddie could sniff out an off-licence as well as you or I could. It will be good for him to maybe cool off a bit."

The two sat in silence for what seemed like an eternity. Eventually Lorna spoke.

"Eddie really is determined to play matchmaker between you and his brother, isn't he?" she said. "Do you think that's why he turned up here in the first place?"

Daisy shot up on the couch like a bullet. Suddenly the penny dropped with a painful thud in her head.

"I had never even contemplated that. Do you think?"

Lorna shrugged. "It's possible…"

Daisy was horrified. It all sounded so deliberate. So intended. And she'd fallen for it, big time.

"You could be right. Shit! That little menace. When he comes back here, I'll be waiting on him with the third degree."

"Oh, no, now it'll be my turn to referee. What have I started?" asked Lorna, and she gave out a giggle.

The two girls continued to down their wine like there was a shortage of vineyards in the world.

"And to think I was going to give up my bed for him tonight," said Daisy. "He can bloody well sleep on this couch. In fact, he'll be lucky if he gets a pillow. I am so, so mad."

"I'm sure he *means* well. It's quite sweet, really."

Daisy looked at Lorna as though she'd lost the plot.

143

"Sweet? What's so sweet about that? It's sick! Before he came back from San Fran I was happy enough here, working in Super Shoes…"

Lorna burst out laughing. "Well, that's a downright lie for a start."

"Okay, then. I was *miserable* enough working in Super Shoes but I had no man trouble at all before Eddie dragged me back to Killshannon."

Lorna looked at the clock and Daisy glanced at her watch at exactly the same time. It was 12.22 am. Neither spoke but both were thinking the same thing.

"Should we be getting worried?" asked Lorna eventually. "He left over half an hour ago and the offy closes at twelve. He really should have been back by now."

Daisy forced herself not to panic, but it was quite a dark walk along the embankment at this hour. She had secretly sent him two text messages as she chatted to Lorna, urging him to hurry up. So far, there was no reply.

"He's a big boy," she said, trying to reassure herself as much as anything else. "I'm sure he'll find his way there and back."

Lorna raised a pencil-thin dark eyebrow.

"Okay, then," said Daisy. "We'll wait five more minutes. He's probably flirting with the guy behind the counter in the offy. Isn't he gay too?"

Lorna recalled a twenty-something, attractive young lad with blue tips in his hair. "Oh, Stephen? Nah, he left a few weeks ago."

"Ah. That rules that theory out then," said Daisy. Lorna thought for a second.

"Oh holy shit!" she squealed suddenly. "Now that I remember, the reason Stephen quit his job was because he'd been getting abuse from a group of drunken homophobes who used to call before closing time!"

Daisy's blood ran cold. She grabbed her jacket and sped down the stairs of her apartment block with Lorna following her closely.

As they walked past the Mini, Daisy thought she was in danger of bursting into tears. If anything happened to Eddie she would never forgive herself. Why had she let him go off alone in the first place? This was a city, and Eddie seemed to think every part of Ireland was like Killshannon. He may have known the way of the streets of San Francisco, but he thought Belfast was a small town in comparison and didn't have a clue of his way round it.

"Did you try his number?" asked Lorna, trying desperately to keep up with Daisy's manic strides. Celebrity keep fit DVDs were shit, she decided. It was back to the gym on Monday for her.

"Three times. There's no answer. Oh, Lorna, I'm almost afraid of walking around this corner."

The girls linked arms and Daisy prayed silently to herself for Eddie's safety. She prayed to her granny and to the Virgin Mary and she prayed to Danny and Brendan up in heaven that Eddie's blond mop of hair would be the first thing they would see when they turned the corner onto the main street.

Eddie's hair *was* the first thing they saw when they turned the corner. But blond it wasn't. Daisy gasped as she saw his head slumped on the pavement just outside the off-licence. His head was doused in bright-red blood, and a group of passers-by gathered around him as he lay unconscious on the cold ground.

"Eddie!" shouted Daisy and she raced over to his side, pushing herself through the crowd. She threw herself down on the pavement and hugged his poor beaten body. "Oh, Eddie, no. NO! NO!"

"The ambulance is on its way, love, so it is. That's a nasty beating he got. Better get him to the hospital pretty quickly."

Daisy looked up to see what seemed like a hundred faces staring down at her and shaking their heads. After that, everything was a blur. Even the sound of the ambulance sirens screaming from the city centre sounded out of sync and surreal. She felt Lorna's hand on her back and she burst into tears.

Chapter 17

Shabby Birthday

Jonathan awoke the next morning to the shrill ringing of the telephone. It was 7.15 am. He didn't *feel* any different. He didn't *look* any different either. Perhaps turning thirty wasn't as bad as everyone made it out to be. In fact, he was actually looking forward to the challenge of maturity. Yesterday he'd still been in his twenties. Today, everything had changed. It was scary in a way, but quite exciting. He had come of age.

He scuffled down the hallway to answer the phone. Was it his imagination or had the phone been ringing all night long?

"Hello," he said and noticed how gruff his voice sounded first thing in the morning. Maybe he had grown older through the night.

"Hi babe, it's me. I'm outside in the car so hurry up and get ready. Don't worry about breakfast. I have everything under control."

"Christ, Shannon. I need a shower at least. Can't you come in for five minutes?"

Shannon sighed. She had the whole day planned so meticulously, although five minutes wouldn't really make that much difference, she supposed. Nothing or nobody was going to ruin her day with her fiancé. She had spent a fortune on treats for him. A few hours at a spa hotel at the Lough Eske Castle Resort was waiting to be enjoyed followed by a round of golf at his favourite course. Then an afternoon of pleasure back in the honeymoon suite of the hotel would follow a long, liquid lunch.

If everything worked out according to plan, she would convince Jonathan to spend the night with her and leave Eddie to pick up the pieces at home for a change. She had it booked already, so Jonathan would just have to stay.

"Okay, okay. But hurry up. Like I promised, this is going to be your best birthday ever. After all, it is your last as a single man," she tittered. "Not that I'm complaining."

Jonathan unlocked the front door of his mother's house to let Shannon in and noticed Maggie's curtains were already opened across the way. Immediately he thought of Daisy, but he decided to push her back out of his mind. He hadn't intended on leaving so early that morning, but since Maggie appeared to be on her way over already to watch Isobel, he could do just that.

The phone rang as soon as he stepped into the shower.

"Can you get that, Shannon? Just take a message," he shouted. "It's probably Eddie calling to let us know when he'll be home. Tell him I'm going to kick his sorry ass if he doesn't get back here soon."

"Okay," said Shannon. She didn't want to talk to Eddie right now. If she did, she just might give him a piece of her mind as to how selfish he was being. The cheek of him gliding off with Daisy to Belfast when his brother needed to celebrate his birthday! She lifted the receiver, and then sat it back down again without saying hello. Then, she carefully pulled the telephone connection from the wall and walked into the living room with a satisfactory smile plastered on her made-up face. That would teach him.

To her delight, she spied Jonathan's mobile on the mantelpiece. What a gift! She switched it off too and slipped it up her sleeve.

"Mum, I'm off now," called Jonathan a record-breaking ten minutes later. "Maggie will be here soon to fix you breakfast and

I think Eddie just phoned. He should be on his way home from Belfast in a few hours' time. If there's anything you need, you can reach me on the mobile."

"Have a lovely day, son," Isobel whispered from the bedroom. "And don't be worrying about me. I'll be fine. Now come in here and let me give my birthday boy a big hug."

Jonathan walked into the bedroom and noticed the tears in his mother's eyes as he approached. He sensed she was thinking exactly as he was; that this would be his last birthday that she'd ever be around for. He felt as though he was being torn down the middle. He didn't want to go away for the day. He had lots of birthdays ahead with Shannon if he wanted them, but this was his last birthday with his mother and he wanted to spend as much precious time with her as possible.

"Jonathan, are you ready to go? We have an action-packed day ahead of us," called Shannon when she heard his footsteps cross the hall.

"Mum, if you'd rather I stayed with you…" he began.

"No, no, go and enjoy yourself. I'll be here when you get back this evening. I'm looking forward to spending the day with Maggie and then I'll have an evening of Eddie fussing around me to contend with. Now off you go."

Reluctantly, Jonathan made his way to the hallway, where Shannon was waving her car keys impatiently.

"All set?" she asked with a grin. "I am *so* excited. We haven't spent time alone in weeks, Jonathan."

"Well, let's go then. Do I have everything I need?" he asked with a forced smile.

"Yes, yes, you do, now come on! Quickly!"

Jonathan gave the house a final glance.

"Oh, by the way, was that Eddie on the phone earlier?"

"Huh? Oh, no. It was just a wrong number," said Shannon, hurrying him out through the door. "Now, please come on and let's have a day out to remember."

As her fiancé led the way outside, Shannon casually slid his mobile phone from her sleeve and onto the hall table. So far he hadn't noticed it was missing.

****

Christian Devine yawned and stretched his arms across the pillow beside him.

"Ow," said a voice, making him almost jump out his skin.

"Jesus, I'm sorry! Did I hurt you?" he asked in horror.

Eloise giggled and wrapped a long, slender arm around Christian's body. He was so warm and she felt like lying beside him forever.

"Er, isn't your sister going to wonder where you are?" he asked, lifting her arm from its resting place and climbing out of the bed.

"I can look after myself. I'm a big girl now," said Eloise. "I'm twenty-one in a few weeks time so I can stay here all day if I want."

Oh no, a cling-on, thought Christian. *That's what I get for messing around with juvenile strangers.*

"Well, I really wish you could, Eloise, but I promised my sister I'd be with her first thing this morning, so I'm going to have to get out of here myself pretty soon. Babysitting duties."

Eloise pouted and reached out her arms.

"Babysitting? Come into bed and babysit me," she said in the tone of a two-year-old.

"I really can't," said Christian, grabbing a towel from the end of the bed and wrapping it around his waist. If there was one thing Christian couldn't stand, it was a woman imitating a baby voice. "Now, I really need to have a shower and then make tracks. You will be working in the bar over the weekend, I presume, so I can contact you there?"

Eloise stood up and Christian blinked at the way she paraded around his apartment naked. She was certainly beautiful, but brazen, as she marched over to the bedroom window and opened the curtains.

"What? Is that it, Christian?"

She put her hands on her hips and stood in full view of passers-by outside. To Christian's shock he noticed the window was open so not only could she possibly be seen, she could also no doubt be heard by everyone on the street outside.

"Jesus, Eloise, will you pull the bloody curtains? The bar is just across the way and I know the couple who live above it. They can see straight in here."

Eloise stood on top of the bed and shouted louder.

"You weren't so shy last night, Christian! Come on, tell me," she yelled. "Don't you want me?"

"I do, I do, but I really have to go…" Christian's voice was in a whisper. It was like reasoning with a child. Hell, she practically *was* a child.

"I don't believe you! You just want rid of me, don't you." Oh no, the baby voice again. "You pick me up in a bar, take me to your house for coffee, a bit of what you fancy all fucking night and then you want to just kick me out on the street! I don't think so!"

Christian tied his towel tighter around his waist and climbed on top of the bed to pull the curtains, but Eloise wrestled him onto the mattress and straddled him at the waist, pinning her hands on his forearms. He had fantasized about moments like this in the past, but in reality it was bloody scary. This was crazy shit and he didn't have a clue how to react.

"Eloise, please, I am telling you the truth. I promised my sister I would baby…OW!"

"You have made a fool out of me," she screamed, leaning harder on his arms and digging her nails into him.

Christian had had enough. His fear of hurting her was quickly replaced by a fear of Eloise hurting him more. He pushed himself upwards and she struggled under his grasp, screaming and shouting obscenities at the top of her heavily accented voice.

"You want rid of me!" she squealed.

When he finally wrestled free, he reached for the curtains and drew them tight. Eloise was a psycho, and a naked Danish psycho at that. The last thing he needed was the entire neighbourhood witnessing her throwing a wobbler.

"Right, Eloise." Christian was breathless. "This has gone far enough. I'm really sorry if you misunderstood me earlier. I was *not* trying to get rid of you. I am merely running *late*. Now please, I really need you to go!"

To his relief she started to gather her clothes from the floor and slowly began to get dressed, while muttering in her native language. Finally she stood up, fully clothed again in the same dangerously tight little jeans that had first attracted his gaze, and shimmied her way towards the bedroom door.

"My sister warned me about men like you," she spat towards him on her way through the apartment. "She said I'd never believe how nasty a horny man can be after he takes the sex. Well, now I know. You take the sex, but you don't want *me* in the morning. Selfish, selfish, sex thief!"

She reached the door and Christian prayed she would walk out through it and suddenly get an attack of amnesia so that she wouldn't remember where he lived later on.

"Goodbye, Eloise!" This was definitely a shag that would cost him dearly. The experience would stay in his mind forever for all the wrong reasons.

"Oh, and by the way….," she screeched.

Jesus, this girl is relentless, he thought, when he saw her pause again at the doorway to make sure she had the last word.

"What is it now? I told you I was running late."

Eloise stood with a hand on her skinny hip and gave an evil laugh.

"I think someone killed your precious fucking cat."

****

151

"What a day you've had!" exclaimed Christian's sister as she wiped down the counter of her pine kitchen in Belfast's Malone Road later that afternoon.

"Tell me about it, Jess! Believe me, no matter how crazy you think your house is with two toddlers, I am ready for a night away from the single life. It's not all it's cracked up to be," said Christian, nestling a cup of tea in his hands as though he was holding on for grim death.

"Well, maybe you'll be more careful in your choice of women from now on," said Jess's husband, Michael, on his way through the kitchen. "You deserve all you get, Casanova."

Jess threw her eyes up. "Oh, do you hear the voice of reason? I'm sure you picked up the odd psycho yourself in your single days around Belfast. That was obviously before you had the good fortune to meet me," she said with a giggle.

"I sure did," said Michael, winking at Christian behind his wife's back. "Speaking of psychos, I hear there was a young lad badly beaten up last night outside an off-licence out in Stranmillis direction."

"Really?" said Christian. "I suppose that's city life for you. Does that sort of thing happen a lot?"

"Not around those parts, no. I hear he's been brought to hospital. It was a bad kicking he got, that's for sure."

Christian shook his head. Donegal had its anti-social areas too, but thankfully he knew them like the back of his hand. He also was well enough travelled to know that cities were the same the world over. There were thugs in every town.

"Uncle Chris, can you play with us now, please?"

Jess's daughters, Lara and Molly, were playing Cowboys and Indians in the background and impatiently waiting for Christian to be their horse.

"I'll be there in a second, kids. I'm just saddling up here. How about some cartoons while you're waiting?"

Jess looked at her brother with a smile and Christian swallowed hard.

"Please ask them to go easy on me, Jess," he joked. "I've already been injured by a juvenile nymphomaniac today and it wasn't pretty."

"Sounds pretty good to me," said Michael from behind a newspaper. "Most men have dreams about stuff like that. Count yourself lucky because once you're married you'll be crying out for some excitement like that, won't he Jess?"

Jess threw a cushion at her husband, who was on a roll now he had a bit of male company.

Christian stood up to emphasise his point. "I'm telling you the truth, Michael. The only dream I have is that she doesn't come near me again. In fact, at the moment I'm dreaming of her on a one-way flight back to Denmark. Now, please excuse me but I'm going to have to entertain your children while you two get ready for your night out on the tiles."

Christian crawled on his hands and knees towards his nieces, who screamed playfully as he approached their playroom but then his phone rang, much to their disappointment.

"Sorry, girls," he said and they groaned as he took the call. "Hello?"

"Christian? Christian! Can you hear me?"

The line was bad and the voice on the other end was breaking up. Jesus Christ, he thought. How the hell did Eloise get this number?

"Who is this? I can't hear you very well," he said, panicking.

"Christian? It's Daisy. Daisy Anderson. Do you have any idea where Jonathan is?"

Christian paced the floor of the house. "Sorry, Daisy. I don't know if it's a bad line or the noise in my sister's house, but I didn't recognise your voice. You're looking for Jonathan?"

"Yes. I need to find him urgently. There's no answer at Isobel's, I don't have his mobile number and I can't get in touch with my mother. I need to find him quickly."

Christian sat down on the back doorstep.

153

"Wait a minute, Daisy. Where are you? What's happened?"

"I'm at the Royal Victoria Hospital in Belfast," she said, and Christian could hear her sob between words. "Eddie has been beaten up really badly and I haven't been able to reach anyone all morning. I found your number in my pocket and hoped you might tell Jonathan to get here as soon as he can. Or try to reach him on his mobile. Or give me his number and I will. Shit, I don't know what to do!"

Christian could feel his heart thump in his chest. Daisy was so distressed. This sounded bad. He had to think fast.

"The thing is, Daisy, I'm not in Donegal. I'm in Belfast like yourself, but I'll phone Jonathan straight away. I'll be with you in twenty minutes and we'll figure something out."

****

Daisy stroked Eddie's hair as he slept. The only noise she could hear was the faint bleep of the heart monitor and the odd moan from her friend.

She needed to find Jonathan quickly, but every avenue she tried was coming up blank. Apart from her own mother and the Eastwoods, there was no one else she could think of to contact in Killshannon. She couldn't remember Shannon's surname, nor did she know the elderly folk who lived on either side of her mother. She didn't even know who ran the local pub these days. Daisy had run away from her old life and now when she desperately needed it back, she couldn't find it.

Finding Christian Devine's number had been a real scoop. At least he was on his way over and should have contacted Jonathan by now.

Lorna, in her kindness, had offered to drive to Killshannon to find Jonathan, but Daisy had put her off. Sooner or later, he would be located, and besides, she needed Lorna to stay with her and reassure her that Eddie was going to be alright.

"How is he now?"

Daisy looked around to see Christian standing beside her and she automatically fell into his arms at the relief of seeing a familiar face.

"He's not so good, Christian," she sobbed. "He woke for the first time about an hour ago and he's just gone back to sleep now. I don't think he knew where he was. I just kept talking and talking to him and even my friend Lorna couldn't get through to him. So far, we've had no response. What am I going to do, Christian? What am I going to tell Isobel and Jonathan?"

Christian smoothed Daisy's hair and let her cry for a moment. Eddie was almost unrecognisable, lying on the trolley bed. Whoever did this to him deserved to be locked up. His face was black and blue, his arm was in a sling and his eyes, though closed, were swollen horrifically and had turned all colours of the rainbow.

"First of all, we have to find Jonathan. But his mobile is going straight to voicemail, I'm afraid."

"Oh, no…"

"Now, let's think. It's his birthday today, so if he's not at home, he's most likely gone away somewhere with Shannon. Did he mention to you at all what his plans were?"

"No. The last time I saw him we were talking about you. He had this silly notion that something was going on between us and that's why I left for Belfast. Eddie came with me and now this has happened. It's all my fault."

Christian sat Daisy up straight and looked her in the eye.

"It's not your fault, Daisy. It's nobody's fault except the thugs who did this to Eddie. It could have happened to him in Donegal, or it could have happened to him in San Francisco, so don't even go there. Now, how about your mum? Is it likely she could find out where Jonathan is?"

Daisy's head was thumping sore. She hadn't slept all night. She hadn't even been able to eat anything despite being offered tea and toast by nursing staff around the clock. She just couldn't

155

think straight. What time was it now, even?

"For some reason, there's no reply at my mum's. There's nobody at Isobel's either and Eddie's phone was stolen so I don't have a contact for Jonathan. Can you try his mobile again?"

"It's no use, Daisy. I've been ringing it constantly on my way here. It must be either switched off or the battery has gone flat. It's almost six now. Will your mum be home now? You could try her again."

"I suppose. The mobile signals are so bad in Killshannon I don't know why people bother to have them at all. I'll try her landline again but I've already left her three messages. Oh God, I hope nothing has happened to Isobel. That would really make this the worst day ever."

Daisy's fingers slipped off the phone's tiny digits and her hands shook as she tried to dial her mother's number. Please, please pick up the phone, she prayed. On the fourth ring, her prayers were answered.

"Mum, Mum is that you?"

"Well, of course it's me, Daisy. Who else would be answering the phone in this house? How did your doctor's appointment go?"

"Mum, didn't you get my message to contact me urgently? I have been trying to get you all day!"

With a mixture of frustration and relief, Daisy found herself starting to cry again. She dropped the phone by her side and Christian swiftly caught it before it dropped to the floor.

"Mrs Anderson, please don't panic. Daisy is fine. It's Christian here. Yes, Christian Devine. We've been trying to get in touch with Jonathan for some time now. Do you have any idea where he is? I'm afraid something terrible has happened to Eddie."

****

Shannon Cassidy pulled her long blond hair above the nape of her neck and tilted her head to one side. The lights were low and she thought she looked pretty good in the hotel bathroom mirror. The morning on the golf course had left her hair sticky and out of shape so she expertly twisted it into a loose bun and pinned it up high, leaving a few loose tendrils hanging around her slim face. Her red lips needed an extra coat and she pouted into the mirror, congratulating herself on a job well done.

Jonathan hadn't stopped whingeing the whole day about the fact that he had left his mobile phone at home. She didn't know what his problem was. After all, years ago people survived just fine without being constantly tracked down. However, she had felt ever so guilty when he'd used the hotel phone to ring his mother and found there was no reply. Whoops. That was just because she had forgotten to put the connection back in that morning before they'd left. No need to worry.

It had been a blissful day apart from all that, but the best was yet to come, she decided. Shannon had big news for Jonathan. She had been counting down the days to his birthday and saving her big announcement until now. Just as she had promised, this was going to be his best birthday ever and she couldn't wait to see the look on his handsome face.

"Hey, honey. What's up?" she asked when she returned to the restaurant. He had hardly touched his champagne and was staring into space from his window seat, looking miserable.

"What? Oh, nothing. Sorry, Shannon. I was miles away. I didn't see you come back in."

She leaned across the table and gave him a peck on the cheek, then rubbed the lipstick stain off his face with her thumb. She could have sworn that he flinched under her touch but she didn't worry. His form would soon change for the better once he heard her good news.

"So, as I was saying earlier, I'm not too sure about the apple-green dress for Marissa," she cooed. "I mean, it's not that she doesn't suit it, quite the opposite really, but I do think the bride should be the star of the show, not the bridesmaid. In fact, I almost regret asking her to be bridesmaid in the first place. What do you think, Jonathan? Is it too late to put her off?"

Jonathan fiddled with the cuff of his shirtsleeve. It just didn't feel right sitting in the lap of luxury, discussing a wedding he had no interest in planning, with somebody who was not the person for him.

"I think we need to talk, Shannon."

"We do? Do you think I'm over-reacting? Maybe I am. Ah well, it *is* supposed to be the most special day of your life so I want to make it perfect for both of us. Daddy says…"

"Shannon. We need to talk. Not about the wedding. We need to talk about *us*."

Shannon rolled her eyes.

"You know, Jonathan, I heard this really weird story about a man and his wife sitting in this very restaurant and when the husband asked the wife what she would like for dinner she said 'I'll have a divorce, dear.' You're scaring me, Jonathan. You're talking like there's something wrong. Are you getting cold feet? It is perfectly normal. Even Mummy said when Daddy proposed to her…"

Jonathan struggled to find the right words. All the words he'd practised over the past few hours didn't seem so fitting now. They were either too soft or too harsh. He didn't want her threatening to throw herself into a lough. And considering the geography of where they were, water was a bit too close for comfort.

"I'm a little bit stressed right now, Shannon. I think I need a break."

She looked at him puzzled, screwing up her face. "But we're already on a break, darling. Isn't this place wonderful? I thought you'd love it!" she cried.

Jonathan could feel his heart sink. This wasn't going to be easy.

Shannon suddenly seemed to get it.

"Oh… you mean, *we* need a break. Not you. *We*."

Phew, he thought. For a second there he'd feared he was going to have to be harsh. Finally she'd caught his drift.

158

"Yes," he said quickly. "I just need a while to sort my head out, Shannon. We need to postpone the wedding. Just for a while. Please understand. I have so much going on at the minute."

Shannon could feel her bottom lip twitch as her whole world seemed to collapse around her. The last thing she wanted to do was cry in the middle of a packed restaurant. Why was Jonathan doing this to her? She couldn't possibly call off the wedding. She needed this so badly, and besides, what would she tell her parents? How could she explain all this to her bridesmaids, her florists or her wedding singer? It would be humiliating beyond words. Maybe it was time for her to break her news, so that he would have to change his mind.

"No, Jonathan. I'm afraid it isn't quite as simple as that."

She took a deep breath and stared at him with a cold smile. "I'm going to walk out of here now, and you will follow. Then we'll drive home, since you haven't even bothered to touch the champagne I bought, and on the way home I will tell you why postponing our wedding is totally and utterly out of the question."

Jonathan sighed. He wasn't in the mood for one of Shannon's hissy fits. She could stand and stomp her pretty little feet in the middle of this whole restaurant but he had made up his mind. He would not give in to her childish demands.

"I'm serious, Shannon. It's not happening," he said under his breath. "Now, let's pay our bill, leave this place without a fuss and make our way home. We *will* have to postpone the wedding because it takes two to get married and I won't be getting married for at least another year. That's my final word on it. I'm sorry."

"Is that so?" she answered with a confidence that rocked him so much he almost fell off his seat. "Well, I'm actually very sorry too."

"You are? That's good," he said, clearing his throat.

"I mean," she said with a nasty laugh. "How are you going to explain your illegitimate child to your God-fearing mother then?"

Jonathan's heart almost stopped. What was she on about? Was she threatening him?

159

"Wh...what do you mean?" he stammered. How the hell had Shannon found out about Daisy's baby from all those years ago?

"Oh, well, look here," she continued with a smug look on her face. "Has the cat got the birthday boy's tongue?" She patted her flat-as-a-pancake tummy. "Yes, Jonathan. You're going to be a daddy. Congratulations. I was saving the news till dessert but you sort of pushed me into it. So sorry to ruin the surprise. Happy Birthday, darling."

Chapter 18

I Can Feel Your Heart Leap

Daisy continued to watch the bleep of the monitor strapped to Eddie's chest. She felt her own heavy heart sinking deeper and deeper. She was short of breath and felt like she'd smoked sixty cigarettes, when in reality she'd only taken one sneaky puff from Lorna's earlier that morning. It had made her so sick and dizzy that she'd vowed never to pretend to be a smoker again. Anyone who was willing to stand outside in the rain like a second-class citizen while they sucked a little stick of nicotine deserved at least a bit of pleasure from it, but she'd only felt a thousand times worse.

She felt so alone now as she sat by Eddie's bedside. Christian had been sitting with her to reassure her, but he had slipped outside for the first time in three hours. She hoped Lorna would be back soon. She'd only gone home to freshen up and give in to her craving for gravy chips. She'd offered to bring something back for Daisy but food was the furthest thing from Daisy's mind as she sat in numb oblivion.

The silence around her was deafening. She was sure her hearing had improved remarkably since her vigil on the ward. Pretty soon, she reckoned she would be able to identify the other patients by their sighs, breaths and coughs.

"Come on, Eddie. You're taking the piss here," she whispered. But he didn't flinch. Jokes weren't working, nor was being serious. Crying also didn't work but she was willingly trying each method over and over again.

"I can't believe you went to all this trouble just to see if there was anything left between Jonathan and I," she mumbled. "Did you really know our secret, or is it that you hate Shannon so much that you were grasping at straws by bringing me back into the picture? I'll always love him, you know. Always have. But it was too painful to go back, Eddie. I couldn't go back. Every time I thought of Jonathan my heart jumped and I saw our baby's face and I realised how we'd made such a mistake and...well, it became much easier to pretend I couldn't stand him. But I can stand him. I think I'm still in love with him, Eddie. You were right all along."

Daisy leaned across and kissed Eddie's forehead again and then settled back into the silence of the intensive care unit. Medical staff of all ranks had been milling in and out all day, all evening, silently checking notes and pulses and acknowledging her with a pitiful nod.

Sometimes she would acknowledge their presence, sometimes she would just stare at them in a hazy gaze and sometimes she would ask them something random such as, what the weather was like outside.

"Can you hear me, Eddie? Squeeze my hand if you heard what I just told you" she whispered into the empty silence of the cubicle. Her words echoed in her mind, but then a voice from behind her unexpectedly answered her vacant question.

"I hope he did. Christ, Daisy, how the hell did this happen?"

Daisy turned to see Jonathan. Her Jonathan. Oh thank you God, she thought. His eyes were tired, stunned almost and she couldn't find words to express her joy at seeing him again. At last somebody had managed to track him down. It must have been much later into the night than she thought.

"I'm so glad you're here," she said and wrapped her arms around

162

him. "I've tried all day and all last night to get in touch with you. I'm so, so sorry, Jonathan," she said, her voice rusty with emotion and she began to weep uncontrollably.

Jonathan pulled her closer and Daisy sank her head into the security of his broad shoulder. He smelled of something from her childhood. Ice cream or milk shakes or chocolate buttons. Whatever it was, it was homely and reassuring and she was so relieved to see him. She wanted to nestle her head into his arms and hide there forever.

"He has some head injuries," she whispered. "How severe they are they can't say yet. He woke up earlier but only for an hour or so and there was very little response. I'll never forgive myself for letting this happen..."

"Ssh", said Jonathan, rubbing her back gently, his cheek resting in her hair. "How could you have known? If I ever find the bastards that did this to him, I swear I will do time...."

Daisy looked up to see anger seeping from behind Jonathan's sad eyes.

"Don't, Jonathan. The police are onto them. They reckon they've a good chance of having them locked up; it should have been caught on CCTV. Have you told your mother?"

Jonathan shook his head and held Daisy's shoulders. "You've been through a lot today. Don't worry about telling Mum. Let me worry about that." He softly lifted her chin so that her eyes met his. "You're shattered, Daisy. Why don't you get yourself home for a few hours? Shannon and I can take over here for a while?"

Daisy gulped and looked over Jonathan's shoulder like a rabbit caught in headlights. The room where Eddie lay in intensive care looked out through venetian blinds onto a corridor where Daisy could make out Shannon's lithe figure and two others she assumed were Christian and Lorna who seemed to have just arrived back. The hospital had a strict "two person by the bedside" rule so Daisy took Shannon's arrival as her cue to get offside.

"Of course...Shannon is here... I'll get out of the way then,"

163

she said. "I thought you had come by yourself."

Jonathan's heart leaped. He didn't want to chase Daisy away from his brother's bedside. He wanted her to stay in his arms. He wanted to feel every movement of her, every longing beat of her heart but he knew now he had to ignore his feelings and hers. He now had to face up to the same responsibilities with Shannon that he and Daisy had failed to live up to before.

"Your friend Lorna was asking for you outside," he said. "Go on, you need some rest. The nurses said you've been here for almost twenty-four hours."

Daisy looked at Eddie's broken face and the bleeping of the heart monitor grew louder and louder in her brain. She couldn't leave him. She wanted to be with him when he opened his eyes, when he laughed at her and told her it was all a joke. She wanted to turn back time to when he had come tumbling into her apartment with that futile bottle of wine under his arm and a magic pack of cigarettes for Lorna, ready for another debate or argument on the price of fame, or fried bread versus toast. She just wanted him to wake up. She wouldn't leave him with Shannon, whom he had tried so hard to dispel from his brother's life.

"I don't want to go, Jonathan. I want to stay with you and Eddie. I want to be with *you*."

Jonathan looked at her with sorrow, tears pricking his eyes and he shook his head slowly.

"Jesus, Daisy, don't say that. Please don't say things you don't mean. And Shannon…"

"Like you said before, you can explain to her. Tell her you're sorry, tell her anything. Just make this all better, Jonathan, I don't want to leave you now. We're supposed to be together. It was what Eddie wanted all along."

Jonathan pushed a stray lock of Daisy's hair from her damp face and drew a deep breath. He sat down on the clinical green armchair and held his head in his hands.

"I'm afraid things with Shannon are a bit more complicated

now, Daisy."

"What? How?"

Jonathan's face crumpled and he stared at the floor. There was no easy way to break this news.

"I'm...I've just found out that Shannon is pregnant."

Outside the room in the corridor, Lorna, Christian and Shannon sat in silence, each staring at the floor. Lorna had taken a good long look at Jonathan Eastwood's fiancée when she could get the chance. She was a very glamorous girl, there was no doubt about it, but she seemed distracted and irritable, like her mind was far, far away. She kept checking her phone and sighing deeply, exhaling as loudly as she could, which was driving Lorna mental.

To her right sat the most outrageously handsome man she had possibly ever seen in real life. He had introduced himself quietly – in fact they all spoke in whispers as if they were at an Irish wake. Lorna played with the hem of her skirt, not knowing whether to strike up conversation or not. She glanced to the side and saw that Christian was looking at her. They made eye contact and he smiled and then looked away, giving Lorna the perfect opportunity to drink in his drop-dead gorgeous dark stubble that sprinkled so evenly across his strong, tanned jawline. She looked at his hands, which were clasped in front of him and her mind went into overdrive just looking at those hands and imagining them all over her body.

Holy Mary, mother of God, she said to herself, closing her eyes. *Please forgive me for thinking such sexual thoughts outside an intensive care ward. If you send me to hell I will totally understand, but if you don't mind, before you do, could I just have one night with that big mad ride beside me.*

She opened her eyes again, disgusted with herself for not being able to even finish a silent prayer without thinking of him naked and was awoken to her senses when he started to laugh.

"What's so funny?" she whispered. "Did I say that out loud?"

165

"Say what?" he whispered back, still laughing, still smiling. Oh good Lord he was a picture, as her mother would say!

"My prayers," said Lorna. "I was saying a prayer…for Eddie, of course."

Oh God I'm a liar now too, I'm sorry, she thought.

"I thought as much," said Christian. His dark-brown eyes were so alive. "I'm sorry, I don't think that praying is funny at all, in fact, fair play to you, but I find all this silence a bit unnerving and it just got me a bit giddy. Sorry. You just looked so…"

"So what? Looked so what?" asked Lorna. She was extremely paranoid now. Did she look stupid or something? What?

"Angelic," said Christian, his eyes squinting slightly as he spoke. "Like an angel but with an edge. You looked like you were thinking something you shouldn't have been."

Lorna was impressed but a bit spooked at the same time.

"I was thinking the most inappropriate thoughts," she whispered back to him. "I think I am going to hell."

"I'll see you there," said Christian. "I'd say we'd have a good old time."

He winked at her and licked his lips quickly, then went back to his silent pose, his hands clasped again under his chin as he leaned his elbows on his strong thighs.

"Now you look like you're the one saying your prayers," said Lorna. "Say one for me because my last effort went straight to the gutter."

Christian turned his body to face her and leaned his arm on the back of his chair. He looked more serious now.

"You will look after Daisy, won't you," he said, glancing back and forth to Shannon, who was now filing her nails across the corridor. "She's going to need a lot of support after all this."

"Oh I will," said Lorna, forgetting for a second that she was face to face and eye to eye with a man who looked like he had stepped out of a Calvin Klein advertisement. "She's my best friend. I will make sure she gets through this as best she can."

"Do you mind if I give you my number?" asked Christian. "I'd like to keep in touch with…well, with how things are going…with Daisy. And I'd like to know if you go to heaven or hell the next time you decide to say a prayer."

He was serious about Daisy, Lorna had no doubt about that, but there was a slight twinkle in his eye that she picked up on instantly.

"I am sure I can keep you up to date," she said as he wrote his number on the back of a business card for a pizza place he found in his wallet.

"Great, I'd appreciate that," he said.

He gave her the card and Lorna held it in her hand, looked at his neat handwriting and slid it into her coat pocket.

"I think it's about time I got Daisy home," she said. Drop-dead gorgeous or not, she wasn't going to fall for Christian Devine's charms just that easily.

Daisy stared at Jonathan, speechless as she felt the room spin. Dizzily she held onto the side of the bedside locker and tried to find the power to respond. If Eddie was ever going to wake up, he would have done so by now. He would have screamed at the thought of his matchmaking plans slipping slowly down the drain. But he didn't. He just lay in his own silence, a machine making noise on his behalf.

"No matter how much I want to, I can't be with you, Daisy. I'm so, so sorry."

Daisy's stomach gave a leap, just like it had when she was a teenager and she had seen Jonathan talking to another girl. She felt like she was going to choke as his words registered slowly and painfully. All of Eddie's efforts had been wasted. She just had to accept the irony that while she had given away Jonathan's baby, and his love once before, Shannon was now giving him the new chance of a life with a family.

"Oh," she said. "I…I'm so sorry. I've been so stupid."

She let go of the bedside locker and walked slowly out into the cool corridor, where Lorna was now chatting quietly to a perfectly made-up Shannon. Nodding back a wall of tears, Daisy nodded obviously in Shannon's direction, before pulling Lorna by the arm into the nearby lift.

"Can I go in to be with Jonathan now, Daisy?" called Shannon after her.

"Yes," sniffed Daisy as the lift doors closed and Shannon disappeared from sight. "You can be with Jonathan all you want now. You can be with him forever. You've got your own way now."

Chapter 19

Confessions Of An Idiotic Mind

Neither girl spoke very much as they weaved their way through the night-time city traffic to their apartment. As they passed through the Ormeau Road, Lorna noticed Daisy stare coldly through the window at the off-licence where Eddie had been brutally attacked. All sorts of people were going in and out through its swinging doors carrying crates of beer, wine or spirits. Some were laughing with groups of friends while others just nipped in and out quickly on their own.

"What day is it?"

"It's Saturday night," said Lorna, shifting gear on approach to their apartment block.

Daisy let out a fourth deep sigh in a row. "I forgot to wish Jonathan a happy birthday. Can we go back?"

Lorna didn't respond. She veered her Clio into a minute parking space outside the apartment and got out of the car, then walked to Daisy's side, opened the door and helped her out. Daisy's canvas handbag was lying half-open and her eyes were half-closed. She was still in severe shock and her ramblings had become more and more incoherent as the day had progressed.

"You aren't thinking straight, Daisy. Come on, let's get you

169

inside to the warmth and hopefully you'll get some sleep. You look like shit."

Lorna recalled hearing Daisy speak to Eddie in the hospital about a child whose eighth birthday was just around the corner. At first she had referred to the child as Matthew, and then she called him James. Concerned, Lorna had been on the verge of buzzing for a nurse to check her friend's sanity levels. But then she had decided against it and simply let out a raspy cough so Daisy would know she was in close vicinity and come back to the land of the living. The child who was called James or Matthew wasn't mentioned again.

Lorna led the way into the apartment and closed the door properly when Daisy left it ajar. Taking off her coat, she flicked on the kettle to make her friend a warm drink as she had refused all day to eat anything.

"Here, put your feet up and relax, Daisy," she said, slipping off the other girl's trainers and resting her feet on top of a cushion. "I'm going to make you a cup-a-soup and you can just sip it. I won't make you drink it but I think you need some nourishment. You're as white as a ghost."

Daisy's eyelids were starting to fall already.

"Shannon's pregnant," she mumbled, half staring, half squinting towards a corner in the room. "I left it too late with Jonathan, like everything else in my life. You snooze, you lose, once again Daisy Anderson."

Lorna almost dropped the cup she was holding in shock. Had she heard Daisy correctly? Surely not? If this had been a normal day and a normal bit of news, she and Daisy would have gossiped galore at the thought of someone finding out they were pregnant only months before their wedding. But this latest revelation was disastrous. No wonder Daisy looked devastated.

Lorna bit her lip and struggled to find the right response. She figured that the more they talked, the longer Daisy would stay awake and would therefore be tempted to drink the soup.

170

"Daisy, remember, if you hadn't left here for Killshannon last Monday, Jonathan would never have declared his undying love for you, and you would have been happy enough in your own life here in Belfast, with Jonathan nothing more than just a faded memory. I'm sorry, love, but you're going to have to realise that maybe you and Jonathan were never meant to be."

Daisy's stare was cold. "You don't know what you're talking about. I was brought back to Killshannon this week for a reason…"

"Yes, you were. You were brought back to help out an old friend."

"No, Lorna, it was more than that. Much more than that." Daisy was starting to cry now and Lorna instantly regretted her forthright approach. But Daisy had to be realistic.

"Nobody else knows what we had between us back then. Jonathan and I have a special bond, you know. We'll always have a bond. Not even long legs Shannon Shilliday can break."

Lorna paused before speaking.

"Shannon Shilliday? Is that her surname?"

"No, it's not, I just made that up. I even don't remember what her stupid surname is but she'll soon be Shannon Eastwood anyhow, won't she?"

Lorna was baffled. Without a doubt, her friend's behaviour was becoming stranger and stranger since their Spanish holiday plans had fallen through at the weekend. Maybe this was the opposite of sunstroke, thought Lorna. Or else it was the Killshannon fresh air that had made Daisy so crazy. Now she was, after all, only used to city smog since she'd fled the countryside life nearly nine years ago. Daisy had always sworn she'd never go back to Killshannon because it reminded her of her father, but Lorna had smelled a rat. She was sure that Daisy's decision to leave her home village in the back end of Donegal was to escape something else.

And that something was obviously to do with Jonathan Eastwood.

"Why *did* you leave Killshannon, Daisy? And don't tell me it was because you wanted to become an actress because I know that's just a cop-out. Truthfully, was it because of Jonathan?"

Lorna waited patiently for an answer, but when she looked across Daisy was fast asleep with her cup of soup still grasped between her hands. Her long, blond lashes were damp with tears and she looked pitiful. Lorna carefully prised the cup away and pushed Daisy's hair from her eyes.

****

Christian tossed and turned in Jess's cosy spare bedroom. He had phoned the hospital earlier to check on Eddie's condition, but despite pretending to be an uncle and then a work colleague, the staff said they could only release information over the phone to immediate family.

Lara and Molly were sleeping soundly in the room above and his night of babysitting had thankfully proven to be an easy sail. By the time he'd returned from the hospital that evening, Jessie and Michael had put the girls to bed and were ready to walk out of the door, so all plans of Cowboys and Indians had been shelved.

Eddie Eastwood was a mess. Nobody deserved the beating he had received. Christian didn't envy the fate of the culprits who did it if Jonathan ever got his hands on them. Jonathan was a tough nut to crack, but when it came to his mother and his only sibling, he would walk to the ends of the earth for them.

As he tossed and turned in sheer unsettlement, Christian remembered he had Daisy's number from earlier that day. Maybe he should give her a call. He reached to the floor to where his mobile lay and scrolled through his received call list until he found her number. It rang three times and then was answered.

"Hi Daisy, it's Christian. I'm just phoning about Eddie. How is he now?"

"Oh, I'm sorry Christian, but Daisy is asleep," said Lorna. "This is Lorna. Jonathan called earlier to say that not much has changed, I'm afraid."

Christian remembered Lorna well and the sound of her voice made him smile, much to his surprise. She had caught his eye, but not in the way a woman normally would. Her hair had been dyed the wildest shade of red. Only a blind man could have missed it but she was striking in her own, very individual way and her humour was very attractive.

"Lorna, of course. I hope you are still saying your prayers, like a good girl?" he laughed.

Lorna blushed, remembering her illicit thoughts from earlier.

"Yes, of course. And still looking like…what was it? Oh, angelic," she said.

"Yes…yes, angelic," he said. "It was kinda cute."

Lorna felt a flutter inside and tried to shake it off. The one and only Christian Devine, he of the velvet voice, inky dark eyes and his "click your fingers and we're in bed" magic was working on her and getting under her skin already. But no. Lorna was *so* not going to let him do so that easily.

"So, anyway, Christopher…" she said in the coolest tone she could manage.

"It's, er, Christian, actually. Not Christopher."

As *if* she didn't know!

"Sorry, *Christian*. Daisy is so, so worried about Eddie. It's terrible, isn't it?"

"Eddie's a strong lad. He's had a bad beating but I have high hopes he'll pull out of this before we know it. I still can't sleep a wink thinking about him, though."

"Me neither," admitted Lorna.

She pulled her feet under her knees and settled into the comfort of the sofa, while on the other side of Belfast city, Christian sank further back into his pillow. Neither of them had any intention of hanging up just yet.

"At least Jonathan has Shannon with him to keep him company," said Lorna, hoping that the conversation would steer towards Daisy and Jonathan. "I mean, she is his fiancée after all, and the closest person he has under the circumstances."

"I suppose."

Shit, that wasn't the answer Lorna was hoping for.

He cleared his throat. "Look Lorna, I'm not sure how well you know Daisy …"

"I've lived with her over four years. We're very close; like sisters," she said protectively.

"Well, then, you know her better than I do at the minute," said Christian. "But it's my opinion that if Jonathan had his way, Daisy would be by his side at the minute, not Shannon Cassidy."

"Really?" said Lorna. "I hadn't realised they'd been so close." She was hurt at being kept in the dark. She had thought she knew everything about Daisy.

Christian pondered for a moment before answering. "I think Jonathan's hasty engagement to Shannon was a cry for help when Isobel got the bad news. They work together but really haven't been seeing each other for that long. Daisy's arrival back home made him realise that no matter how much time had passed, Daisy *is* the one for him. I just hope he doesn't leave it too late to tell her so."

Lorna faltered. She still had so many questions to ask Christian Devine. So many, that she didn't know where to start.

"But Jonathan did tell Daisy during the week that he would call off the wedding if she wanted him to," said Lorna. "Sadly now it's too late because Shannon has just announced she has a bloody bun in the oven. Poor Daisy."

Christian fell silent.

"Oh. Shit. I didn't know *that*. Well, that does complicate things, doesn't it? Talk about déjà vu."

"How do you mean?"

Christian knew he had put his foot in it.

"Oh, nothing."

"Go on, how do you mean? You can tell me…"

"It was just a rumour, that's all. A rumour at the time when Daisy left Killshannon, not long after the car accident, that she may have been pregnant."

Lorna's heart skipped a beat. Everything made sense now. But was it true?

"To Jonathan! And did she have the baby?"

"Dunno for sure," said Christian. "I heard she gave it up for adoption and then went to university. She hasn't been back in Killshannon much since. I'd imagine with having the baby so soon after her father was killed, things have been way too painful. They never really gave themselves time to deal with it. They both, sort of, ran away from each other instead."

Lorna rubbed her forehead.

"Oh, Christian, I think I've made a big mistake," said Lorna. "I think Daisy would have stayed in Killshannon this week for longer if I hadn't convinced her to come back to Belfast. I was sure she was going to be labelled a marriage-wrecker if she split up Jonathan's engagement."

Christian could sense Lorna's despair down the phone. He was guilty himself in the past of coming between Jonathan and Daisy. He knew how she felt.

"Look, Lorna, Shannon is pregnant. You can't change that and Jonathan won't walk away from his own child again. Maybe you've saved Daisy from a harder heartache in the long run."

Lorna looked over at Daisy, who was fast asleep on the sofa.

"Maybe I did. Oh shit, I don't know, Christian. I hope I've done the right thing."

"Time will tell, Lorna. It's out of your hands now. And mine."

Chapter 20

A Mother's Work Is Never Fun

"Maggie? Maggie, are you there?"

Maggie Anderson scurried down the corridor to answer Isobel's calls. It was almost noon now, and she hadn't heard any word about Eddie's condition since the night before. No news was good news, though, she reckoned.

"I'm here, Isobel. Are you okay, love? What can I get you?" asked Maggie, peeping her head around the bedroom door. While she was there to supervise her friend, she didn't want to fuss around her or cramp her in her own home. Therefore she had taken to pottering around the house, doing light chores, and taking advantage of Isobel's spacious garden when the sun came out.

Isobel patted the bedside in a gesture for Maggie to sit down, her face etched with worry. Did she sense something was wrong?

"I've been thinking, Maggie," she said. "Thinking really hard about some of the things going on around me and I wanted to sound some of my feelings off with you now that my boys are away partying."

Maggie gulped. She felt like such a cheat but until she heard some good news, she didn't feel the need to knock Isobel back any further.

"Of course, go ahead. You know you can tell me anything."

Isobel swallowed hard. She was determined to lay her cards on the table. "I know you're terribly lonely, Maggie."

"Oh, Isobel, don't be silly…"

"But you are. I can see it in your every move. The way you talk, the way you carry yourself lately. I can tell. I've had a lot of time to think lately, but my time to *say* things is quickly running out."

"Really, Isobel, you have no need to worry about me," said Maggie with a forced laugh. "How could I be lonely? I have Daisy, and of course Richard and Jennifer who call whenever they can. And I have you."

Isobel looked at her friend with sad eyes.

"Maggie, you won't have me for very long. I want you to listen to me carefully, and if you can find the strength, please do what I say."

Isobel's frail hand reached for her neighbour's and gave it a light squeeze. She drew a rattled breath and then slowly spoke again.

"We have lived beside each other through the hardest years of our lives. When Brendan and Danny died and the police arrested Jonathan, I thought my world was over. But eventually the truth came out, my son was cleared and slowly things started to fall back into place. I have never gripped on to anything in my life like I have to my children and even though they've both moved on, they are always close to me, in my heart, the same way Richard and Daisy are to you."

Maggie had a feeling she knew what her dear friend was angling at. Despite her illness and old-fashioned views, Isobel Eastwood knew exactly what needed to be done to sort out the lives of those around her.

"I am saying this to you for a number of reasons, Maggie. Firstly, I know it is breaking your heart that Daisy and Richard don't visit Killshannon as much as you'd like them to…"

"But they both lead such busy lives. It can't be easy for them…" Maggie interrupted.

Isobel continued. "It's time you sat your children down and

177

gave them a reality check. You're their mother and you deserve to be happy."

"But I am happy, Isobel. Really, I am."

As she said it, Maggie felt her eyes prick with tears. She couldn't argue with a woman on her deathbed.

"Are you? When was the last time that you laughed or smiled or went out dancing?"

Maggie didn't have the answer.

"I thought so," Isobel pointed out. "Now, that nice man in Donegal who sold you that silly yellow t-shirt? Do you have his number?"

"Geoff? Er, yes." Maggie's eyes widened with disbelief. She had told Isobel of her encounter with Geoff only in passing.

"Now, pass me your mobile phone, please."

"What? But Isobel, you've never even held a mobile before."

Isobel raised an eyebrow. "Oh, but I have. Don't write me off just yet, Maggie. Now give me the phone."

Maggie handed Isobel the phone, afraid of what was to come, yet excited at the same time. She watched as her friend's bony fingers held the mobile to her ear, waiting for Geoff to answer. It went straight to voicemail and Isobel panicked slightly, then cleared her throat and spoke aloud in her most practiced, polite telephone voice.

"Hello. Geoff. My name is Isobel Eastwood. I believe you know a friend of mine, Maggie Anderson? She would be delighted to take up your offer of dinner this weekend. Oh, and by the way, she also loves to dance. Her address is 9, Ivy Cottages, Killshannon and I believe you already have her number. Many thanks. Bye."

Isobel hung up and handed the phone back to Maggie with a smug grin and Maggie burst out laughing.

"Isobel Eastwood. I didn't know you had that in you! You amaze me, sometimes."

"You should have seen me as a sprightly teenager!" laughed Isobel. "I wasn't always a fuddy duddy, you know. Matchmaking

178

was my speciality. I think Eddie takes after me in a way."

Maggie leaned over and gave her friend a light hug.

"Thank you, Isobel. You are absolutely right. I will pull those two children of mine together sooner or later and Richard can stomp his feet all he likes, but it's about time he realised that I have a long life ahead of me and I intend to live it to the full." She stopped suddenly, realising what she had said. "Oh, I'm so sorry, Isobel. That was insensitive of me to make such a remark."

Isobel smiled and shook her head, a loose grey curl making its way to the side of her face. "Why do you think I'm so determined to sort the lot of you out? If I can make a difference before I go, I'll die one happy lady. Now, since we've sorted the problems with your brood out, I'm going to need your help in sorting my two boys. *That* could prove to be a little bit more difficult."

****

Daisy had tried and tried for two hours to get through to Isobel's landline, but to no avail. The phone was constantly ringing out. Eventually she concluded that there must be a fault on the line. As a last resort she sent her mum a text message and hoped for the best.

She was glad that Jonathan and Shannon had left the hospital at daybreak, leaving space for her to take over first thing that morning. It had been awkward to meet them again, but the news that Eddie was making consistent recovery kept everybody's spirits up.

"It's Sunday now, Eddie, and we still have two days of fun together before we officially split up," said Daisy, following the doctor's instructions and talking to Eddie as though he was awake. During the night he had squeezed Jonathan's hand when asked to and his eyes had flickered open for minutes at a time. "Did you hear you're going to be an uncle?" she asked. "Isn't that exciting? I wonder how Fanny, the wedding-planner, will take that news. Hardly on her 'to do' list, was it?"

179

"Now, now, Daisy don't be polluting young Edward's mind like that," said a welcome, familiar voice. "He'll be able to bitch enough about the whole situation when he pulls himself together."

Daisy looked up to see the handsome face of Christian Devine across the bed, a box of chocolates in one hand and a huge bottle of fizzy drink in the other.

"I know. I can't help it. Who are the goodies for, Christian?" asked Daisy. "I hope they're not all for you."

Christian tilted his head, his tall body casting a cool shadow over the hospital bed. "I thought we'd start stocking up for Eddie's waking-up party. We'll give the cigarettes and alcohol a miss on this occasion though, eh? That's what got you into this whole mess in the first place, isn't it Ed?"

Daisy tutted at Christian but she could sense what he was trying to do. The more they spoke normally to Eddie, the more likely he'd respond. A bit of Christian's banter was just what the doctor ordered. All he needed now was a touch of Lorna's cheeky ways and high opinions, and Eddie was sure to wake up.

"So how did your evening with the tiny tots go? Any scars or war wounds?" asked Daisy.

"Would you believe, it was actually quite relaxing," he said, pulling up a chair. "I took them for a walk in the park this morning – around the Botanic Gardens. Belfast is a beautiful city, you know. Very refreshing."

"Christian Devine!" said Daisy, realising she was smiling for the first time in ages. "I don't believe for a second that you found it so easy playing Daddy day care. You're a big kid yourself. I'd say you had them hanging from the rafters. Were they full of fizzy drink and junk food?"

"Well," laughed Christian. "I sort of cheated 'cos by the time I got back from here last night, the two babes were in bed, fast asleep. Jessie and Michael left around nine and I spent the evening on the couch with Sky Sports for company and the family cat at my feet. I seem to attract cats lately, for some unknown reason. Though the last one who came my way ended up dead. Poor Buddy."

Daisy laughed, wide-eyed and marvelled at how Christian always managed to put her at ease.

"I wouldn't leave as much as a goldfish in your care, Devine," said a hoarse voice from the bed.

Daisy and Christian stared at each other in disbelief. Eddie had spoken. Yes, Eddie had muttered something out of the blue.

"What did you say, Ed?" asked Christian, his eyes now wide. A broad smile crept across his face. "Are you questioning my capability of looking after a little pussy cat?"

Eddie's eyes were like half moons and his pupils were abnormally dilated but his speech, though mumbled and restricted, was clear enough to his audience, who had risen to their feet.

"I never once mentioned the word pussy," he mumbled. "Filthy beggar."

Daisy leaned over and gently kissed Eddie's forehead, but Eddie recoiled under her touch.

"On a scale of one to ten, how repulsive do I look?" he muttered. "I'm hoping for a four-ish."

"Don't you worry, love," said Daisy. "You'll be back to your old gorgeous self in no time. You scared the life out of us."

"Ed, just think Quasimodo meets Gordon Brown and you're on the right tracks," said Christian. "It's all good."

Daisy didn't know whether to jump and shout with glee or remain calm for fear of over-reacting.

"Don't listen to him, Ed," she whispered. "He's just the warm-up act before Lorna comes in and then you'll really have to take some slagging. Tell me, how do you feel? Do you remember what happened?"

Eddie was quiet and his eyes closed momentarily. Both Daisy and Christian glanced at each other for fear that he would slip away again.

"Bastards called me a poof," he muttered. "I answered them back. Can't remember what I said. That's about it."

His voice was sore and broken and he spoke in a whisper.

"The police are onto them already, Eddie. The same gang tried it before on another lad who used to work at the off-licence. He came forward yesterday and reported their previous threats to him when he heard what happened to you," said Daisy, her own voice filled with emotion and relief.

"And Jonathan is onto the case, big time," added Christian. "I met him in the foyer earlier and he's on his way to the station now to check the progress with the officer in charge. You know your brother, Eddie. There'll be no stone unturned until he sees those thugs get their come-uppance."

Eddie closed his eyes again, for longer this time. He drew a shallow breath and the pain in his face showed how fragile a state he was in.

"So, tell me the truth. What's the damage? Did I lose any teeth? I have the most horrible taste in my mouth."

"Broken ribs, left arm and collarbone," said Daisy. "Heavy bruising to pelvic area..."

"Ow!"

"...and face. But thankfully, your teeth are intact and they've ordered another brain scan to check that everything's in order upstairs. You're a very lucky boy, Ed. In the strangest sense, if you know what I mean."

"Does my mum know about this? Please say she doesn't."

Daisy and Christian shot each other another glance.

"She doesn't," answered Christian, "but as soon as you're trans-ferred closer to home, it may be a good idea to tell her what happened and that you're going to be alright, thank God."

"No, she can't know," said Eddie. "I can't tell her why I was..."

Daisy stood up and patted Eddie's hair.

"Hush, love. That's enough conversation for now. Rest again and we'll go and let the nurse know you've woken up. You've a long way to go yet, but we'll be with you every step of the way."

Eddie nodded ever so slightly and closed his eyes again while

Daisy and Christian quietly left his side and slipped out onto the corridor.

Daisy turned to Christian the second they reached the door of the side ward. "He's back. Thank God, he's back. Oh, Christian I really feared the worst. I thought he was never going to talk to us again."

Christian put his arm around Daisy and let her head rest on his chest. "The only thing now is to decide whether or not to tell Isobel," he said. "You go and find some staff and I'll give Jonathan a ring at his hotel. He's staying not too far from the hospital. We can let him decide whether his mother needs to know about all this."

****

Killshannon was eerily silent but Maggie still couldn't concentrate on the crossword puzzle in the daily newspaper. Crosswords had once been her and Danny's favourite pastime on the weekend, but today she wasn't getting any of the clues. Isobel was fast asleep now. The visits of the care nurse were becoming more frequent as the days went by and Maggie was anxious. She knew her friend's health was quickly deteriorating. It had been fascinating listening to Isobel earlier. They had discussed everything from dinner with Geoff to her guidelines on her own sons' future and what was to happen at her funeral. It was a bit too much to take in.

Just then, Maggie noticed a new text message on her mobile phone. It had to be Daisy. She hoped the message wouldn't be as cryptic as her crossword clues, but thankfully it was crystal clear. Her daughter was asking her to check Isobel's telephone connection as she still couldn't get through.

Maggie leapt from her kitchen chair and ran out to the hallway. Sure enough, the phone cord had been pulled from the wall. She quickly put it back in its place, then dialled Daisy's mobile number frantically.

"Hello?"

"It's me, love."

"Oh Mum! It's good news. Eddie has woken up and I've been speaking to him. Thank God!"

"That's fantastic, love!" said Maggie with a deep sigh of relief. "Can I tell Isobel now? She'll be starting to ask questions when the boys don't arrive home this evening."

Daisy paused. "Not yet. I need to talk to Jonathan first. Eddie doesn't want her to know why he was attacked, or even *that* he was attacked at this stage, but I suppose you can only hold it from her for so long before she'll get suspicious."

Maggie rubbed her head. "Right. She asked if I could arrange a special dinner for the boys tonight but I put her off, suggesting that after a night out on the town they may just prefer to grab a takeaway."

Daisy laughed with surprise. "Quick thinking, Mum, but you are not meant to know about hangover cures! Where do you get your up-to-date information from?"

"Aren't I your mother? Mothers know everything. I remember a time when you used to believe that."

Daisy bit her lip. "I still do believe that, Mum. You certainly know what's best for me…well, most of the time."

Maggie sensed her opportunity and forced herself to seize the moment before she could change her mind.

"That I do. Which leads me to my next suggestion. I'm holding an Anderson family reunion…."

"A family reunion?" sighed Daisy, visualising a host of cousins and aunts and uncles she barely knew.

"Just you and I and Richard," said Maggie with strength. "There are a few changes to be made in our family, and I want you both to be present when they are announced. Then we can all start afresh."

There, she'd said it. Maggie hung up the phone feeling a huge weight had been lifted off her shoulders.

184

Chapter 21

Dirty Chancing

Jonathan was ecstatic for the first time in ages. According to Christian, Eddie was to be moved to Letterkenny General once the MRI scans were clear. The police had been fantastic and were on their way to nailing the culprits. Eddie's attackers would swiftly get the justice they deserved.

"Jonathan, have you seen my blue sundress?" called Shannon from the Belfast hotel bathroom. "I was sure I packed it in my case for Lough Eske yesterday."

"I didn't see it, Shannon, but the hospital is hardly the correct setting for a fashion parade. Hurry up and let's get out of here. I can't wait any longer to talk to my brother."

Shannon reappeared from the bathroom in baby-pink underwear, with one hand on her hip and her toothbrush pointing towards him.

"Just because that silly cow Daisy Anderson arrived on the ward this morning looking like she'd slept on a bed of nails doesn't mean I have to follow suit. I, unlike others, like to look my best *all* the time."

Jonathan flicked off the television and reached for his shoes. "The difference, Shannon," he said, "is that Daisy happens to be equally as distraught as I am about Eddie. I believe that when you truly fear for someone's life, things like perfume and make-up don't enter the equation."

Shannon came storming out of the bathroom again, this time with a mouth full of toothpaste and her retrieved blue sundress over her arm.

"You know something, Jonathan. Sometimes over the past few days I have really questioned which brother Daisy has her gritty little eye on. I can see through her pathetic game with Eddie, pretending to fool your mother with their 'soon-to-be-engaged' story. At least I don't pretend I'm something I'm not. I'll be your wife in less than five weeks and our wedding seems to be the furthest thing from your mind."

"Oh, you sure are honest, Shannon. Don't hold back. Go ahead, speak your mind."

"I will," she continued with a vengeance. "The way that girl looked at you in the hospital yesterday, all doe-eyed and sorrowful, would have made anyone sick. It was so damn pathetic I felt like crawling under the covers of the nearest bed and calling for a nurse myself!"

Shannon wiped her mouth on a towel and flung it onto the bed, then pulled her dress over her head and stepped into a pair of strappy silver sandals.

"How can you be so damn selfish?" shouted Jonathan. "My mother is dying, I don't know how long she has left, and yesterday I almost lost my only brother too. However, all you can talk to me about is a wedding. I can't take this anymore, Shannon. I can't. Can you please come back into the real world?"

Jonathan paced the floor and then poured himself a glass of lukewarm water. Part of his built-up anger was with Shannon's ignorance and selfishness, but most of it was because of his family situation, and the fact that Daisy Anderson now seemed further from his reach than ever.

And now Shannon was starting to weep.

186

"I'm sorry, Jonathan. It's my hormones. They're all over the place," she sobbed. "I've a feeling you don't want this baby. Do you want it? Be honest."

She held her stomach and gave her fiancé a most helpless look.

"It's all just happening so fast, Shannon. Please try and understand. There's so much going on in my head at the minute. It's hard…"

"But you haven't even spoken to me about the baby since yesterday. Then, when I saw you last night at the hospital with Daisy, so gentle and loving, it scared me. You never act like that with me anymore and it just made me hate her even more."

Jonathan sat down on the bed again. "Look, Shannon, the Andersons have a long family connection with us. I've known Daisy since we were teenagers but please don't hate her. You don't know enough about her to make such a rash judgement."

"Huh," sniffed Shannon. "I know that she pranced into Killshannon last week like she'd never been away. Suddenly it was all 'Eddie this and Daisy that' and our wedding was totally forgotten about. All anyone wanted to do was throw a party for Daisy, or have a special dinner for Daisy, or do this and that just because Daisy was home. It was ridiculous."

Jonathan knew that part of what Shannon was telling was the truth. Daisy did tend to get the red-carpet treatment when she came to Killshannon every once in a blue moon, but still, that was hardly a reason to hate her.

"Daisy is a good girl, Shannon, and she and Eddie have always been a popular duo," he said, trying to reason with his fiancée. "They go way back. When you get to know her, she actually really is good fun. A bit stubborn, mind, but she has a good heart."

Shannon turned to the mirror, wrestling with the buttons on her dress. "Oh, do give over, Jonathan," she scoffed. "Little Miss Daisy isn't as pure and good as she makes out to be at all. She doesn't exactly have a clean slate around Killshannon after all, does she?"

Jonathan shot a look towards Shannon in disbelief. What was

she getting at?

"Just who have you been talking to about Daisy? Is there something you'd like to share with me?"

Shannon's eyes widened, the picture of innocence.

"What? I haven't been talking to anyone. What are you looking at me like that for? Wait a minute! Is there something *you* want to tell *me*?"

Jonathan was sure he saw a smirk creep across Shannon's pretty face. "There's nothing I want to tell you whatsoever," he said.

Shannon dabbed powder under her eyes, leaned into the mirror and then swept a deep shade of red lipstick across her lips.

"Fine, honey, but Miss Daisy and I are even now. In fact, when it comes to having a claim over you, I'm ahead of the game since I happen to be the one with the ring on my finger *and* your baby on the way. You wouldn't make the same mistake twice, would you now, *Daddy*?"

Jonathan felt sickened. Shannon certainly knew how to get a rise out of him. Not only did she guess his feelings for Daisy, but she had done her homework on his past too. Suddenly he felt an overwhelming urge to get away from under her clutches. He was on the verge of saying something he might regret later.

"Don't threaten me, Shannon," he said steadily. "I'm going to leave you now to doll yourself up in the mirror while I go and visit my brother in hospital. Have a nice afternoon, whatever your plans are."

Shannon dropped her lipstick in a panic and shouted after him, but Jonathan was gone, striding down the hotel corridor and ignoring her pleas for him to wait.

"Jonathan, please. I don't care about any of that. I don't even believe it. Forget everything I said. I want to go with you to see Eddie. Jonny! Wait!"

But Jonathan marched on down the corridor and into the awaiting lift without looking back once.

"I'm so angry, Jonathan. I'm so fed up with being made to feel I am doing something wrong and having to pretend to defend myself from ignorance."

Eddie's eyes were rimmed with rainbow colours and his hands gripped the bedclothes as he spoke.

"We'll find out who did this to you," whispered Jonathan.

"This is how hard it is to be different. I hoped those days were gone but scum like the people who did this to me still exist. How can I explain this to Mum? How?"

"Ssh, Eddie. Close your eyes. You don't have to pretend anymore, nor should you feel you have to. This is not what you deserve. No one deserves this. No one."

Jonathan waited and watched his brother fall into a light sleep, and then he took the opportunity to grab a coffee in the canteen.

The corridor walk was lengthy but Jonathan welcomed the opportunity to gather his thoughts. Faces passed him along the way, some withdrawn with worry, while others were visibly pleased on their way to visit a new arrival. Jonathan had dreamed of the day when he would come to visit his wife on the maternity ward. He now hoped that a new baby might help pave over the cracks in the relationship between himself and Shannon. He promised himself he would be the best father in the world when the time came. But on the other hand he still couldn't shake off his feelings for Daisy. Shannon's last words to him, and the look on her face in the hotel room earlier that morning, had put the fear of God in him. Her steely determination to marry him as soon as possible was suffocating, and she had gone to great lengths to ensure he had no room left to breathe by suddenly announcing her pregnancy.

She had it all well planned. And now that she knew the history of himself and Daisy, there would be no stopping her. He would never be free again.

Jonathan noticed Christian and Daisy, who were huddled in a

189

far corner of the canteen sharing a sandwich. He tried his best to ignore any pangs of jealousy at how friendly the pair had become once again. Visiting Eddie seemed to have helped them form a strong bond. Oh, well, what could he do about it? He had no hold over Daisy now. She could do whatever she wanted to. At first he pretended not to see them, but Christian waved over. It burned Jonathan inside to even look in Daisy's direction, let alone hold a sensible conversation with her. And as for Christian! Well, he still hadn't properly apologised for making those recent, and perhaps unfounded, accusations.

"Hey, Jonathan," said Christian, sheepishly. "Great news about Eddie, isn't it?"

"It's fantastic, Christian. And thanks so much for being here with us through all of this. I can't tell you both how much I appreciate it."

Daisy lifted her head and Jonathan noticed her face flush at the sight of him. He felt uncomfortable too, but he pulled out a chair and forced himself to join them. He had to get used to the fact that Daisy could never be his.

"I'm sure you can't wait to get him moved to Donegal," said Daisy brightly. "If they decide to keep him for another night here in Belfast, you're very welcome to crash on my sofa. And Shannon is too, of course."

Jonathan nodded and played with a set of cutlery, avoiding eye contact with either of his friends. "I know you mean well, Daisy, but I don't think that would be a very wise idea."

Christian could feel the tension mounting and decided to make a swift exit.

"Do you know something?" he piped up. "I think I'll go out the front and see if Lorna has arrived, folks. What did she say in her last text, Daisy?"

"Er, I think she said she hoped a gorgeous handsome man with the initials CD would meet her at the door!"

Christian laughed. "Very, very funny. Did she say she was making

190

her way over?"

"Yes, she did and I'm sure she would really appreciate the welcome. Do you even know what she looks like?"

Christian stood up and a huge grin took over his face, flashing his pearly whites and creasing up his light stubble.

"How would you describe her tactfully? Bright-red hair? Tick. Not exactly light on her feet? Another tick…"

Daisy was astounded but Jonathan burst out laughing.

"Sounds spot-on to me, Christian. You know who you're looking for," he guffawed. "From what I gather, she'd eat you up and spit you out, Devine. I double dare you."

"You've never even met Lorna. Don't be so rude, Jonathan!" said Daisy, slapping his arm playfully.

"I saw her last night," he said. "That was enough to make a sound judgement that Christian couldn't handle her. Go on, Devine, you big stud. I dare you."

"No way. I think both you and I have had our fingers burnt with dares. Anyway I've had my fill of women so you can forget all about that. I'll catch you two up on the ward. Later."

Jonathan and Daisy sat in silence for a few minutes, neither knowing what to say, or what was left to say.

"I found out why we couldn't get through to your mum's house," said Daisy tentatively.

"You have? I've been trying to check in with her all morning but there's been no answer. For some strange reason I left without my mobile yesterday. I was sure Shannon had it."

Daisy's mind was going into overdrive.

"The cord of the land line was pulled from the wall," she continued. "Maybe someone tripped over it. Anyway, it's sorted now so you should be able to get through from now on."

"Good."

Now it was Jonathan's turn to think of something to say. He stirred his coffee, longing to drink it despite it being piping hot, if only for something to do with his hands.

"Daisy?"

"Yes?"

"Did I ever tell you that I loved you?"

There. The question had just tumbled out of his mouth. Now he stared into her eyes and waited for her answer.

Daisy looked shocked. "Please don't say that. It's too late," she replied sadly and looked away as her heart somersaulted in her chest.

Jonathan dropped his head again and continued to stir the froth at the top of the paper cup.

"I just want you to know that. You're right; it's too late. I'm sorry."

"Are you going to marry her?" Daisy suddenly asked, already knowing the answer but asking nevertheless. She found herself completely unable to utter Shannon's name.

"She knows, Daisy." Jonathan forced a mouthful of coffee down his throat. "Shannon knows about our baby. About Matthew."

"What?" Daisy's heart sank. She thought she was going to be sick. Even to say Matthew's name was painful enough for either of them. As far as Daisy had been concerned, nobody else on this earth had known for definite about Matthew's existence, despite all the rumours.

"How the hell did she find out?"

"I don't know. She more or less threatened me this morning. I have no choice, Daisy. I have to marry her."

Daisy was startled. It just didn't make sense.

"But how did she find out? Maybe you're just being paranoid and you're assuming she knows?"

Jonathan shook his head dolefully.

"I'm sure. Look, there was big talk at the time. After you left Killshannon, people assumed that you blamed me for the accident. Then there were undercurrents that you were pregnant and Shannon has obviously used her time in Killshannon to investigate."

"Shit. I actually don't believe this is happening."

The pair sat in silence once more, both absorbing the fact that their secret was out.

"I'm sorry for all of this," Jonathan said eventually. He sounded so helpless, so broken.

"Don't be. We have nothing to be ashamed of."

"But I *am* ashamed," he persisted. "And I'm sorry. I keep wondering what he's doing now. I wonder whether he looks like you or me…"

"For Christ sake, Jonathan!" Daisy couldn't bear to listen to him any longer. "I was eighteen years old and could barely look after myself let alone a baby. Our hands were tied. You'd just finished your teaching degree and had your life ahead of you. Because our fathers argued so much over what was best for us, they caused a fatal accident in the car that night and almost left you with the blame."

"But we were wrong. *I* was wrong," cried Jonathan. He really felt this was his last chance to discuss what had happened and express his regret.

"Bringing a baby into that environment at such a young age would have been cruel and foolish," said Daisy. "I couldn't have gone through with an abortion, but James is with a good family now. I know for a fact that they cherish him in a way that we never could have done."

"James? You said you named him Matthew."

Daisy swallowed back a lump in her throat.

"The adoptive parents changed his name to James. It sort of helps me to think that he's not really mine any more so I'm glad they did. You should try to think the same way."

Jonathan's heart felt heavy, but in a strange way he was comforted from Daisy's logic.

"James is my middle name," he whispered and suddenly he felt cold.

"I know," whispered Daisy. "So maybe he does have a bit of his old dad in him after all."

Daisy reached out for Jonathan's hand and they held each other under the table, both lost in peaceful thought for the child they never got to know, and both knowing in their hearts that it would be too much for Jonathan to go through all of that again.

Shannon had got her way. The wedding of the year was very much on.

Chapter 22

Super Dooper Trooper

Daisy leaned on the counter of Super Shoes and stared out of the window onto Belfast's busy Cornmarket. She hated Mondays and was counting down the hours until home time. Maybe she should have listened to Lorna's advice when she had suggested writing a begging email to her ex-agent Mervyn to fix her up with an audition for the Opera House Christmas pantomime… or maybe not. Her agent, like her ex-boyfriends, were exes for a reason. She had to look ahead, not backwards and the events of recent days had proven that to her more than ever.

Yes, Daisy Louise Anderson was determined to make changes in her life and had made a good start, which made her feel better inside. She'd made up a new CV, fidgeted with some movie-making software so that she had a fairly basic but effective show reel and she'd sent it out to every single agency she could find across Ireland, north and south and a few in London too.

"Onwards and upwards" was her new mantra. She just hoped if she repeated this phrase enough times, she might start to believe it.

Eddie had sent her a weird text message that morning to say that the morning suits for Jonathan's wedding had arrived and that the colour of the cravat matched the tiny scar on the side of his face. Sickly pink. Nice. He also reported that he'd dyed his hair blonder than ever and that the pins in his left arm kept sending off the robber-catcher bleeper every time he went to lift his mother's widow's benefit at the corner post office

Daisy was sure this was a big fat lie as there was no way there was any room in the post office in Killshannon for anything, let alone a security bleeper, but she knew he was trying to give her some light relief as the wedding date loomed.

Daisy also knew that Eddie's own days in Killshannon were numbered. He was fast on the road to recovery, and if it weren't for the wedding and his mother's illness, he would have been on the first plane back to San Francisco.

The shrill ring of the shop phone made Daisy jump. She was back into the world of shoes and stockings once more. She picked up the receiver and sang in her most chirpy, shop-assistant voice.

"Hello, Super Shoes. Daisy speaking, how can I help?"

"What a waste of talent for a girl of your capabilities to be working in a discount shoe store! It's despicable. But never fear, my darling dear, for I have got news for you!"

Daisy got a strange sense of déjà vu, which reminded her of the same day some weeks ago when Eddie had caught her unawares with his strange phone call.

"Who's calling?" she asked. She wasn't in the mood for guessing games. But maybe it was a reply to one of her CV send outs? Already?

"It's Mervyn, remember?" said the voice. "Many moons ago before you grew indefinitely lazy and resigned yourself to a life of wedges, peep toes and slip-on sandals, I used to be your agent."

Oh, Merve the Perve. Of course.

"You dumped *me*, Mervyn, after you'd sent me to twelve ridiculous auditions in a row, remember? Why didn't you call my mobile? Did you lose my number?"

Mervyn faked an over-the-top sneeze down the earpiece.

"Bless *me*! Look, Daisy, let's not get into an unnecessary fluster.

196

I bumped into your very forthright friend, Laura…"

"Lorna."

"Whatever. She said I'd find you on this number, so that's why I rang. She tells me you'd like to get back into the swing of your acting career…"

"Did she now?"

"She mentioned you were interested in an audition at the Grand Opera House for this year's panto with your man from Big Brother?"

Daisy sat up straight in her chair. Despite her grievances with Mervyn, she was willing to give him a second chance.

"Oh, yes I know the one you're talking about. Sorry, I can't remember his name just at the minute… I'm afraid I've been missing out on reality TV lately. My own life has been a bit of a drama…"

Mervyn was quick to interrupt. "Anyway, that's all totally irrelevant as there's *no* way I can get you as much as a toenail through the door of the Grand Opera House, my dear."

"What?"

Mervyn actually sounded like he was enjoying her disappointment.

"To cut a very long story short," he continued. "I had a blazing row with one of the board members at a casting party for a play last week and he vowed never to show me the light of day again. So, we'll strike that one off our list now, shall we?"

Daisy sucked the top of her pen. What was Merv playing at?

"So, please remind me why you're phoning after all this time?"

Mervyn faked a cough. "I'm ringing because I *can* get you a super audition at a little theatre outside Ballymena for the role of Peter Pan's mother. I think you'd be perfect for the part."

"Peter Pan's mother?"

"That's the one. It's a gem of a role."

Daisy felt a slight rush of excitement. Ballymena wasn't that far away. She could always borrow Lorna's wheels each evening and a minor role would at least get her back into the swing of things. She *was* pretty insulted, however, that she was being pencilled in to play someone's mother…then again it was time to accept that her days of Tinkerbell were well and truly over. She was willing to give it a go if the price was right.

"Sounds fair enough, so far. How much would I get paid?"

Another sneeze.

"Bless *me*. That, I'm afraid, is where you have to be fairly flexible, Daisy. They're a very low-budget theatre group, amateur in fact, so their ability to pay their cast is highly…"

"*Unlikely?*"

"Yes, that's the word I'm looking for.

"Well, it's *unlikely* that I would audition for a role in Ballymena where I won't be getting paid a brass penny."

Daisy could sense Mervyn wincing on the other end as her mood changed. She imagined him pushing his little thick black-rimmed glasses further back on his oily nose.

"My days of charity roles are long over," she sighed. "I have bills to pay, believe it or not, so I'm sorry, but it's my turn to give you the heave-ho. Call me back when you've some real work in the pipeline. Oh, and go easy on the sherry at the next casting party, wont you? Now, cuckoo!"

Daisy slammed down the phone and almost jumped out of her skin when her mobile bleeped at exactly that same moment. It was her mother, speaking in a whisper in a voicemail message. Daisy knew instantly it wasn't good news.

"Darling, it's me. I thought you might like to know that Isobel hasn't very long. Days, maybe less. It may be a good idea to come home. I mean, home to Killshannon, when you can. For Eddie's sake. And mine. Thanks, love. Bye."

Goosebumps rose on Daisy's arms and the hairs on the back of her neck stood up. This was the message she had been dreading for days. She could only imagine what the boys were going through. In a blind rush to be with her own mother at such a harrowing time, she called for her colleague to take over on the checkout.

She had only been back in work for a week and now she was going to have to ask for more time off, but Daisy had made up her mind to hand in her resignation if they wouldn't let her go home.

****

Isobel Eastwood waited for her youngest son to come to her bedside just as she'd asked. The room was bright and a light summer breeze drifted in through the open window. The priest had called for the second time that afternoon and had said some quiet prayers. They had comforted her greatly and the support nurses had been by her side since dawn. Maggie, of course, had been a rock, wetting her lips and burning gentle oils in the bedroom, or simply sitting with her in silence. However now all Isobel wanted to do was talk to her boys individually. She needed to say goodbye to them properly before it was too late.

"Oh, Mum," said Eddie, his lip quivering before he even reached the centre of the room. "How are we going to get through all of this?"

"Now, Eddie, come and sit with me," she whispered, her throat so dry she found it extremely hard to speak. "I'm not fit to talk much, as you know, but I wanted to tell you how much I love you."

"Yes, Mum, I know all that. But there's something I have to tell you. Please let me. I've tried so hard to tell you this all week. In fact I've tried all my life, but I haven't had the courage. I've always been such a baby. I'm so sorry."

Eddie gripped the side of the bedclothes as perspiration seeped through his hands. He didn't want to have any regrets, but the thought of letting his mother down in her final hours was wrecking him and he needed peace of mind.

"Hush, my love. Please don't cry," said Isobel. "I wanted to tell you about some of the great joys you have brought to my life while I still can…. The day you were born I knew you'd be as lively as you are now. You're so handsome, so funny, so much my precious son." Isobel drew a long breath and Eddie laid his head on her hand, holding it to his face. "I'll always love you for who you are, for everything you are. You don't need to be any different for anyone's sake. It's the person inside that counts. Promise me, darling, promise me that you'll never change. No one will ever beat you again for you'll soon have a new guardian angel in heaven who loves you exactly the way you are."

Eddie lay holding his mother's hand to his face for a few more minutes until he could hold back his emotions no longer.

"Thank you, Mum. You don't know how much that means to me. Thank you for being so understanding and for defending me down the years when it must have been so hard for you..."

"You're my son and I love you. That's all that matters. Always remember that," whispered Isobel and her eyes closed once more.

Eddie kissed her forehead gently, his face sodden with tears and then left her room quietly to find a quiet space. The house was already full of whispers from well-meaning neighbours, relatives and nurses, who had each built up their own special rapport with Isobel during her short, cruel illness.

In her own gentle way, Isobel Eastwood had eased the burden of worry her son had carried for years, only hours before he would be granted the angel she had promised him.

****

Jonathan looked at his watch. It was almost seven and still daylight outside. He longed for it to stay that way, knowing that when darkness fell, his mother would no longer have the strength to hold on any longer. She loved the daytime, the outdoors and the summer, and he feared that when night came she would give up her fight. He couldn't even bear to think of it.

A few minutes beforehand, Jonathan had cleared the few scattered wedding presents from the kitchen table and left them in the garden shed out of his sight. He had also taken the opportunity to grab a breath of fresh air. He still couldn't get his head around the fact that he was getting married in a few weeks. If truth be told, he felt like his purgatory had already begun a fortnight ago, the minute Shannon had dropped the pregnancy bombshell on him. He felt smothered, trapped and most of all, downright foolish.

"Jonathan, love. Your mother is asking for you."

Jonathan turned to see Maggie Anderson standing at the back door, her eyes hooded and dark. For the first time since he'd known her, he could see her age etched in her fine face.

"Thanks. I'll just be a second."

"If you don't mind, love," said Maggie. "I was thinking I might phone the priest again. I think it's important he is here. Your mother would want that."

Her words blurred into the distance and Jonathan tried to pretend this wasn't happening. He'd heard stories of his father's wake and funeral only from his mum as he had been in hospital over the entire period. But judging by the tales, he dreaded to think of what the next few days would bring.

"Daisy's on her way home," added Maggie softly.

At the sound of her name, Jonathan felt comfort and pain simultaneously.

"That's good. That's really good of her. I can't wait to see her."

Maggie walked towards him and stopped only a few feet away. He was a sensitive soul, and despite what Isobel had asked her to do, she didn't feel it was her place to meddle in his wedding plans.

"Jonathan, I need to say something to you. I haven't spoken of this to Daisy, not once since it happened. It was my way of dealing with it, I suppose. I was terrified of pushing her away even further, but I don't think either of you should beat yourself up over the decision you made when you both were so young."

Jonathan stared at the sky. It was still as bright as a summer afternoon, just like the day Daisy had left Killshannon with her bags packed for Belfast, and a tiny concealed bump under her red knitted sweater. So Maggie had known all along.

"I've made such a mess of everything," he sighed. "They say what goes around, comes around, and now I know what that means. I should never have let Daisy leave back then. We could have got through it. Other people have…"

Maggie longed to say what was on her mind, but she couldn't interfere, no matter what.

"But you have a new life with Shannon now. You're getting married in three weeks."

"I know…"

"At the same time, don't be hasty. Before you make any decisions about your future, please make sure you've thought them all through. That's all any of us want for you. That's what I've always told my own children."

Jonathan looked at Maggie and then around the house he had grown up in. He wondered what would become of his home when the heart of it was dying inside.

"Thanks, Maggie. I know you mean well, but I will do what I have to do. I really should go inside and see my mother now. Perhaps you will phone the priest? Like you said, Mum would want that."

****

In Belfast, Daisy stuffed half the contents of her wardrobe into a holdall and searched frantically in the bathroom cabinet for her new toothbrush. On finding it, she filled her toiletry bag with other essentials and then did a double check to make sure she'd packed everything. She reckoned she'd probably packed too much but at least the zip was able to close.

"Are you sure you don't mind driving me, Lorna? It is a bit of a trek. You really don't know what you're in for," she shouted into the sitting room.

Lorna stretched herself off the settee and switched off the

202

television. "I don't mind at all," she said. "Sure, won't it give me a chance to see the famous Killshannon for the first time? And anyway, I have a bet to settle with Christian Devine, so I might just bite the bullet and give him a quick call when I get that far."

Daisy walked towards the sitting area in disbelief.

"You have a bet with Christian? Are you crazy? No one ever beats Christian in a bet."

"I just have," said Lorna, looking extremely proud of herself. "Remember the night at the hospital, before Eddie was moved back to Letterkenny General?"

"Yes," said Daisy, and a shiver went through her body as she remembered Jonathan's words to her that same night.

"Well, he gave me his number and bet me that I would call him within a fortnight. That was much more than two weeks ago so now he owes me twenty quid. And I'll be taking sterling from him, not euros, since the bet was made in the North. He doesn't know who he's messing with now."

Daisy threw her eyes up. Lorna definitely wasn't Christian's stereotypical kind of girl. She was over thirty for a start, but one thing was sure – he wouldn't make a fool out of her. Of that, Daisy had no fear.

"Right, okay Miss Gamblers Anonymous. Let's go and face the music in the bright lights of good old Killshannon. You can claim your fortune when you get there."

Chapter 23

Never Can Say Goodbye

Isobel Eastwood passed away at 9:15 pm just as dusk settled on the fishing village where she had reared her small family. Her dear friend Maggie stopped the clocks and drew the curtains. Then she phoned for Seamus O'Hanlon, the local undertaker, just as she'd agreed to. Isobel's two sons sat at either side of the bed, motionless, not wanting to let go as the warmth left their mother's tiny hands.

"Why did this happen, Jonathan?" asked Eddie. He had lost weight and his face was long and gaunt, as despair and shock waved through his body. "I want to know why. *Why*?"

Tears dripped down his face but he couldn't bring himself to wipe them away. His sweet, gentle mother was gone.

"I don't know, Ed. I don't know," whispered Jonathan. "What are we supposed to do now? I mean, practically, what do we do? Do you remember much about Dad's wake and funeral? I don't know which is worse, being here or not being here. Oh God, I just can't take this in."

Eddie reached for a tissue and dabbed his face, which still had some bruising. His jaw hurt badly. "Don't say that. You have to leave that behind you. How many times can we tell you it wasn't your fault?"

Jonathan had kept his strength until now, but he felt a new rush of emotion overcome him now. In his last, private conversation with his mother she had told him the same thing. He was trying so hard to respect her wishes.

"Do you remember your football final in Monaghan when you were sixteen?" she'd asked with a soft smile, her thumb rubbing the back of his hand as she spoke. "I've never seen your father bursting with pride as much as I did that day, Jonathan. 'My son' he shouted to the rest of the spectators. 'That's my son,' as if you were the only player on the field. He could see nobody but you and he hugged you on the sidelines so tightly I thought he'd never let go. He loved you so, so much, Jonathan. You were his 'big man' he always said. Remember the good times, son. It's important.'"

Jonathan stood up and stared out of the bedroom window onto the quiet cul-de-sac where cars were beginning to arrive for the wake. Aunts and uncles carried trays of sandwiches and the local priest stood in the garden chatting to family members as they gathered on hearing the news of Isobel's death.

"Did I ever tell you I have a son, Eddie?"

Eddie lifted his head and gulped. Jonathan had never mentioned this before.

"No. No you haven't... But I...well to be honest Jonathan I sort of knew. One night, when you thought I was asleep," he said, "I heard you and Daisy talk on the phone. It was after Dad's funeral and you sat at the bedroom window, while she at hers across the road and she was crying, asking you what the two of you were going to do. I was too afraid to mention it to you afterwards, afraid of what you might say about me eavesdropping, but I've known since then that there was a baby. I remember Daisy leaving. I remember that she wore red that day and that you didn't speak to anyone for weeks and weeks after she went."

Jonathan was stunned. All along, he'd been so positive that nobody could have possibly known about the pregnancy. Both he and Daisy had thought they'd had everything well covered, but

Eddie knew, Maggie knew and now even Shannon had found out.

"Follow your heart, Jonathan," his mother had told him during her parting words. "Follow your heart but always look after what is yours. Always."

The boys were interrupted by a gentle knock on the door. It was Maggie. She didn't come in, but whispered around the door instead.

"Boys, the undertaker has just arrived," she said. "And Jonathan, Shannon is here too. No hurry, you just take your time."

The brothers looked at each other and both felt numb. So this was it, then. The waiting was over and the formalities were about to begin. The house was filling up and there were people to see, hands to shake and shoulders to cry on. Jonathan knew he had to be strong for Eddie, who was visibly crumbling. He took a deep breath and wiped his eyes.

"Let's go, Eddie," he said, taking his younger brother from their mother's bedside. "We'll get through this together. Let's go out here and make Mum very proud of her two big sons."

Eddie sniffled and obeyed his brother's command. "You go first," he said, nervous of what lay ahead.

"I will," said Jonathan and he opened the door, ready to face up to the hardest day of his life.

****

"Are we nearly there yet?"

Daisy vowed if Lorna asked her that question once more she would yank her red hair really, really hard.

"Nearly. We're about ten kilometres away."

"Jesus! I'd heard that Killshannon was in the back of beyond but at this stage we must be nearly on another planet!"

Daisy laughed. "I did warn you. You'll know for the future if you ever again take a fit of blind generosity. Perhaps there is another motive for your little excursion out northwest though? To do with one Mr Devine?"

Lorna turned down the window of Chloe, the green Clio, and fanned her face with her hand.

"I don't think so. Unless I lost two stone overnight and dyed my hair a brassy shade of blond, I doubt very much that the Devine one would even acknowledge my existence, let alone ask me out on a date. So there. It was his ego that made him give me his number and I don't do ego."

Daisy smiled to herself and Lorna swiftly changed gear as they approached the country road that led to Daisy's home village.

"You're only human, Lorna. I was mad about Christian for years. Most of our high school and our village were too. He's a good guy, don't get me wrong, but his heart went on a plane to Copenhagen four weeks ago and no matter what he says, it hasn't found its way back to Ireland yet."

Lorna turned up the volume of the Scissor Sisters CD. She didn't really feel like dancing either so the song suited her just fine.

"Really? He never mentioned that to me. So who was the lucky girl, then?"

Daisy tried to remember.

"Anna someone, from Leitrim, I think. I don't know much about it to be honest. She dumped him over the phone a few days after leaving for Denmark."

"Ow. Poor guy. That must have hurt." Lorna checked her rear-view mirror and took a left turn.

"Don't feel too sorry for him. He did give you his number, remember, so he can't be all that heartbroken. You may be in with a chance."

Lorna snorted.

"He gave *you* his number not so long ago too, if I recall. Oh, it was just a silly joke. I think he found me too outspoken for my own good, but as much as it kills me to admit it, he *is* one goddam sexy bit of stuff. I wouldn't kick him out of bed."

The girls laughed aloud until the smell of the sea invaded the car and Lorna held her nose, much to Daisy's defence. She barely noticed Killshannon's fishy aroma any more, and she quite liked the fact that she didn't find it as potent as she had during her last few visits. In fact, the smell almost made her feel at home now.

"You're bound to be knackered, Lorna. This is a long drive after a day's work."

"I am," she yawned. "I could sleep on a hen's knee right now."

"I know, I know. Before you say it, I really ought to get my act together and buy a car of my own pretty soon. I really do need to get my act together, literally."

Lorna laughed at the double entendre.

"Er, I hate to mention such a minor detail, but wouldn't you need to get a job first? You have just resigned from Super Shoes *and* turned down the offerings of your agent despite my best intentions of trying to get your acting career back on track."

Daisy scoffed at the mention of Merve the Perv. The quick, recent thud back to unemployment actually hurt more than she'd like to admit.

"Can you imagine what my dear brother would say? *'So how's the five-year plan going Daisy? Have you got your foot on the property ladder yet?'*"

"And you'll say, 'not even as much as a toe on the bottom rung, dear Richard,'" laughed Lorna.

"Dear Dick, you mean. Boy, but he was aptly named."

Lorna shook her head. "He can't be *that* pretentious. Are you sure you two even share the same genes? You couldn't be less focused if you tried, yet he sounds as if he was born with his life plan tucked under his arm and the word 'property developer' written on his birth tags."

Lorna nosed Chloe into the nearest parking space at Ivy Cottages. Daisy suddenly fell silent at the sight of Jonathan Eastwood standing on the front step of his mother's house. He looked drawn and distracted as he chatted to the small crowd that had gathered at the garden gate. Daisy's skin went cold as she realised that they were too late. She hadn't made it in time to say goodbye. Isobel was already gone.

She longed to run towards her childhood sweetheart, to hold him and to make everything better, and she was certain she could physically feel his pain. Her face went a cool shade of white as Shannon came behind him and draped her arm around his waist. She seemed to be dressed like someone fresh from London Fashion Week, clad in designer black from head to toe, and sporting a pair of huge sunglasses perched on top of her platinum hair. There would have been more remorse and feeling in a mask at Hallowe'en.

"I'd say he'll be glad to see you, Daisy, despite Minnie the Minx there and her false affection," said Lorna, sensing her friend's heartache.

"Do you think so? Oh, I so want to be with him, Lorna. I just want to be with him. Why can't I be with him now, when he needs me so much?"

Lorna grasped Daisy's hand. "I can stay with you if you want, to try and help you get through this. After all, what's a sickie between friends?"

"You know, I'd really like that," said Daisy. "I think I'm going to need all the help I can get. This brings back so many painful, horrible memories. I can't even bear to think what those two boys are going through."

Christian Devine heard of Isobel's death at around 9:40 pm that evening. He decided to head for Killshannon immediately. He ran himself a bath and then went to his bedroom to lay out some clothes for the next few days. It would be best for him to stay with his own parents over the wake and funeral. His chic bachelor pad in Donegal just didn't feel like home at the moment.

The loud ring of the doorbell shook him unexpectedly. It was now after ten on a Monday night. Who the hell would be calling on him at this time of the evening? Wrapping a bathrobe around his naked body, he walked towards the front door of his apartment and opened the door, expecting a random ticket seller or someone wanting directions to Bundoran.

But it wasn't a stranger at all. He had to look twice, wondering if the recent bad news had made him hallucinate. What on earth was Anna doing here? His Anna.

Standing in his doorway, arms by her side, her long, straight, dark hair was as silky and soft as it was the day she left him for Copenhagen a month ago. Her lightly freckled skin, her green eyes and everything he had loved about her was back.

For once, Christian Devine was truly lost for words.

"Hi babe. Can I come in?" she whispered seductively, looking upwards at him from beneath her long eyelashes.

"Jesus, Anna. What's going on? I…"

Anna leaned forward, held Christian's face with her cold hands, and then kissed him passionately on the mouth. She then brushed past him and made her own way through to the tiny sitting area of his apartment, flung her coat on the settee, sat down and lit up a cigarette.

"So, aren't you glad to see me?" she asked. "You're so quiet. I thought you'd be pleased."

"I am. I am. This is…this is amazing. I just wasn't expecting you back so soon. What happened?"

Anna slipped off her shoes, exhaled a ring of smoke and put her dainty bare feet up on Christian's coffee table.

"Oh, I think I just got bored. Copenhagen was fab but after a while it was like any other city. I'd seen enough. It wasn't as happening as I thought it was going to be."

"Happening? How do you mean? I thought it was the best place you'd ever been to?"

Christian sat down on the armchair opposite her and tried to take the whole scene in. This unexpected visit had left his mind racing.

"I dunno. It's hard to explain. It was so new, so exciting at first and I thought it would stay that way. I need excitement, Christian. I want to live a little."

210

"So," Christian was confused. "Why did you come back here, then? This is hardly the hub of *excitement*..."

"I had to be sure. Maybe you and I haven't finished yet. Maybe we can have a good time for another while, eh?"

For another while? Christian let Anna's words sink in and thought back to the day she'd left him. He recalled how he'd watched her walk away out of his sight and out of his life without so much as a backward glance. He was sick of doing things "for a while."

"You know what, Anna. I'm not sure we want the same things in life anymore," he said eventually. "You want excitement and you want to throw aside anyone, including me, who doesn't fit in with your plans. I used to be like that. Don't get me wrong, I did enjoy myself, I even made mistakes, but I learned by them and I grew up."

"My God, Christian," said Anna in disbelief. "What has happened to you? Why have you become so settled and sensible all of a sudden?"

"I haven't, I'm not. I'm just getting tired of living for the moment, of everything being so short-term."

Anna shrugged her shoulders and packed her lighter and cigarettes into her handbag. "I just thought you might want to grab a few drinks and chill out back here afterwards. Have a bit of fun. No pressure."

Christian thought of Eloise, the young Danish girl from a few weeks ago and a shiver ran down his spine. He thought of the way he and Anna used to be. No pressure. Is that how she thought of him? He looked at Anna carefully; the same Anna he had pined over for the past four weeks. The gorgeous, sexy Anna who he'd truly thought he'd loved. He couldn't just let her go again.

"I'm afraid I'm not much fun tonight, Anna, but my God it is so good to see you again. You see, Jonathan's mum died tonight..."

"Oh, I'm sorry. Bad timing for my surprise then, eh?" she shrugged.

"Well, I was just about to leave for Killshannon. Look I don't want to leave it like this. Can I see you tomorrow? We can talk then."

Anna's mobile phone rang and she rummaged in her handbag to find it.

"Charlie! Hey, how the hell are you?" she sang. "Sorry, just give me a second...I'm with somebody here..."

She looked at Christian and grimaced to him in apology for the interruption, then paced the living room talking in what might as well have been another language. Christian watched her every move as she chatted and made her plans with this Charlie guy, whoever the hell he was.

"So, where were we?" she asked eventually when she'd finally finished her call.

"Er, I was telling you about Jonathan's mum? And suggested that we might talk tomorrow?"

"Oh, of course. Yeah, that's fine, Chris. I gotta go now, but if you change your mind about going for that drink, you know where to find me."

Anna leaned towards him, stood on her tiptoes and gave him a quick peck on the cheek. Then she answered her mobile for a second time with a girly giggle and walked through the front door.

"I sure do," mumbled Christian and he watched her disappear into the hubbub of the busy town, across the street. Horns were blowing and cars screeched outside The Chocolate Bar, whose music spilled out into the night-time air. It was only Monday, but still, it was a Monday in July. Donegal would be ready for Anna, who was just back from one holiday and ready to start straight into another.

Christian stood pensively at the steps of his apartment and waited for her to look back, but she didn't. So he waited for the stabbing pain in his heart to return, just as it had at the airport on the same day four weeks ago.

But it didn't.

Closing his door, Christian walked back to where he'd been

when his doorbell rang. He pulled on his clothes, checked his hair in the mirror, and then grabbed his overnight bag and keys. He decided he wouldn't call Anna tomorrow after all.

Christian Devine was now prepared to close that chapter of his life and looked forward to whatever the next chapter might bring.

Chapter 24

Making Up Is Hard To Do

"I hate funerals," said Daisy to her mother as they slipped into the left pew of St Agatha's Chapel in Killshannon, "even though I know that's a bit of an obvious thing to say."

From their seats, Maggie and Daisy could see two priests scurrying around in the vestry as the bells tolled and the church choir sang Sweet Heart of Jesus. The very sights and sounds were so haunting and final.

It was cold in the chapel, but then again, Daisy had never known it to be any different. Despite the sun splitting the trees outside, there was a fitting, deathly chill in the air.

"Excuse me?" said a deep male voice and Daisy sighed as she realized her brother and "Posh Wife" were squeezing themselves into the row behind her. Her mother gave her a nudge to turn and acknowledge their arrival but Daisy clasped her hands firmly and closed her eyes tight, pretending to pray.

In fact, she didn't have to pretend at all. She did pray very hard until she heard the congregation shuffle as the cortege passed slowly by them, up the centre aisle. Time stood still for a few seconds as the piercing voices of the choir echoed off the stone walls. Jonathan carried the coffin at the front, with three of his cousins in assistance, while Eddie followed behind with Shannon and various aunts and uncles. A few of the boys' old school mates stood in the chapel gallery, some with one or two children in tow. Everybody looked solemn for the sorrow of Jonathan and Eddie Eastwood, who had buried their father not so long ago in the very same churchyard.

Daisy noticed how Jonathan stared at the floor of the aisle as he carried his mother to the front of the church. She wept at how Eddie had once done the same for their father without Jonathan by his side. Now Jonathan was carrying the burden alone, so to speak, while his only brother followed, unfit to carry his own mother to her final resting place because of his injuries.

After the emotional ceremony, the sun came out to shine a little as Isobel was finally buried by her husband's side in the tiny churchyard. Crowds queued to pay their last respects.

Daisy glanced over at Shannon, whose dark glasses were worn on her eyes this time instead of on top of her head. She kept patting her tummy as if to make a point. Beside her, Eddie looked like a lost soul. His scars were still visible from his assault and he looked gaunt and withdrawn, lost in a world of his own. Many of the gathered crowd stood with him momentarily in sympathy, quizzing him on his wellbeing and shaking their heads as to how he would need all the strength in the world to get over his terrible loss.

"At least Jonathan's wedding will take your mind off things in a few weeks time," Daisy heard an old dear say to Eddie. "Sure isn't it strange how life works out? Time is a great healer, eh?"

Daisy noted how Eddie swallowed hard. She went up to him and squeezed his hand silently. They were no longer pretending to be something they weren't; Daisy and Eddie's friendship was as strong as ever and nobody would change that.

"Have you spoken to Jonathan yet?" asked Eddie in a low voice.

"No. I haven't had a chance yet with the Immaculate Conception standing beside him like superglue," whispered Daisy. "If she looks at me once more with that forlorn face and sneaky smirk I'll knock those dark glasses down her throat."

"I'll help you," laughed Eddie as another neighbour shook his hand. "Oh, thank you Mrs McManus, you're very good to come."

"It was a lovely ceremony, Edward. Your mother would have been very proud of you both today," said the old lady and she shuffled along, wiping her eyes on a handkerchief.

****

Over a hundred mourners must have arrived back at the Eastwood house for tea after the funeral, Daisy reckoned. Lorna was boiling the kettle ten to the dozen while Daisy served the tea and sandwiches kindly supplied by the Credit Union committee. A few other ladies from the Parish Council had also offered to help out and everyone was working systematically as if they had rehearsed the occasion a thousand times.

"Mum, please go and sit down," Daisy begged Maggie, who was trying to help, but was only getting in the way. "You've done enough. Now go and find Dick 'n' Posh and I'll bring you over a cuppa."

"Daisy, I can't just sit around," said Maggie emphatically. "I need to be doing something and please don't call your sister-in- law by that name. I'm afraid it might stick."

"Well then, go and mingle. Go on. You're exhausted. Please do what I say for once in your life."

Secretly Maggie was glad to be told to go and sit down. She was feeling completely drained after the past few weeks and knew it was going to take a long time to adjust to life without Isobel.

"I dare you to go over and hand Shannon a pair of rubber gloves," said Lorna when Daisy returned to her duties. "Has she not stopped weeping once since we came through the doors of this house?"

"She makes me sick, Lorna," said Daisy in a sour tone. "But I'm trying not to think about her. I heard her saying to somebody how much she was going to miss Isobel, but I could count on one hand how many times she darkened the doors of this house when Isobel was alive. What a bloody hypocrite! I would love to…"

"Daisy, do you have a second?"

It was Eddie. He pulled her to one side and leaned into her ear.

"Jonathan is in the back garden, down the far side by the swing. I sat with him for a while but when he broke down I couldn't watch him any longer. I just don't know what to do."

"The poor thing," said Daisy when she noticed Eddie's genuine distress. "It's only natural, though. You have to let him have his time alone…

"I think he'd like you to go and talk to him."

Daisy gulped. Shannon had been glaring at her for the last hour so how could she realistically go out to speak to her future husband alone?

"I think it would mean a lot to him," insisted Eddie.

Daisy took a deep breath. "Right so, I'll go out. You keep an eye on the black witch for me. She is not one for missing a trick from beneath those crocodile tears."

Daisy squeezed herself past the people in the small kitchen and made her way through the back door, which was already opened in order to create some space. She pardoned herself as she threatened to knock cups out of hands in her haste to reach Jonathan at the bottom of the garden. She could see him now, and was longing to hold him as he grieved for his cruel loss but when she finally reached him she found herself lost for words.

"Daisy, this is all wrong. This is all wrong," he repeated, shaking his head helplessly. His eyes were red and swollen and his face looked puffed and sore. "Why did things turn out like this? Why did I have to lose so many people in my life? My father, my son, my mother and now… you."

Daisy just stared, but Jonathan continued regardless. "Yes, it looks like I stand to lose the one woman I love more than anyone else in the world. You know that's you."

217

Daisy kneeled in front of him and leaned on the stone bench on which he sat. "I don't know what to say to you, Jonathan. Only that no matter what happens from here on in, I will always be there for you. No matter where I live, no matter who you marry or who I end up with in years to come, you'll always be in my heart. You always have been."

Jonathan reached out and grasped Daisy's hand. "But I want more than that with you. Right now all I want is to put an end to all of this nonsense. I want to have the strength to tell Shannon that it's over, but then I think of my unborn child and it's tearing me apart."

They sat in silence for a few moments, both too afraid to speak any further. It was too late.

A rustle in the branches let them know that they had company. Daisy stood up and rubbed her hands on her black funeral trousers, trying her best to act as though the world wasn't crashing down on top of her.

"Jonathan, baby," purred Shannon. "There you are and if it isn't Daisy Anderson by your side. Quelle surprise! Can't you even leave my fiancé alone for one minute?"

Shannon stood stony-faced in front of Daisy, glaring at her like she was scum on the bottom of her designer shoe.

"I was just leaving," said Daisy pathetically, fighting back the tears.

"Good," said Shannon. "Jonathan and I have matters to discuss. Private *family* matters that you don't need to be part of. Anyway I think there are more dishes to be washed in the kitchen."

"Shannon!" Jonathan gasped.

To say Daisy was stunned by Shannon's rudeness was an understatement. *Don't rise to it*, she told herself, taking a deep breath. *Don't cause a scene. You'll get her in the long grass.*

"It's fine, Jonathan," she said, as tears stung her eyes. "I'll just go and make myself useful. Happy chatting."

****

The look on Richard Anderson's face said it all as his little sister entered the family kitchen later that evening. He knew that Daisy was terribly upset, but he felt he had at least had to broach the subject, and try and talk some sense into her.

"I see your old flame has gone and got engaged to Shannon Cassidy? Don't worry, Daisy. There are plenty more…"

"Please don't say there are plenty more fish in the sea, Richard. I'm not in the mood and quite frankly, you don't have a clue what you're talking about," snapped Daisy, reaching for a bottle of cola from her mother's fridge. "And how do you know Shannon anyhow?"

"Well, I don't know her. But I know a lot about her. Her brother is one of our 'dentist' friends. She's a pretty girl but a bit of a climber. She's been around the block a few times. All the good that it did her – I mean, look where she's ended up after all her social crawling!"

Daisy was tempted to punch his smarmy face but gripped the bottle of cola instead. "Why don't you like Jonathan, Richard? For someone who claims to be so intelligent, you really are a poor judge of character."

"I just think Shannon could do better for herself. Who would have thought she'd end up with a little boy racer type? She'll learn, though, possibly when it's too late, like everyone else."

Daisy's mouth tightened.

"Daisy, darling! There you are!"

Posh Wife's entrance and the perma-surprised look on her face that yelled *Botox!* managed to save her husband's bacon.

"Hi, Jennifer. Good to see you," said Daisy through gritted teeth. "Sorry I haven't been able to chat with you until now."

"Oh, don't worry wee pet. Your mother has been filling us in. I had no idea that you were so close to those poor Eastwood boys. You really are so kind. I don't think I could pretend I was the girlfriend of a gay man just to please his dying mother. You deserve a medal."

Just count to ten, thought Daisy.

"No, believe me, Jennifer. If there's anyone who deserves a medal around here, it has to be *you*," she cooed, giving her brother a disapproving glance.

"Daisy and I were just speaking of Jonathan's engagement," said Richard. "I was just telling her not to worry about him. She can do much better."

"You shouldn't be so judgemental," snapped his wife.

"Huh," said Richard. "You were the one who said earlier that you didn't like the look of Jonathan's fiancée. And now you're accusing me of being judgemental?"

Daisy was all ears. Could she and Jennifer possibly have something in common – a bad feeling about Shannon?

"What do you know about Shannon?" asked Daisy.

"Not much at all, love," said Jennifer. "I've just seen her around over the years. She was the type of girl who always had a richer, older man on her arm from the age of about sixteen. I don't know her personally but she had quite a reputation in my circle."

"And then she goes and settles for a teacher from Killshannon!" laughed Richard. "You're so intuitive, Jen, but if she was such a minx, why would she be marrying *him*?"

"Because she loves him, possibly," said Jennifer. "Oh, I don't know."

Daisy felt her blood chill. How dare her brother insult Jonathan in this way?

"For your information, Jonathan is head of his department in school. He has a very respectable job."

"I'm not knocking his profession at all," said Richard with a cough. "Actually, speaking of work, I hear you've given up your latest job. It really does baffle me how you manage to pay your bills, Daisy."

"I manage quite fine," she lied, taking a gulp of her cola as she felt her face burn. The truth was that she was skint. And at the moment her only future career prospect was on the end of a lengthy dole queue.

"Do you need a bit of help on the old finance front, sis?" asked Richard. "You know you only have to ask."

I'd rather slam my tits in the door, thought Daisy.

"If I wanted charity, I'd busk in the city centre. Thanks, but no thanks."

Jennifer cleared her throat gently and tried to lighten the mood. "My friends have some great contacts in the drama industry, Daisy," she said. "Are you acting at all these days?"

"From what I hear she put on quite a fine act when she pretended to be Eddie's girlfriend," laughed Richard. "I suppose that was just practice for your art, mind you."

Daisy knew Jennifer was trying her best, but enough was enough.

"Look you two, I really can manage my own life, thank you. There is no need for concern. I'm just at…a bit of a crossroads, you could say."

Where the hell was her mother? She needed an excuse to get away from this pair.

"Never mind the crossroads – you need to find the highway," said Richard, wagging a finger in her direction. "That's my motto in life, and look how far it's got me. A fine house in the country, a thriving business, a beautiful wife…"

Daisy zoned out as he rambled on. The only highway she needed right now was the M1 to Belfast, away from Richard, away from Jonathan, and as far away from Killshannon as she could possibly go.

"I'm just going to pop down to the shops to grab something for dinner," said Jennifer as she stood up. "I'm sure your mum will be ready for something when she gets back from next door. Please don't murder each other when I'm gone."

Daisy managed a slight smile in Jennifer's direction and received a wink in return.

Maggie Anderson looked sullen when she arrived back home after the final visitors had left Isobel's house. She was pleased to see that Richard and Daisy were chatting together at the kitchen table.

"Hi all," she said wearily and sat down at the table. "Be a honey, Richard, and put the kettle on. Where's Jennifer?" she asked.

"She went out to fetch something nice for dinner," said Richard. Make yourself comfy Mum and I'll make you a cuppa."

A voice in the back of Maggie's mind told her that this might be a good time to make her announcement. It was a rare occasion that she had her family all to herself.

"Richard. Daisy," she said with a strength she never thought she had within her. "I need to discuss a few things with you, now that I have you both here."

She looked at her two children, as alike as chalk and cheese as they were, determined to have her say.

"What is it, Mum? Is there something wrong?" asked Richard with concern.

"Yes. Well, no. It's just that, Isobel's death has forced me to look at the rest of my own life very seriously."

"Mum, I don't like the sound of this…" Daisy trailed off.

Both her children looked at her as though they had seen a ghost. It wasn't like their mother to address them so formally. This *must* be serious.

"Go on," said Richard anxiously, leaning on his hands.

"Richard, you and Jennifer have made a wonderful life together in Sligo and I am very proud of you for that. And Daisy," she said, directing a more gentle tone towards her only daughter, "I am also so proud of you the way you've helped Jonathan and Eddie over the past few weeks. Your loyalty to your friends has always been your strongest point, and I am confident that whatever path you choose in life will be the right one."

"Mum, have you been drinking?"

"No, Daisy. Indeed I have not. But after I've finished my speech I would be most grateful for a rather large brandy, if you don't mind."

Richard and Daisy both laughed, before Maggie continued.

"Since your father died I have been putting up a very brave front, running here and there and, of course, worrying about you two. But I've decided that it's time for some 'me' time at long last."

"I thought you were a real social butterfly," said Daisy, trying desperately to lighten the mood. Her mother was beginning to frighten her with this weird, deep behaviour. Perhaps she had decided to change her religion after all.

"Don't you have everything you need, Mum?" added Jonathan. "I bought you a car, and you have all your mod cons in this comfortable home."

"Jonathan, that is *exactly* my point. You can buy me all the riches in the world and I might look and seem like I'm the life and soul of the party, but inside I'm screaming. Deep inside, I've been screaming for a long time."

"Oh, Mum," said Daisy as her mother began to sob.

"No, no, I'm okay," said Maggie, taking a deep breath in a bid to compose herself. "I've tried to tell you this before, Richard, but you managed to put me off. Not anymore. You see, lately I have found great company with the most wonderful man."

"A man?" asked Richard in astonishment. "Isn't this a bit rash? Who is he?"

Maggie watched as her children took her news to their hearts. To her surprise, Daisy looked almost accepting. Richard, however, looked as though he'd just been stabbed in the back.

"As long as he's good to you," said Daisy. "That's the main thing."

"Oh, he is, pet. I'm sure you'll like him very much. In fact I *know* you will as you've met him before. His name is Geoff. He's an artist and he's taking me out to dinner at the weekend."

Daisy racked her brains trying to figure out why that name was so familiar. And then the penny dropped as she remembered her Brigitte Bardot picture.

"Mum, I am so, so happy for you. Geoff is a wonderful man," said Daisy, reaching out to hug her mother.

"I'm not sure about this at all, Mum. An artist?" said Richard in disdain. "Does he have a real job? Might I know him through the galleries?"

Daisy rolled her eyes at her mother, who burst out laughing. As much as she dearly loved her only son, he could be such a snob at times. However she'd made her mind up. He was not going to control her private life any more.

"I'm not sure if you've seen him at all before, Richard," she said. "But if I have my way, you'll be seeing a lot more of him in future. And that's the end of it."

Chapter 25

Where There's Light, There's Hope

Lorna had just driven through Killshannon village on her way back to Belfast when her mobile flashed a text message from Christian. She smiled to herself but decided to refrain from replying for at least another ten minutes. There was no harm in making a man sweat.

Just before the ten-minute test was up, Lorna's phone rang. It was him. She hit the hands-free option and flicked her hair back.

"Hi Christopher," she said breezily.

"Hi Laura."

"Very funny. What can I do for you, my dear?"

"Ah, Lorna," replied Christian. "What could you *do* for me? Well, that would take me quite some explaining and I wouldn't want to distract you when you are driving. I just thought I'd phone to say hello. It's been a tough few days and I need a laugh."

Lorna threw her head back. "Is that all I'm good for? A laugh?"

"No, no I didn't mean it like that. I didn't get a chance to speak to you much today at the funeral and I think I owe you twenty euros. I have to hand it to you Lorna – you're a woman of your word."

Lorna gave a smug grin. "I think you'll find its twenty pounds *sterling* you'll be paying up, Mister. The bet was made in my part of the country and quite frankly the euro isn't much good to me."

She could hear him sigh, albeit in a nice way, on the other end of the line.

"You're a hard woman, Lorna. But why don't I start with buying you a drink in *my* part of the country this evening? You're the first person to beat me in a bet so that in itself deserves a celebration."

"I'm sure I could fit you in. Where is your local watering hole?"

Christian thought for a second. The Chocolate Bar should be fairly quiet at this time of the evening, but Gerry, the know-it-all barman, and Eloise, the psycho Dane, had recently made it a no-go area.

"I'll tell you what. Meet me in the Diamond and we'll take it from there. You can park on the street and we'll go into the first bar that takes our fancy. In fact, it can be your choice."

"Sounds good," said Lorna, changing Chloe's gear with a broad smile. "I'll see you there then."

****

Back in Killshannon, Eddie Eastwood burst in through the doors of the Anderson household with an animated smile. He had just woken up after a few hours' kip to receive a text message from Brad in Los Angeles. This had definitely managed to brighten up what would have otherwise been an extremely dark day, the worst of his life, in fact. He was looking forward to telling Daisy, but instead of bumping into his best friend in the hallway, he was met abruptly by a frowning Rick, the Dick.

"Eddie, mate. How are you feeling? You've been through the wars."

"I'll be fine, Richard," said Eddie fidgeting with his fingers. There was something about Daisy's brother that made him incredibly nervous. He could feel a ramble coming on. "At least I have the chance to get away from it all soon when I fly back to San Francisco.

It's Jonathan I feel for more to be honest. He has a wedding to go through in a few weeks' time and as he lives close by, he'll be surrounded by constant reminders that Mum isn't coming back."

For a second, Eddie was certain he could actually see remorse for Jonathan on Richard's face.

"He's marrying Shannon Cassidy, eh?" said Richard, folding his arms and leaning on the doorframe. "Funnily enough, I always thought he'd win my little sister over eventually."

Eddie was shocked to the core at Richard's reference to Jonathan and Daisy. That was supposed to be a no-go area. Maybe Richard Anderson did have a heart somewhere after all. Or maybe he knew more than he was letting on?

"To be honest, I'd always *hoped* he would win her over too," said Eddie. "I tried my best...they have a very deep bond but unfortunately it's just not meant to be. I have another two weeks to work on him, though, so you never know. He hasn't taken the jump just yet."

Richard's face turned to stone and Eddie's stomach gave a leap.

"My sister isn't a bargaining chip, Eddie," he said firmly. "If Jonathan wants her, he can fight for her himself. He can prove to us all that he's a man who knows what he wants and how to get it. I'd advise you strongly to leave him to his own devices, don't interfere and let nature take its course. Good or bad."

Eddie's face flushed and he stuttered and stammered through a jittery response, but Richard had already walked back into the kitchen, leaving Eddie muttering and shrugging to himself and his reflection in the tall hallway mirror.

Daisy came out to greet him with a concerned look on her face.

"Eddie, hi there, love. Did you have a good sleep?" she asked.

She looked a bit fresher than before, noted Eddie, and if he wasn't mistaken she seemed to have an unusual glow about her.

"What are you so chirpy about?" he asked.

"Oh, I'm sorry. It's nothing." Daisy said suddenly, realising it was much too soon for good humour with Eddie. "Has the house settled down now? I was waiting for the witch to leave so I could go over and help you move the furniture back into place. I know how hard it is to see the house so quiet again after the wake and funeral. Believe me, I remember it too well."

Daisy felt a shiver and Eddie linked his arm with hers.

"I know. Look, I did come over here for a reason, well, for a number of reasons. Firstly, to tell you that you are welcome to come over to our house anytime and that the witch's presence should not make any difference."

"But..."

"Let me finish," he said as they strolled out into the warm evening sunshine. "Secondly, I want to say thank you for all that you've done for me over the past few weeks and to tell you that when you're ready, there is an all-expenses-paid trip for you to come and stay with me in San Fran."

"Wow! Who died and made you a millionaire?" blurted Daisy, and then she gasped at her own stupidity. "Oh, I'm sorry, Eddie! That just came out. Remember we used to say that all the time? Sorry..."

"Give over; I know you didn't mean anything by it."

Daisy was relieved and cursed herself for being so insensitive.

"Oh, gosh, I am so excited!" she gasped. "I've never been to the west coast of America. Will I meet any celebs?"

"Aha! Which brings me swiftly to my next reason for calling over..."

"Go on..."

Now it was Eddie who was bursting with excitement.

"Remember when I picked you up in Belfast and I told you about my friend, Brad?"

"Yes," said Daisy, with caution. "Brad the youngster?"

"Shut up. Okay then, Brad, the youngster. You're right. Well, anyhow, Brad's father is coming to the little old Emerald Isle soon to film a Hollywood rom-com starring proper A-list actors!"

Daisy drew a breath. There was more. There had to be more.

228

Hollywood movies were filmed on location in Ireland all the time.

"That's great, Ed. But why is it so exciting for you, or me?"

"Daisy, my dear! I have managed to secure you an audition for a part…"

"What!" she screamed.

"Hold on, hold on! When I say 'a part', I actually mean a non-speaking part that is an inch above an extra, but Brad's dad has agreed to meet you on set personally and I just know he will love you instantly."

Daisy didn't know what to say. On the day of his own mother's funeral Eddie had set aside his own grief for a moment just to give her good news. His selflessness knew no bounds.

"Brad's dad! I'm going to meet Brad's dad! The movie director! Eddie, I can't even respond. This is amazing."

Eddie wrapped his arm around Daisy and kissed her on the forehead.

"They start filming in four weeks' time in County Cavan and I just know you'll wow the pants off them."

"Wait a minute; did you say they start filming in four weeks?"

"Yes, why?" said Eddie with a smirk.

"That means I'll be terribly busy when Jonathan is getting married."

"Exactly," said Eddie. "Funny the way things work out, eh?"

Daisy let out a huge sigh of relief. She had been secretly fretting over Jonathan's wedding, but now Eddie had handed her the most incredible option.

"Eddie, have I told you lately how great you are?" she said, sitting on the small summer seat that overlooked the lush greenery of her mother's garden.

"I don't think you have actually. Tell me again!"

"Don't overdo it, Spud."

The two sat arm-in-arm in silence, listening to the sounds of the summer and thinking of what the future might bring. Seagulls flew overhead en route to the shoreline and a horn from the fishing port blew in the distance.

"You know something, Daisy?" asked Eddie. "My mother always told me, when God takes something from us with one hand, he gives us something good with the other. My mother is gone, but I have a really strong feeling we're all going to be okay."

****

Christian waited in the Diamond for the red-haired girl with the funny laugh who had bowled him over the first time they had ever spoken on the phone some weeks ago. He couldn't quite understand why, but over the last few days she had occupied his mind more than any young sex siren. Not even Anna or Daisy could compare.

He had mentally recorded the registration of her car, he had savoured the sound of her voice, and right now he was waiting in eager anticipation of just one hour in her company.

"Hey, Stud," came a loud raspy voice from the opposite side of the road and Christian looked over to see a dark green Clio park neatly in a narrow space. Lorna emerged from the driver's seat with a radiant smile that took his breath away.

"Do you come here often?" he bellowed back.

"How bloody original," she answered with a giggle as Christian drank in her lively appearance, her long legs and bright smile. He was smitten.

The funny thing was that she wasn't really his type, yet she presented a challenge to him that he found irresistible.

"Right, Devine. I've just decided on our drinking den. Let's go and then you can show me the money," she said.

The bar Lorna chose was heaving with tourists who wanted to drown their shamrocks till the wee hours. So they squeezed past the gathered crowds and finally found a spot where they could chat together in peace without gangs of European or American visitors wanting a piece of their Irish charm.

230

Lorna quizzed Christian on Jonathan and Daisy. She wanted to know how he had once, and almost twice, come between them. "Did it ever occur to you, Christian, that there is more to life than a quick how's-your-father and then an even quicker goodbye in the morning?"

Christian did a double-take. This girl had really done her homework.

They were seated so far apart they had to shout above the lilting Irish rock music and no matter how much Christian tried to move closer, Lorna shifted an inch further away. It was driving him insane.

"I have learned some very hard lessons, believe me, Lorna. But the hardest one of all has been realising that what I thought was…"

His redemption speech was interrupted by a high-pitched squeal from across the bar. "Christian Devine! I don't believe it. The fucker! The sex thief!"

Christian was mortified as Eloise and a group of her friends gathered in front of him, scoffing and shouting insults in his direction.

"Er, Lorna, I think it's time to get out of here," he said and Lorna stood up instantly, shaking her head. Being a drinking buddy of the legendary Christian Devine was obviously going to be a cross to bear.

They stepped out onto the cobbled street and though it was still warm, Christian removed his jacket and placed it over Lorna's shoulders.

"Are you trying to be all romantic with me, Christian? You really don't have to make the effort. I've met guys like you before," she said.

Christian sighed. Obviously he was going to have to try extra hard to get into Lorna's good books. He hadn't exactly got off to a great start, had he?

"I'm doing my best here. Give me a break," he said, genuinely. "Now, I suppose a nightcap at mine is out of the question? At least

231

we'll have some peace there."

Lorna stopped in her tracks and studied her options. Should she give in to his charm, or else turn his offer down and risk never hearing from him again?

"I must be crazy," she began, "and I know I'll probably regret this in the morning, but okay then, I'll go to yours for a nightcap."

Christian duly offered her his arm and they strolled back to his apartment, where he hoped for some pleasant conversation, and a peaceful evening. Anything after that would be a bonus.

Chapter 26

Oh, What A Tangled Web We Weave...

"This is way too nice a day to be inside," said Richard Anderson as his family finished a well-earned full Irish breakfast the morning after Isobel's funeral. "Anyone fancy catching a few rays with me in the back garden?"

"No thanks," Daisy muttered as she snuggled deeper into the sofa. "I think I'll have a bit of a nap."

"You know, that idea sounds appealing to me as well," said Maggie, patting her tummy. "Thanks for breakfast, Richard. I could get used to having you around to fuss over me like this."

"And how about you, Jen?" said Richard to his wife. "You could really top up your tan out there today. I'm sure I told you before how the back of Mum's house is a real sun trap."

"I'll be with you in a second, darling" said Jennifer. "I'm just going to have a shower and pack our bags first of all. Remember, we're meeting Alex and Noelle tonight for supper so we'd better be going soon."

"Alex and Noelle? Are they new friends? I haven't heard you mention those names before," said Maggie with interest.

"Oh, Alexandra and Noelle are a fabulous couple we met on holiday on the Algarve in May," said Jennifer. "They've invited us

233

to their partnership party on a yacht in Marbella later this month."

Daisy rolled her eyes in surprise.

"Right, well I'll go and make the most of the sunshine while you ladies busy yourself showering and, er, napping then," said Richard. "You could do with some colour in your cheeks, Daisy though. You're very pasty-looking these days."

"Thanks, Rick. You always know how to make me feel so good about myself," said Daisy, burying her head further into the cushion.

Richard shrugged his shoulders and lifted the local newspaper from the armchair on his way outside. He opened the patio doors and inhaled the scent of the bluebells that engulfed his mother's overgrown paradise. The garden of Ivy Cottages was one of his favourite places in any season, but on a summer day like this, it was heaven.

Redirecting the deckchair so that it faced the heat of the sun, Richard settled down to read his paper. He scanned a news article on a planning application for a hotel a few miles outside Killshannon and the sale of a nearby restaurant, which was owned by one of the town's more affluent families. He re-read the headlines and the first paragraph of the restaurant story but the distinctive voice of Shannon Cassidy wafting through the fence from next door was invading his concentration.

He shook the newspaper and in a fit of frustration started to read the same passage for the third time, but just as it finally began to penetrate his brain, he overheard his sister's name being flung around throughout Shannon's conversation.

Richard sat up straight and laid the newspaper quietly under his chair so he could listen closely.

"That stupid Anderson bitch is out to wreck everything for me," said Shannon in a high-pitched screech. "No, no, I think I can deal with it, but the quicker Jonathan's queer brother gets out of my face the better. She has no chance of winning Jonathan back after my little baby bombshell. It's hilarious yet so pitiful at the same time."

Jennifer slid back the patio doors and Richard waved at her to be quiet and to join him quickly in case he missed what was coming next.

"Please, Mr McKenzie, just trust me on this, okay?" said Shannon from the other side of the fence, her voice dropping once more into a frantic whisper. "I know you've heard this all before, but I mean it this time, it's in the bag. Jonathan believes everything I say and in just a few weeks you'll get every penny owed to you, I swear."

Richard's eyes widened and Jennifer's mouth dropped. Shannon was leading Jonathan Eastwood in a merry dance and the poor man's mother was only barely cold in the ground. Nobody, not even Jonathan Eastwood, deserved this.

"Look, I'll meet you as planned in The Granary and I'll tell you everything then," continued Shannon. "Yes, be there at noon and I'll bring you two grand. Okay, okay, three then. Yes, yes and the relevant papers. Bye, Mr McKenzie. Bye."

Richard and Jennifer exchanged glances of sheer disbelief. Jennifer covered his mouth to prevent him from saying anything until the sound of Shannon's high heels had completely faded into the distance.

"What the hell could that little bitch be up to?" he hissed when his wife finally allowed him to speak. Jennifer led the way back towards the deckchair and sat on its edge. "And who could Mr McKenzie possibly be?" he asked, rubbing his temples.

"Whoever he is, he seems to be pulling Shannon Cassidy's purse strings and Jonathan obviously has no idea his marriage is just part of a well-thought-out plan," said Jennifer.

"Should I tell Daisy what I heard?"

Jennifer thought for a second. "No. Let's just take our time, darling," she said. "You don't know enough about it and you aren't exactly top of Jonathan Eastwood's Christmas card list from what I can see. Besides, what could Daisy do about it anyway? Shannon would only convince him it was all lies."

Richard nodded and Jennifer linked his arm. "I think Daisy still loves him, Richard," she said.

Jennifer felt her husband's body stiffen as her words sank in. This was not what he wanted to hear and she knew it.

"What? Who?"

"You know quite well who. *Jonathan*. Maybe that's why you could never take to the boy," she continued, knowing a bit of tough love was just what was needed on this occasion. "You want to protect Daisy, you want to be her father figure, but you'll end up just pushing her away."

Richard took Jennifer's hand in both of his. "I just hate to see her hurt so much over a man who will marry someone else very soon. It's pointless."

Jennifer gave him a tight hug. Sometimes Richard felt he had the power to change the world and it took some straight-talking to sort him out.

"You may be able to advise your baby sister on her career, her money, her five-year plan and whatever else," she added, "but when it comes to affairs of the heart, she'll make up her own mind no matter what you say. It's time you accepted that, once and for all. Now let's see what we can find out about Shannon and her stinking plans, eh?"

****

The tiny cemetery in Killshannon was always blissfully peaceful and Jonathan knew his way around its corners and crevices like the back of his hand.

Some people felt great remorse when they stood over their loved ones' graves, and in Jonathan's case, it succeeded in ripping his heart in two every time. Nonetheless, he still felt a powerful longing to visit there, despite the pain he always felt afterwards.

When he reached the Eastwood family plot, he hunkered down

at its side, fingering the fresh soil on the surface of the square of land where his mother and father now lay side by side. The undertaker said he would arrange for Isobel's name to be carved on the headstone shortly, but Jonathan had asked him to wait a while longer. To put her name on her grave would be like confirming the obvious. It was too definite.

He breathed in deeply and pinched his eyes when an overwhelming urge to cry engulfed his body. When he finally regained his strength, he blessed himself slowly, despite not having said a single prayer, and made his way towards the iron gate at the foot of the hill on which the cemetery lay.

It had been his same routine for the two days since Isobel's funeral, now. Each morning he would find himself at the cemetery, and only a few minutes later he would make for the gates like he had been dragged there kicking and screaming in the first place.

A girl waved at him from a distance but Jonathan stared at the ground for fear of catching her eye as she came towards him, clutching a huge bouquet of flowers. He decided to nod a quick hello as she came closer as he couldn't bear the thought of small talk with a well-meaning parishioner right now. Killshannon was full of those. He glanced up mournfully in the hope of making a swift greeting and then stopped in his tracks in recognition of the girl who was making her way over to him with a wary smile.

It was Daisy.

"Hey, Jonathan," she said quietly.

"Hi," he said, and shifting from foot to foot like a nervous teenager.

"I was just going to lay some flowers on your mum's grave before I went back to Belfast."

Jonathan looked at her with his head still bowed and a light smile grew from the side of his mouth at the glorious sound of her voice.

"That's nice of you. I have a feeling I won't be very good at doing that sort of thing myself, so I'll be glad of friends like you in future."

The pair stood opposite each other awkwardly.

"I'll never forget the good times," said Daisy and Jonathan had to look away as his mother's words echoed around him.

"Lilies?" he said, nodding at the flowers. "You remembered her favourites. That's nice of you."

"Yeah, I have two bunches, actually," said Daisy, lifting each bouquet. "I couldn't have old Danny Anderson mumbling to his best buddies upstairs that I gave the Eastwoods flowers and forgot all about him, could I?"

Jonathan laughed and touched her shoulder.

"I can just hear them bickering and Mum playing referee as usual," said Jonathan. "I hope each bunch is the same size!"

Daisy laughed. "They are. To be honest, I'm not very good at the whole cemetery thing either. In fact, this is a place I normally avoid if I can when I come home. It tears me apart."

Jonathan noticed Daisy was shaking, despite the blistering heat that had swept the Northern coast over the past few days. He reached out his hand to comfort her but then stopped suddenly, realising it was too late for such amicable gestures now. He shoved his hands in his pockets and looked at the ground again.

"I'll walk with you, if you like?" he said. "To the graveside, that is. My last visit didn't really come up to much."

Daisy squinted in the sunshine. "I'd like that," she said. "I'm leaving for Belfast shortly, so that would be perfect."

She gripped the flower stems so hard she feared they would break before they reached their resting place on Isobel's grave.

"You'll always hold a special place in my heart, Daisy. You do know that?"

Daisy laughed in a bid to shrug off Jonathan's sentimental proclamation.

"You sound as if you're about eighty years old!" she said, and Jonathan laughed back, realising that she was right. "In a few weeks you'll be a married man with a baby on the way. Isn't that wild?"

"It is pretty crazy," said Jonathan, seriously now. "If only things were different…"

"But they're not, so let's not dwell on what could have been, okay?" said Daisy firmly, trying to convince herself to be logical and practical about the entire situation. Thinking that way would help numb the pain she was feeling through every inch of her body. "I have a busy life to get back to in Belfast and soon you'll be back at work teaching the geniuses of tomorrow at St Benedict's."

Daisy began to walk again as she spoke, determined to keep her last meeting with Jonathan light-hearted and realistic. There was no point living in the past when the future had such different plans for both of them.

"You have it all well-planned, that's for sure, Daisy Anderson. I do hope it all works out for you," said Jonathan, casually ruffling the end of her golden hair as they reached the Eastwood graveside. "I've really made a mess of things for both of us, haven't I?"

Daisy looked at him and forced a smile. "We've both made some huge mistakes, but maybe it's time we closed the door on that part of our past. I think that's all we *can* do."

Daisy kneeled and carefully laid the bunch of lilies on Isobel's grave while Jonathan stared at her every move, knowing that what she said was true. He reached his arms behind his head and stretched them high in a bid to release some of the anger and hurt he felt. Then he noticed how tears were streaming down Daisy's face, how she was trying to hide that she was crying and he couldn't hold back any longer.

"Daisy," he said, his voice trembling with emotion and pent-up fury. "I can't pretend any more. I can't do it. I'm going to tell Shannon today it's over, once and for all. I love you, Daisy. I love *you*."

Daisy stood up to meet him, shaking her head and wiping her tears with her bare arm. She spoke in a whisper, hoping he would sense the plea in her voice. "No, no, Jonathan. You can't. Shannon is having your baby."

Jonathan took Daisy's hand in a desperate grip. "But I don't love her. Isn't it better to tell her now, instead of making her suffer in a marriage that only one of us wants to be in?"

Daisy stared into his face, which was only inches from hers. How she longed to pull him closer to her, to inhale every inch of him and to stay like that for as long as they both wanted to, but she convinced herself it was all wrong.

"Sorry, Jonathan, but I have to go. I'm going to leave you now. Please don't be so hard on yourself, you don't deserve it."

She leaned forward and kissed his cheek, her lips lingering perhaps more slowly than they should have. She then prised herself free and walked away.

Chapter 27

Devine Interventions

Lorna opened one eye and absorbed with horror the unfamiliar surroundings of Christian's bachelor-style bedroom.

"Oh holy sweet mother of God in Heaven," she mumbled. "Please tell me I didn't do anything stupid 'cos I missed the pill on Saturday and Sunday and I'm as ripe and fertile as a bunny rabbit."

But she breathed a huge sigh of relief when she opened her two eyes and realised she wasn't actually in Christian's bedroom at all, but in a spacious spare room. She was fully clothed as well. Phew. She felt as pure as the driven snow and very, very proud of herself indeed.

"Oh thank you, God. I swear I won't miss Mass for a whole month," she blurted. "You have been so good and kind to make me such a good girl and not allowing me to commit such a sin with such a gorgeous man when I haven't even met his mother," she chanted and blessed herself once to show her almighty thanks and then did it again a second time, just for luck.

She lay under the cool, grey cotton bed covers that smelled clean and fresh. Pale walls and black and white posters tastefully framed the bedroom. All of the posters were of beautiful women, of course – Marilyn, Greta, Bette, Grace. They were all looking ultimately gorgeous as they stared down at Lorna, challenging her to get out of bed and face their timeless beauty and elegance.

"Hey gorgeous, fancy a Devine special?" said Christian, peeping his head around the door of the bedroom.

"And what would that entail?" *You absolute sex god*, thought Lorna. *My days of playing hard to get are coming to a very swift end, don't you worry.*

"Bacon and toast with lashings of brown sauce," said Christian with a warm smile. "The perfect cure for the rotten hangover you are about to suffer for resisting my manly charms last night."

Lorna leaned her head on her hand and tried to look as sexy as the gorgeous women on the wall. "There is a first time for everything, Christian Devine. Now off you go and tend to my needs while I go and freshen up. I need a shower like I've never needed one before."

Lorna teetered down the hallway into the bathroom as the smell of grilled bacon filled the air. Her tummy rumbled and she whistled a happy tune to herself. She wasn't doing too badly for a fine filly of thirty-three. She had Christian Devine dangling like a carrot under her nose and the more she flirted and teased him, the more he wanted her. It felt damn good. She twisted the shower knob and sighed with joy as the water pumped out over her head and down her body, and washed away the cobwebs from the night before. She was ready for Christian's next move now. She wouldn't turn him down a second time – that would be just so cruel. Lorna sang a pop song loudly, hoping he would hear the joy in her voice and perhaps come and join her. Now that would be nice.

Christian's own thoughts were distracted by the sound of the doorbell. He turned the grill down a little, and then made his way to the door. When he reluctantly opened it, his heart stopped as Anna Harrison stumbled into his apartment. Her normally timid voice was hoarse and much louder than usual.

"What the hell has happened to you, Devine?" she croaked. "Where did the old party animal I once knew go to? Is he hiding in here somewhere? Come out, come out wherever you are!!"

Anna marched into the living area, pulling Christian by his linen shirt.

"I know my old friend is in here somewhere," she said, unbuttoning his shirt and staring up at him through bloodshot eyes.

"No, Anna!"

"I know you want me. You've always wanted me. You love me, remember? You told me on the phone…"

Christian gently eased Anna's sticky hands off him and spoke to her in a forced whisper, praying that his tone of voice would give her the message and that Lorna wouldn't hear.

"Look, Anna, why don't you run along and catch up with your good-time friends? I don't really fit into that category anymore. I have changed, believe me."

"You absolute saddo!" said Anna in a huff, and Christian realised she was still obviously drunk from last night. "I don't believe for one second that you'd rather mess about with *her* than come out on the piss with me. Yes, you *have* changed."

"With who?" Christian's heart stopped as he realised Lorna was standing behind him.

"Am I interrupting something?" asked Lorna, her face flushed with anger and embarrassment. She was wearing nothing more than a towel and a sweep of lipstick and now she felt like such a fool.

"Believe me, Anna was just leaving, Lorna. You are *not* interrupting, I can assure you."

So this was Anna, thought Lorna, and her stomach did a flip. Anna who took Christian's heart to Copenhagen.

"I'll just leave you to it," she murmured and stumbled back into the bathroom, where she locked the door and quickly got dressed.

"No, don't go, Lorna!" said Christian.

"Yes, do go, Lorna. Christian and I are going to a party," laughed Anna.

"I want you to leave, now," shouted Christian. "There was a time when I would have begged you to stay, but not anymore. I want more from life than partying around the clock. I've been there, done that, but you go right ahead. It's your time for partying, so go and enjoy yourself. You don't need me. You never have."

"I am going nowhere. There are CDs of mine here, and my exercise bike. I'm not going without them."

Enough was enough. What was it lately with him that he had to chase women out of his apartment? He couldn't be bothered with this shit anymore.

"Take your CDs, take anything you want, but don't come knocking on my door unannounced like that again, Anna. You finished this a long time ago."

Anna stood up in a stumble, then steadied herself and made her way to the door.

"Fine, fine, fine, I'm leaving," she mumbled. "Your playboy reputation will die with this one, Christian Devine."

Anna sauntered towards the door and Christian shouted after her. "You don't know how happy that makes me to hear you say that. Enjoy the party. I know I did."

Christian walked back into the living room, where Lorna sat, staring at her nails and feeling like a prize idiot. He sat down beside her and reached for her hand, but she pulled away.

"I don't know what you want from me, Christian, but I can assure you I'll never be one of your floozies," said Lorna, her steely exterior showing a crack of emotion. "I'm way past that and I don't feel the need to compete with your little friends calling for you to come out to play. I'm a bit past that nonsense, if you don't mind."

Christian looked sincerely into her brown eyes. How could he convince this wonderful, beautiful woman that he was tired of chasing skirt around nightclubs and bars and that her company meant so much more to him than bedding any young thing ever again? With the reappearance of Eloise and now Anna, he hadn't got off to a great start in earning her trust.

"Believe me, Lorna. I am happy to take things as slowly or as quickly as you want. I love being with you. You make me laugh,

244

you make me want to scream and the scariest thing is that the minute I leave your company, I can't wait to see you again. Surely all of that deserves at least one more chance?"

Lorna looked up at the gorgeous vision beside her, with his unbuttoned shirt that had seen better days. She wanted to reach for him right there and then, but deep down she knew she was much, much safer playing all of this very cool. This was a man who once would have got up *on* the crack of dawn, so there was no way she was going to fall where others had before her had perished at the first hurdle.

"What's that smell? Is it bacon?" she asked when a waft of burning interrupted her train of thought.

"Oh, shit! So much for your breakfast! This isn't working for me at all this morning," said Christian, racing to salvage the bacon but sadly it was burnt to a crisp.

"Listen, why don't we start our morning off again?" said Lorna with a giggle. "I'm sure we could find some old greasy spoon around the corner where we can feed ourselves. I'm famished and it's almost noon. If I was at work I'd be getting ready for lunch at this stage."

"*If* you were at work. Small word, big meaning," said Christian, pulling her towards him.

"Shut your face, I'm going back tomorrow!"

"Yeah, yeah, you're going nowhere…"

"I am," said Lorna. "It's your fault for getting me drunk last night and giving me a fright this morning when I woke up in a strange room all alone."

Christian raised an eyebrow and laughed.

"Now let's go and get some food. I'm wasting away here and you wouldn't like me when I'm skinny."

****

The town centre café was as busy as always and Christian and

Lorna were lucky to find a seat. They nabbed a snug in the back corner of the airy room, which was dotted with sporting memorabilia and football trophies.

"I could eat the face of a baby," said Christian as he scanned the list of paninis, wraps and deli sandwiches on the menu.

"Yuk! How could you say that?" said Lorna, her nose wrinkled in disgust.

"I could."

"Well, I could eat the snot of a corpse," said Lorna, in a bid to match his humour.

"Now, that was just totally uncalled for," said Christian. They both tittered like schoolchildren as they read the menu, then waited impatiently for some service.

"Hey," said Christian. "Don't look now, but do you recognise that woman hiding behind a magazine over there? Yellow scarf."

Lorna casually looked around. She spotted an elegant lady who sat with her head cocked up to one side, barely visible from behind the latest edition of Vanity Fair. She wore a canary-coloured headscarf, a black v-neck top and a slim black pencil skirt.

"If I could see her face I would decide. Why do you ask?" said Lorna.

"She looks either very suspicious, or somewhat familiar to me. I can't decide," said Christian, stealing another glance.

The woman eventually caught him watching her and she busied herself with her handbag and keys, then reached for a pair of oversized sunglasses and shuffled out of the café with her head down, as if she didn't want to be recognised by anyone in her vicinity.

"Weird chick," said Christian.

"Who?" asked Lorna as she waited impatiently for someone to come and take her order. "Oh, right, I see who you mean now."

Lorna nodded over to the far corner of the café, where none other than Shannon Cassidy was shaking hands with a smartly dressed silver-haired man.

"I actually meant the other woman who was sitting at the corner table, but I wasn't expecting to see Shannon here either. Don't let her see us," said Christian as Shannon glanced around. "She'll start talking about weddings and babies and I can't be bothered. Wait a minute. I think I know the man she is with."

"Who is he? Mr McKenzie?"

"Yes, Mack McKenzie, that's his name," said Christian. "Do you know him?"

"No, but I have ears like Mr Spock. I heard her say it a few times just now."

Christian leaned over the table and whispered from behind his menu.

"If I'm not mistaken, Mack McKenzie used to own The Chocolate Bar years and years ago before Gerry took it over. It was a shit-hole back then. Mack's known as one of the shrewdest gangsters in this county and yet he always seems to keep his hands clean. What the hell is going on? How does Shannon know *him*?"

"Shit. Smile," said Lorna as Shannon bounded towards them, all white teeth and fake tan. "She's spotted us. And she looks like she's as glad to see us as we are her."

"Christian, baby! How are you?" beamed Shannon through gritted teeth as Mr McKenzie left The Granary with a fine leather case under his arm. "And it's Laura, isn't it? You own the apart-ment in Belfast where our Eddie was beaten up and left to die on a pavement?"

Lorna refused to rise to the bait and kept her silence.

"Anyhow, Christian, are you looking forward to the wedding?" asked Shannon. "I've just had the most wonderful meeting with my florist and everything is going to be divine. Ha, ha. Get it? *Divine*? Though not *half* as divine as you are, honey."

Christian tried to pretend he was listening but his mind was racing miles ahead of where it should have been. Why was Shannon meeting a man like Mack McKenzie? He used to run a seedy brothel and had disappeared into the gutter years ago. Lorna kicked him sharply under the table, bringing him quickly back to reality.

"Anyhow, must dash," said Shannon, her eyes narrowing. "I have my bridesmaid dresses to pick up and my cake is on its way from Paris. You know how it is, all go, go, go in the run-up to such a happy occasion. Anyway in my condition I don't want to be leaving it all to the last minute. I'll see you around, darling."

She kissed Christian quickly, leaving a deep stain of red lipstick on his cheek and a waft of Chanel in her wake. "Nice to see you again, Laura."

Christian and Lorna sat in awe and disbelief at Shannon's sheer arrogance.

"What a cheeky, jumped-up little cow!" hissed Lorna, unable to wait until she was even out of earshot. "She knows my name fine and well. Didn't I have coffee with the wee bitch in the Royal Hospital when Eddie was in there only a few weeks ago? Didn't I serve her tea until it was coming out of my ears at Isobel's wake as she wept her crocodile tears? I'd love to slap her orange face until it turns to slush. Christian, are you listening to me?"

Christian stared at the plates of food that had just arrived to the table.

"Eat up quickly, Lorna. I have a bit of investigating to do and I don't have much time to do it."

Lorna looked at Christian, horrified. She wasn't abandoning her precious panini for anyone.

"Nobody meets with Mack McKenzie for the good of their health," he continued, "and for the life of me I can't think why there would be a connection between him and Shannon Cassidy, but I plan to find out."

Chapter 28

Sibling Chivalry

"Are you sure you're happy enough to take the bus to Belfast, Daisy?"

"Honestly Mum, I don't mind."

"But Richard has offered to drive you," said Maggie as her daughter fought with the zip on her battered green suitcase. "And if you're going to be coming home more often, as you promised, I think you should learn to pack just a little more lightly. There really is no need to lug such a huge suitcase around with you every time."

Daisy looked at her mother and sighed, then pushed the case to one side and plunged herself onto her bed.

"Mum, if you don't mind, I think I've had enough of Killshannon over the past few weeks. Why don't you come and spend the odd weekend with me in Belfast for the next while until I get my head sorted? We could go to the Opera House and catch a musical or to a concert at the Odyssey? Hey, I could even cook Christmas dinner at mine this year for a change?"

Richard's ears pricked up as he passed the open bedroom door to where his mother and sister were chatting.

"Who did I hear mention Christmas on a hot summer day like

249

this?" he said. "Are we planning for the festive season already?"

"I think Daisy is just trying to tell me that she won't be back here for a while, that's all," said Maggie with a heavy heart.

"Mum, *please*," said Daisy. "You know how hard this is for me. I can't just come here and switch off my feelings like you all expect me to. It's bad enough as it is now, but to watch Jonathan playing happy families next door, right under my nose...don't you understand? This is killing me, Mum."

Richard did a double take. "Daisy, how can you still have feelings for someone you've avoided for so long?" he almost spat. "You have your whole life ahead of you."

Maggie cleared her throat to break the deathly silence that followed, but Daisy was soon ready for action.

"Oh shut up, Richard, you really haven't a clue, do you? What the hell do you know about me and my life? All you care about is your precious work and your own packaged friends. You don't care about me. You never have."

"That is not true, Daisy! Don't you dare say that! I only want what's best for you."

"Then I'll tell you what is best for me, Richard. Why don't you listen to me and I'll tell you how I lost Jonathan in the first place? I had to leave him because I was so afraid of what you would think..."

"Daisy, please don't," said Maggie.

"No, Mum," said Daisy. "He needs to know. I loved Jonathan back then, Richard, just as I do now, but we were both so afraid of your high expectations for me. We knew you disliked him because of Dad. I couldn't have possibly told you the truth. I was pregnant, Richard! I was pregnant and I couldn't tell you! I couldn't tell anyone!"

Richard took a step backwards, visibly shocked, and his mother turned to face the window. "Mum? Is this true?"

Maggie couldn't speak.

"I couldn't even tell Mum back then, either. I was so scared," said

Daisy, fearing she was on a rant she would regret but continuing nevertheless as a lone tear escaped down her cheek. "Jonathan and I could have tried back then to make it work, but I was too afraid. I ran away from everyone. I ran away from the man I loved and I gave away our baby so I wouldn't let any of you down or tarnish the memory of our father. If you want to know exactly what happened in that car that night then I will tell you."

"Daisy, *please*. This won't do any of us any good," pleaded Maggie.

"On the evening of the accident I told Dad I was pregnant. He stormed out to find Jonathan, determined to make him pay for ruining my life and high career prospects."

"I can't take this in…" Richard held his head in disbelief.

"Listen!" shouted Daisy. "Jonathan met him on the road and stopped to give him a lift, thinking he was going to the pub, as he normally did on a Thursday night, but then Dad started to shout and Danny was in the back seat and he shouted louder and then Jonathan lost control at the wheel. It wasn't his fault, Richard! It was nobody's fault. It was an accident!"

Richard could feel a huge lump in his throat. "I know that, Daisy," he whispered. "I just had to blame someone at the time, but I know now that I was wrong."

"Anyway I ran away to Belfast, thinking you all would be better off without me. I was petrified. I'll never have my baby back and now I can't have Jonathan back either. It's too late."

Richard sat down on the bed beside his sister but neither spoke. The only sounds were Daisy's heavy sobs.

"Eddie's waiting in the car, Daisy," said Maggie, her voice shaking with emotion. "I take it he's driving you to the bus station."

Maggie feared that if she let go of the windowsill she might fall, but despite the tears, the air felt crystal clear between her children for the first time in eight years.

Daisy stood up and lifted her case. She looked around her bedroom and walked towards her mother to kiss her goodbye.

Maggie held her tightly, managing to physically feel the pain and regret that burst from her daughter's sorry heart.

"So now you know, Richard," said Daisy with a new-found strength and relief. "Now you know why I don't come back to Killshannon as often as you'd like me to. Give my regards to Jennifer since she's not here to see me off."

Richard meekly followed his younger sister through the hallway, his head muffled with all the things he wanted to say, but the words couldn't come fast enough. Should he say what he had overheard earlier from next door? Not yet, he decided.

"Daisy! Daisy, just give me a second," he called as she walked down the pathway towards Eddie's yellow Mini Cooper. He noticed Jonathan standing in the porch next door and how Daisy waved forlornly in his direction. She turned towards her brother as Eddie squeezed her case into the back of the car.

"I meant what I said," called Richard. "I only ever wanted what is best for you. Maybe until now I just didn't know what that was."

****

Lorna's gut warned her that she was destined for the most severe bout of indigestion she'd ever encountered. Besides the fact that green peppers didn't agree with her at the best of times, she had stuffed her lunch into her so quickly that she was sure she heard the chicken scream for mercy as she gulped it down her throat.

"Christian, I have to say how much you really suit this whole man-on-a-mission thing. In fact, I am one hundred percent sure you are wasting your time in the teaching profession," she said as she marched behind him, desperately trying to keep up with his long determined strides. "But can I just ask you one thing?"

"Of course," said Christian, taking her hand and leading her like a child across the road before the green man showed up on the traffic monitor.

"Where the hell are we going? My feet are on fire, you know.

It's hardly a suitable day for a stroll, let alone a power walk around the streets of Donegal."

"Not too far now, Lorn," said Christian, taking a ninety-degree turn so quickly that Lorna almost lost a contact lens in the motion. "Believe me, I think this will be worth our while in the end."

Christian stopped abruptly at a smart townhouse with a yellow door, then lit up a cigarette and took a long drag while staring intently towards the second floor.

"Can I help you, sir?" said an exotic young lady with the longest black hair Lorna had ever seen. Her skin was the colour of milk chocolate and she wore a long, pale-green gypsy skirt that high-lighted her emerald eyes. The girl was a true beauty.

"I'm looking for Gerry, er, Gerry the barman from The Chocolate Bar."

"Ah, I'm sorry, but you have just missed him," she said as Lorna wracked her brain to work out where her accent was from. "He left to take my mother to the airport a few hours ago and then he was heading to work. I'm sure if you make your way over there now, you should catch him within the next fifteen minutes or so."

"Thank you. Thank you very much," said Christian as he hurriedly made off in the opposite direction, leaving Lorna to smile inanely at the girl before rushing off to catch up with him.

"I have never seen such a beauty in all my life, Christian. Who is that girl?"

"I haven't a clue," said Christian. He genuinely hadn't noticed. "I was sure I knew Gerry's rota off by heart by now. I didn't think he started till much later today."

"Maybe he's short-staffed," said Lorna, thinking of her poor sister holding the fort for her back in Belfast at the hair salon with a pang of guilt.

"Well, we'll soon find out," said Christian. "I just hope he's here."

Christian pulled the door of The Chocolate Bar wide open and let Lorna go in front of him. She automatically led the way to a bar stool, but Christian redirected her to a more secluded booth and asked the waiter to bring their drinks to the table. Lorna excused herself to visit the bathroom and the boy returned with two colas and ice on a tray.

"I thought you told me recently that you were through with women," said the waiter, leaving the drinks on the table and catching Christian in a daze. "And you warned *me* to stay well away from them too."

"Huh? Oh, that's right," said Christian, recognising the boy. "I suppose I must have been lying to you. Tell me, what time is Gerry due in at?"

"Oh, he's here already. He's upstairs. Will I get him for you?"

"Good lad, thanks. That would be great."

When Lorna returned to her seat, Christian was still waiting for Gerry and was fidgeting with a beer mat.

"Ah, here he comes," he said a few minutes later. "Hello Gerry, how's it going?"

Gerry shimmied towards Christian and on spotting Lorna, he shook his head with a smile. "And to what do I owe the pleasure of such fine company?"

"Gerry, meet my friend Lorna. Lorna, this is Gerry."

"Hi, Gerry," said Lorna, extending a hand to greet the owner of the infamous Chocolate Bar.

"A Belfast girl? Very nice, Mr Devine. Now what can I do for you two youngsters? I haven't seen you around for ages, Christian. I thought you were avoiding the place."

Christian cleared his throat. He had to be very tactful in his approach to his questions. He knew from experience that Gerry couldn't hold his piss in the best of situations.

"You see, I'm planning on carrying out a bit of research with my form class on the streets of Donegal when I go back to work in a few weeks' time," he said, "and I was wondering if you could tell me a bit about the previous proprietor of this fine establishment and a wee bit about its history."

Gerry sniggered and then let out a mighty bellowing laugh.

"Cut the crap, Devine. If you've any particular questions about Mack McKenzie, just ask. Don't try and flower it up into a goddamn history lesson."

Lorna glanced warily at Christian, who struggled for a way to word his next question. Gerry had seen straight through him already.

"Okay, then. Let's just say, for example, that a certain young lady is in a spot of trouble. Money trouble. What do you think she might owe Mack McKenzie money for?"

Gerry nodded as if the penny finally dropped. "Ah, now we're talking. Are you in some sort of trouble, Belfast girl?"

Lorna sat up straight and tried to speak, but instead she let out a stammer.

"I, eh, I am in no such thing. This has nothing to do with me. I can assure you of that."

"Steady on, steady on. Well, let's just put it this way, Christian. You and I both know what this place was better known for before I turned it around, but don't get me wrong, I have no place to complain. If it wasn't for Mr McKenzie I would never have met my ex-wife, and if I hadn't done that, I wouldn't have a beautiful daughter waiting for me at home today."

Lorna almost choked on her cola. The girl at Gerry's house was his *daughter*.

"I know all that," said Christian, beginning to lose patience. "So, tell me why a girl of around our age would need to meet with Mack? What sort of business does he run nowadays?"

Gerry let out another snigger and ran his fingers through his silver hair.

"Look here, kiddo," he said. "Mack McKenzie has had more seedy businesses down the years than I have had pints of Guinness. He ran a dating agency, wink, wink, for a long time and I heard he had a dodgy modelling agency on the go for a long time too. In fact he might still have one. He's also been known to deal with a few girls at the higher end of the business," said Gerry, glancing again at Lorna. "High-class hookers."

"Christian, will you please tell him once and for all, this is not about *me*?"

"It really isn't," said Christian. "Cheers, my friend. You've given me a bit of a head start and a lot of food for thought. We'll run on now. Thanks again."

Christian and Lorna left the bar and crossed the street towards the apartment. There, Christian grabbed his car keys and invited Lorna to join him in his motor.

"Are you sure you don't want me to take Chloe the Clio?" asked Lorna, jumping into the front seat of Christian's BMW.

"Positive. I'd like to get there today if you don't mind," he said, shifting the car into reverse and speeding down the cobbled street.

"But you haven't told me where we're going," said Lorna. "Where is the next clue on your trail?"

"Killshannon," said Christian. "Where else?"

****

"I shouldn't have told him, Eddie," said Daisy. "If you had seen the look on his face! I swear to you, it was as if the ghosts of Christmas past, present and future had visited him all at once. It wasn't fair on Mum either, the way I just spilled the beans like that. I fairly lost control."

Eddie and Daisy were taking a break and sharing a bag of chips in the Mini Cooper at Killshannon Harbour. All plans of a bus journey home had been abandoned and Eddie promised that he would drive her to Belfast as soon as she had got some food into her belly.

"To be honest with you, he probably didn't take it as badly as you think," said Eddie, dipping a chip into a blob of ketchup. "I mean, hearing that you and Jonathan had a baby together should have knocked him for six. To me, however, he just looked as if everything had fallen into place and that he had finally understood

256

why you two grew so far apart."

Daisy's phone bleeped a text message but she didn't check to see who it was. She couldn't bear to communicate with anyone outside just now.

"I feel like just running away from it all again, Ed, but Belfast doesn't seem far enough away for me now. Where do I go from here? I have no job, no sense of home. Oh, if my mother heard me saying that she'd go mental, but you know what I mean. No *man* even. Need I go on?"

Eddie adjusted the rear-view mirror and picked the sharp edge of a chip from his teeth.

"So then, you *do* want to come with me to San Francisco after my dear brother signs up to lifelong misery with the super-bitch?"

Daisy moved the bag of chips from her knee and turned to face Eddie. "What exactly are you saying, Mr Eastwood? I couldn't afford to go to Bundoran at the minute, let alone San Francisco?"

"We'll sort something out."

Daisy eventually checked her unread text message. "Oh, I've just got a message from Lorna."

"Well, what does she say? Is she ordering you to get back to Belfast?"

"No," said Daisy with a frown. "Quite the opposite really. She's en route to Killshannon with Christian and has offered me a lift back to Belfast. That means you're off the hook, sunshine. And it looks like I can kill another hour or two around here after all. Now, that I'm done with these chips, shall we go feed the seagulls and plan my super holiday in San Francisco?"

****

Christian sped along the windy road to Killshannon so fast that Lorna's indigestion disappeared as quickly as it had arrived. At this stage Lorna had ceased trying to keep up with his latest conspiracy theory regarding Shannon and Mack McKenzie.

"So, she owes him a shitload of money and was meeting him today to pay some of it off," he said. "*That* we do know, but there has to be more."

"Maybe Jonathan knows all about her debt to McKenzie and we're barking up the wrong tree," said Lorna, deciding that if she couldn't beat him she might as well join him in his investigation.

"Good point. But why did she look so caught out when she spotted us? If Jonathan knew, she wouldn't have cared less. She looked guilty as hell. I think we should pay my buddy Jonathan a surprise visit and put Shannon under so much pressure that we'll corner her into 'fessing up."

"You mean, *you'll* put her under pressure," said Lorna. "I think I'll go and visit Maggie while you play Inspector Gadget."

Jonathan Eastwood answered the door after the first ring and was genuinely delighted to see Christian.

"What's the scoop, Devine? Come on in. I was just making a coffee. Will you have one?"

"Sure will," said Christian, pulling out a chair in the Eastwood kitchen. He noted how the house was eerily quiet now, except for faint footsteps from down the hallway. Shannon was obviously back. Great.

He cleared his throat. "So do you have any plans to come back to the bright lights of Donegal this summer, Jonathan, or are you going to stay here in the sticks for another while?"

"I'm happy to hang out here for the rest of the summer at least. Then when Eddie goes back to the US it will be just me and Shannon. I'd love to live here to be honest but Shannon has bigger and better ideas to live in town. She wants to sell up here straight away but I'm not fussed. Not for another two or three years anyway."

Christian's brain clicked into gear and his blood began to boil when he heard the now familiar high-pitched squeal of Shannon from the kitchen door.

"Well, fancy that!" she said with a hint of sarcasm. "Twice in one day. And what brings you here, Christian Devine?"

Christian was thrown by Shannon's casual reference to how they had met earlier, but then again, she wasn't stupid. He should have known she'd have her skinny ass covered.

"That's right, Christian. Shannon tells me you met up today in Donegal. You were with Lorna, right? What's going on there, fly boy?"

Oh no, thought Christian. A diversion. How clever of her.

"We're just getting to know each other. Mind you, Shannon, you *did* have a busy day. What was it – the florist, bridesmaid dresses and cake all in the one morning? You are a fast worker."

Christian noticed her falter, but only ever so slightly.

"I am. So much to do, so little time," she chirped.

"You wouldn't believe how much there is to sort out for a wedding, Christian. Who knows? It could be your turn soon," said Jonathan with a wink.

"You never know. Actually, Shannon, I have been racking my brain all day to try and figure out the name of the guy you were having coffee with. What did you say his name was?"

Shannon eyeballed Christian from across the kitchen and a smirk drew over her face.

"I didn't. Now, I'm going to let you two boys get on with your catch-up chat while I to go for a walk along the beach. No eating for two for this gal! I have a designer dress to squeeze into very soon."

Christian quickly realised he was dealing with an expert. His so-called investigation wasn't exactly going to plan. He couldn't catch a cold, let alone a con artist bride-to-be, he mustered.

"So, did you catch the game last night?" asked Jonathan and Christian hadn't the strength or kudos to try and change the subject.

****

259

Lorna could see from Maggie's weary eyes that the course of recent events had really caught up with her. She wasn't her usual cheery self at all and their conversation was drained and proving to be very hard work.

Meanwhile, Richard fumbled around making small talk and acting like he had a bee up his bum. So Daisy had been right about him after all. He was a bit of a weird cadet and he kept checking his phone as if he was waiting on a call from the President. Way, way above his station, Lorna decided.

When his wife's car pulled up outside, Richard leapt from his chair in the corner of the kitchen and made for the front door.

"So that's what it's like to be a newlywed," Lorna commented to Maggie who sat absent-mindedly stirring her tea. "I hope the man I marry is as glad to see me come back from a morning's shopping."

"Oh, you wouldn't know what is going on around here half the time," said Maggie. "Between you and me, Lorna, I can't wait till everything gets back to normal. Oh, hi Jennifer dear. Did you buy anything nice?"

Lorna gasped when she recognised Jennifer instantly. It was the lady from the café, the one wearing the black pencil skirt, the oversized sunglasses and the yellow scarf.

"I didn't buy anything at all, except for a coffee, Maggie. But I can assure you of one thing," she said, almost unable to contain her excitement as Richard stood by her side grinning like a Cheshire cat. "What I heard today in a little café in Donegal is absolutely priceless."

Chapter 29

Handbags at Dawn

"Jonathan, there's something I have to ask you about Shannon," said Christian, getting straight to the point. "Maybe you already know what I'm about to say, but I feel I have to say it anyway…"

"What are you on about, Christian? I thought we were talking football?"

Christian knew he couldn't go back now. He had started, so he had to finish.

"The man I saw her with today. It was Mack McKenzie."

Christian could see Jonathan swallow hard and he did the same himself. He was trying his best to appear confident on the outside, but inside he was as nervous as a kitten.

"Ah, come on, Christian. What would Shannon be doing with Mack McKenzie? Don't be so ridiculous."

Jonathan set the remote control of the TV down on the living-room coffee table. He had been about to show Christian the highlights of the game he had recorded on Sky Plus. Now he didn't know where to put himself.

"I *know* it was him. Lorna and I were having lunch in the same café and I recognised him instantly. Then Lorna heard Shannon call him by his name. I think she's up to something, or else she's in some sort of trouble."

Christian gulped again and Jonathan sat down across from him with a thud. He joined his hands in deep thought, wondering what all this meant. Being associated with Mack McKenzie meant only two things – serious debt and a sleazy past.

"Are you sure it was him?" he asked again.

"It's the only reason I came here today. I thought you had a right to know," said Christian.

"But, I just don't understand. Mack McKenzie is an out-and-out gangster."

The doorbell rang, but before Jonathan could rise to answer it, Shannon burst through the back door and beat him to it. She opened the front door with a cagey smile and was met by Richard Anderson.

"I'd like to speak to Jonathan, please," he said, a bit too brusquely for her liking.

"I'll just get him for you now," she said with confidence, but her poise was rocked when she looked behind Richard and saw Jennifer standing in the distance.

Shannon had noticed her snooping about in the café earlier but hadn't recognised her at the time. Now she was beginning to feel claustrophobic.

"Jonathan, love," she called, willing her voice not to shake. "Richard Anderson to see you."

Jonathan looked at Christian with a frown and then shrugged his shoulders. "This day is becoming stranger by the second."

"You go and see what he wants and don't take any shit. I'm sure the match highlights can occupy me till you're done," said Christian, reaching for the remote control.

Richard Anderson looked as stern as ever. Jonathan wasn't even sure how to greet him. He certainly didn't like the look on his face. It reminded Jonathan too much of the night Daisy's father found out she was pregnant.

"Jonathan," said Richard. "I'm sorry to call on you unexpectedly like this but I'm heading back down home to Sligo shortly. However I feel it's about time you and I had a bit of a chat about a few things. In private, of course. That is, if you don't mind, Shannon."

"Oh, of course not. I was just heading out. Again," she said with forced cheeriness as she made her way towards the door.

"Maybe it would be better if you didn't go too far, actually," said Richard as Shannon's face turned a deathly white. "I think it might interest you to hang around a while."

"I have to admit, you have caught me quite unawares, Richard," said Jonathan leading the way into the kitchen. "I take it this isn't exactly a social visit. Have a seat."

Richard refused the offer and stood instead with his arms folded. "I have learned a lot today, Jonathan," he said. "I've learned the truth of my sister's past and her earlier involvement with you, not to mention the real reason why she insisted on using an education in Belfast as an excuse to stay away from Killshannon. For almost six months in her first year we couldn't convince her to come home and nor would she let us come visit. Now I understand why."

Jonathan could feel his palms sweat. This was all too much.

"I'm sure it all came as a shock to you, Richard, but it seemed the only option for us at the time," said Jonathan." We know now how wrong we were."

"Please let me finish," said Richard. "I know that Daisy has held on to her regret over that time of her life for many years, and because I was so blind with my own grief and anger, I couldn't see it. To deal with things, I just threw myself into my work, and into the big bad world where a man without money is no man at all. Everything changed today when Daisy told me the truth. I'm afraid I have been blind to my family's needs."

Jonathan walked towards the kitchen door and made sure it was closed tight.

"I'm not sure how to tell you this, so I'll do it bluntly and keep it to the point. This morning I overheard your fiancée chatting on the phone to a man who is out to do you serious harm, Jonathan."

Jonathan's skin went cold.

"Mack McKenzie?"

"The very man. Perhaps you know more than I think you do?"

"I know absolutely nothing, only that for some reason Shannon met with him today in a café in Donegal. Christian saw her."

Richard's voice dropped to a whisper. "Believe me, Jonathan, only that she used Daisy's name a few times, I would have known nothing about this. Call it guilt for how I've treated you down the years, I don't know, but I sent my wife Jennifer to follow her. What she found out will be devastating for both you and Eddie."

Jonathan felt like the walls of his mother's cosy kitchen were closing in on him. What was this all about? He had spent the entire morning moping around after saying goodbye to Daisy. What more could he take? What had Shannon done now?

"Before she met you, which I believe isn't really that long ago..."

"She started teaching in St Benedict's at the start of term. I suppose we started going out fairly quickly after that."

"Well, it turns out that Shannon had been topping up her student loan by servicing a few high-class clients of Mack McKenzie. She owed him quite a lot of money apparently, and when she got her teaching post, his demands became more and more extreme. Now Shannon has to pay him off. And to do so, she's still taking on clients. He's bribing her with photos, videos... you name it."

"Jesus!" said Jonathan, taking a step back in disbelief. "Are you saying Shannon's a..."

"She knew she could never tell her family about this, but when you showed an interest in her she could see only three things – a very sick relative, a house as an inheritance, and a swift ticket to pay off her mounting debt."

Jonathan felt sick to the core. He held on to the table and his head began to spin. "No, no I can't believe this. What about the baby? Don't tell me she lied about that too?"

"When Daisy came back to Killshannon, Shannon knew she was losing her grip on you and so she conjured up a pregnancy to hold you within her grasp. She had done her homework and knew that she had you well and truly by the balls then."

Richard opened a cupboard and found a glass on the draining board. He filled it with cold water and gave it to Jonathan but as he handed to him, Shannon bounded through the door.

"What the fuck is going on here? Would someone like to tell me? Did you send someone to follow me today, Jonathan? Don't you trust me in the run-up to our wedding?"

Jonathan gulped back the water and downed it like he was swallowing nails. He couldn't take this all in. Could she really have been so deceptive?

"Are you really pregnant, Shannon? Tell me the truth! Are you pregnant?"

Shannon's lip trembled. "I wouldn't lie to you! Richard is doing this all for Daisy. She can't cope that she gave up your baby and now she wants you back. Don't fall for their lies."

"Are you fucking pregnant, Shannon? Tell me the truth!"

Richard shook his head and handed a sheet of paper to Jonathan.

"I don't think you should waste your breath with any more lies, Shannon. I think this will prove exactly why you were meeting with Mack McKenzie today. You should be more careful with your paperwork," said Richard. He turned his attention towards Jonathan. "There you go. A full valuation, dated only two days ago, of your mother's house and the appointment of an estate agent to sell it as soon as possible. You must be desperate to stoop to such levels, Shannon Cassidy. Your family would be ashamed of you."

Shannon walked unsteadily over to Jonathan, who sat now with his head bowed on the table. "I'm so sorry, pet. I was desperate."

"No!" shouted Jonathan.

"I just needed to pay him off so I could get on with my life. With you. He is out to ruin me over a few smutty photos and tapes but if I can get rid of him we can be happy together. Please believe me."

"Shannon, if you were in trouble, why didn't you tell me instead of leading me on with all these lies! A baby? Oh you had done your homework well, knowing I could never abandon a child again!"

"I was so desperate. I thought you were going to leave me."

"My mother's house? My family home? Why Shannon? And now I hear that you are sleeping around too to make money? You disgust me!"

"Baby, I love you," said Shannon, darting her eyes around the room. "Can't we talk about this in private?"

"Get out, Shannon," said Jonathan, looking her straight in the eye. "Get out of my house you conniving, lying little bitch. While I was burying my mother you had estate agents tripping through her house according to this paper! Stuff your wedding and your rotten lies about having my baby. Get out!"

Christian ran into the kitchen on overhearing the commotion and bumped into Shannon on his way through the hallway. Her tan seemed to have faded, and her normally flawless face was streaked with black stripes of tears and mascara. She pushed Christian out of her way and ran blindly out of the house.

"Are you okay, Jonathan?" he asked, realising the shit had well and truly hit the fan.

"No. Actually, would you two mind if I had a bit of time on my own?" He gripped the glass of water between his hands and visibly shook with anger.

"I hope you think I did the right thing, said Richard. "I thought you had a right to know. Sorry if you feel I interfered."

Richard and Christian closed the front door behind them and stood in the pathway.

"I'm Christian Devine by the way," said Christian, lighting up a cigarette. "Do you smoke?"

"Not normally," said Richard. "But if you don't mind, Christian, I think I'll join you just this once."

266

Chapter 30

Back to the Future

Eddie and Daisy were skimming stones along Killshannon harbour when Daisy's mobile rang. It was Lorna, who screamed down the line for her to come to her mother's house quickly.

"What's wrong, Lorna? You're scaring the shit out of me!"

"You will never believe what has just happened! Shannon has been caught out as a lying, scheming bitch and Jonathan has sent her packing."

"How? When?" asked Daisy in disbelief. What on earth was going on? A wave of panic ran through her. Had Jonathan done all of this for her?

"It's a long story," said Lorna in a frenzy, "and as much as I'd like to tell you that Christian and I were the Mulder and Scully of the whole operation, it was actually your brother and his wife, or Posh 'n' Dicks as you fondly call them."

"Richard and Jennifer are involved? Are you sure?"

"Yip. They should be secret agents, I'm telling you. I think Eddie should get home to Jonathan as soon as he can. He's had quite a shock, as you can imagine."

Daisy hung up and shouted frantically at Eddie to wait up. He was lost in a different world as he savoured the delights of

Killshannon harbour and remarked to himself how the smell of fish was actually quite pleasant once you got used to it.

"Eddie," said Daisy. "It looks like you don't have to hang around here for as long as you thought you would, after all. The wedding is off."

Eddie looked at her as though she had just sprouted horns. "Come on, Daisy. Let's get back. This sea air is making you delusional."

"I swear I'm telling the truth, Ed. Come on. Get into the car and I'll fill you in as much as I know on the way home

****

Eddie found Jonathan on the swing in the back garden, a bottle of brandy in one hand and a crystal glass in the other.

"Hey, bro. I can't even leave you for a second but your whole life changes as soon as I turn my back. Lucky escape, eh?"

"Grab a glass, Ed, and come and join me for a drink. There's a case of brandy in the garden shed, along with at least four sets of crystal glasses. They were all bought as wedding presents but thank the Lord I won't need them now."

Eddie didn't need to be told twice. "So is this, er, a party?" he asked, tiptoeing around the back of the swing in case he had got the wrong vibes.

"It is, if it's possible to drown your sorrows and celebrate at the same time. You know, I always thought Richard Anderson hated my guts."

"So did I," said Eddie, pouring himself a hefty measure.

"For all the years he blamed me for that damn accident, he certainly made up for it today by preventing Shannon Cassidy from ruining my life. People surprise me, in good ways and bad, that all I'm saying."

Eddie parked himself on a boulder, balancing his brandy glass on his leg. "They sure do. So what happens now? Do you want me

268

to do anything practical like phone relatives and let them know the wedding is off?"

Jonathan tapped his fingers on his glass in thought.

"I suppose we'll have to do that eventually, but not today. I don't feel like talking to anyone or answering questions just yet, if you don't mind."

"Cool, cool," said Eddie.

"Does Daisy know about all this?" asked Jonathan warily.

"She does. She's devastated, of course, that she won't be able to give you that stainless-steel kettle and toaster she'd bought you for a wedding gift. And the lacy table cloth will just have to go back to the shop."

Jonathan laughed. He wanted to run off and find Daisy this very minute, but he knew it was way too early for that. He'd have to settle for the heat of the brandy to give him comfort for the moment.

"I *could* go and get her," said Eddie with a shrug. "She's outside packing that stupid green suitcase of hers into Christian's car now. That old case has really done the rounds recently."

Jonathan had almost forgotten about Christian, who had gone next door to find Lorna earlier. "Oh shit, Ed, tell me what to do. I want nothing more than to hold Daisy and forget about all the mess of recent years and to start all over again, but now that Shannon is out of the equation, I'm not sure it's right to jump straight in."

"Take your time, Jonathan," said Eddie. "You have all the time in the world and I know Daisy will understand. She'll wait for you for as long as it takes. Just don't tear the ass out of it, for God's sake, or go proposing to anyone else in the meantime."

"Ha, ha, very funny," said Jonathan, taking another swig of brandy. "I think I've learnt my lesson the hard way on that one. But should I go out and see her before she leaves?"

"Do you want to?" asked Eddie with a raised eyebrow.

"Damn right I do," said Jonathan, handing Eddie his empty glass.

Richard and Jennifer said their farewells in the doorway of 10, Ivy Cottages. Daisy hugged them both, still in a state of shock.

"I know Jonathan probably didn't say too much to you, Richard, but I'm sure he'll be in touch to thank you both once all of this sinks in," she said.

"Aren't you going to go and see him?" asked Jennifer.

"No, I won't just yet. I think after all that has happened he'll need some space to sort his head out. Mum said she'll pop over later with some dinner and Eddie has my number, of course. I hope he'll be in touch when he's ready but he needs time alone. Where *is* Mum by the way?"

"I think she's on the phone," said Lorna, who was waiting for Christian to finish his fourth cup of coffee in the kitchen.

"Still!" exclaimed Richard. "It must be the artist guy, Geoff. I think I heard her making plans for the weekend. Right then, we'd better go. Remember to look after yourself, sis."

"I will," said Daisy, waving Richard and Jennifer off.

"And when the dust settles, if you and Jonathan ever need to get away from it all, just give us a call. You can have the keys of the holiday home anytime," said Jennifer, as she gave Daisy an air kiss and skipped out to the car.

"Come on, Mr Devine. We should go too. My car is still at your apartment," said Lorna to Christian, who had finally emerged from the kitchen.

"I'll just go and *mime* goodbye to my mother," said Daisy.

"You don't need to, love," said Maggie, racing down the hallway with a rosy glow in her cheeks. "I've all my weekend plans made and I'll see you out properly. Please don't leave it so long until the next time, Daisy."

"Don't worry. I'll be home again soon," said Daisy and she walked down the pathway with a new spring in her step.

"Er, before you go, love, I think there's someone else who wants to see you off," said Maggie, nodding across to where Jonathan Eastwood stood, his hair ruffled and his eyes slightly bloodshot from the effects of the brandy.

Daisy pursed her lips. He looked slightly drunk, yet so utterly gorgeous.

"You know, I couldn't just let you leave," he said as Daisy walked towards him, her hands behind her back. She sucked her cheeks to stop the overpowering beam that threatened to spread across her face.

"You've been drinking," she said. "How do you feel?"

"Alive," he replied, and took her hands slowly up to his mouth. He closed his eyes and kissed her fingertips.

"You have a lot of thinking to do, Jonathan. We both have."

Jonathan shook his head resolutely. "I've been thinking about you for years, Daisy Anderson, and look how far that got me. I'm tired of thinking. Now, can we please stop thinking and start *doing*?"

"Yes, I think we can," said Daisy, her heart racing, and she kissed him slowly in a way she'd once thought she'd never get the chance to again. "I'll see you very, very soon. I promise you that."

****

Daisy and Lorna zoomed up the road from Donegal. They were both tired and weary when they reached the bright lights of Belfast city. They cracked open a bottle of wine to toast their homecoming but neither girl had the strength nor the energy to finish even the first glass before they retired to their rooms and fell into a deep, satisfied sleep. Daisy dreamed of Jonathan Eastwood and how good it would feel to lie in his arms again, something she planned on doing very, very soon.

Back in Killshannon, Maggie folded away her yellow Madonna t-shirt with a smile and placed it in her bottom drawer. She then framed a photo of Isobel Eastwood and placed it on her mantelpiece. She blew out a scented candle and went to bed to dream about her plans for the weekend, so thoughtfully arranged by her dearly departed friend. Geoff was to take her dancing, and she had two whole days to plan what to wear.

Next door, Jonathan tossed and turned until the brandy truly kicked in and he fell fast asleep, promising himself that the next day he would cancel all the wedding plans. Once he had done that he intended driving to Belfast to surprise Daisy Anderson in Belfast; something he knew he should have done a long time ago.

And downstairs in number ten, Eddie was burning the midnight oil in front of a laptop he had borrowed from Maggie Anderson. He clicked online and bought a one-way ticket to San Francisco for himself. Then he re-checked the booking he had made weeks earlier for a certain Miss Daisy Anderson and Mr Jonathan Eastwood to also fly to San Francisco in a fortnight's time.

Luckily for Eddie, everything had worked out just as he had hoped it would, otherwise he would have had a lot of explaining to do.

Next, he visited a smart website and ordered a compact red leather suitcase. There was no way he was going to allow Daisy to arrive in America with that awful green thing.

Then, feeling very smug indeed, Eddie shut down the laptop, polished off the dregs of his brandy and toasted his mother in heaven.

Thanks to her, he had inherited some very sharp female intuition.

Ingram Content Group UK Ltd.
Milton Keynes UK
UKHW042144220523
422178UK00004B/182

9 780007 591619